POSSUM HOLLOW BOOK FOUR

HOLLOW POINT

ERIN RUSSELL

ISBN 978-1-969568-99-2

POSSUM HOLLOW BOOK FOUR

HOLLOW POINT

ERIN RUSSELL

CONTENTS

A Note on Content

Possum Hollow is a fictional small town in rural Missouri. All the roads and surrounding towns mentioned are also fictional, so don't look for them on a map. The world was inspired by real places where I spent some of my childhood. For anyone unfamiliar to the area, there may be moments in this book you find unrealistic or seem exaggerated. I need you to know, from the bottom of my heart, that it's not. The story and the characters are works of fiction, but the amount of anecdotes and incidents that were taken from the pages of my own life is so much higher than you could possibly imagine.

These characters are flawed and so are their choices. The writing is subjective to their thoughts, not an objective observer passing judgement. It's not a fantasy where everyone gets their comeuppance and only the morally upright survive to the end of the book. If that's what you're looking for, then this book might not be for you. These characters learn and grow, and bad behavior is called out, but above all, my intention here was to write something honest. Something that reflects my own experience and the experience of others I know in a safe, fictional context. Purity culture and moral perfectionism has no place in that for me, and never will.

The backdrop for the series is one of rural poverty. Across the series, you'll find common themes of drug & alcohol abuse, family violence, parental neglect, recreational use of firearms, toxic masculinity & violence, cultural homophobia, and untreated mental illness.

This book is similar in content to *Stupid Dirty*, including themes of suicide and post-partum psychosis (off-page) and disordered eating, as well as those listed above.

For a comprehensive list of triggers that includes spoilers for the story, please visit my website:

www.erinrussellauthor.com

CHAPTER ONE

SILAS

I can't stop staring at the picture of me and Cade at Pride. It's a selfie that he insisted we take. He's making a dumbass face and squishing me into his cheek, and while I don't look comfortable, I do look... happy. Relaxed. In love.

Earlier, I noticed how much dust had gathered on the frame, even though we only put it there a couple of months ago. It's harder to see now, which makes me think it might be nighttime. I could look at the window or the time or something, but it seems pointless to waste the energy. I can't change what time of day it is.

I can clean this fucking picture frame, though. And all the shit around it. There's half a dozen little items strewn across the sideboard, all stuff that Cade collected that day and felt like memorializing in our house. Wristbands and novelty condoms and the penis lollipop I refused to eat.

Because of the sugar, not because I didn't want to be seen with a confectionary dick in my mouth. I'm not that fucked up.

I have a love-hate relationship with all the crap. Cade is absolutely the only reason this place feels like a home. Every piece of junk he gets excited over and puts on a shelf or dumb picture he gets a dollar-store frame for makes this place feel more like a home and less like the tomb it always was before. Even just the little stuff, like the way he leaves t-shirts and shoes lying around in every single room, or the girls' school shit and art up on the fridge.

It's beautiful, in a way. It feels like how real families are supposed to be. I could have lived a thousand lifetimes and never would have expected to have this. Even the thought of it right now makes my heart pinch in my chest, half with indescribable love and warmth, half with the terror that one day it will inevitably come to an end. Probably just when I've really come to take it for granted.

The downside to it all is that it makes it absolutely impossible to keep it clean. Along with the pictures and dirty laundry are fast food wrappers and papers that the girls forgot to take with them, plus a million other pieces of garbage. Sky's sticky fingers manage to touch every single surface, and no matter what, disorder reigns in this space.

It bothers me. I try to force myself not to care, but it doesn't work. I have a home that actually feels like home for the first time in my life. Why should I complain about the mess?

The part of me that gets what he wants but still never seems satisfied might be the part of myself I hate the most.

I don't know how long I turn inwards to dwell on that thought. I know I'm standing next to the picture with one hand resting on it, still not really cleaning, and I think it gets darker because the lights turning on feels so abrupt I nearly jump out of my skin.

"Never fear! Your man has arrived, and like a good provider, I come with sustenance."

Cade's voice booms out from the entryway, knocking me back into reality. I blink a few times while my brain pulls itself out of the sludge of whatever I had been thinking about, which is already becoming a fuzzy memory, and my eyes adjust to how fucking bright it is in here.

"Hey baby," he says, his voice closer now, before I feel his warm hand on the back of my neck as he pulls me in for a kiss.

I blink again, and everything continues to come back into focus. Cade's cheeks are pink-tinged from the cold outside, which combines with the brightness in his eyes to make him look so young. So vivacious. I want to siphon it off into myself.

He's smiling at me like I'm the most amazing thing he's ever seen, which is how he always looks at me and I'll never get used to it.

Too many pieces of myself are marked by his fingerprints. Like a subtle, repeating pattern that says *Cade was here* in some infinite, unreadable language. Like I belong to him, and don't exist without him.

"I don't think you count as the 'provider' if we both work but it just happens to be my day off. How was your shift?" I ask.

My voice sounds normal, so I think whatever moment I was in before is being chased away by Cade's buoyant presence.

"It was good. A lady who shall remain nameless because of HIPAA, but I really wish I could name, had a very interesting run in with a hair curler that should not have been plugged in at the time. And now I'm beating Tristan at Self-Induced Sexual Injury Bingo. If I keep this up, he's buying us dinner."

The image makes me cringe, although Cade's unreasonably gleeful delivery makes me want to laugh. He's in the process of breezing past me toward the kitchen, bag of food in hand, when he catches the grimace and stops, his hand resting gently on my forearm.

"Don't worry, she's okay. She laughed about it as well, I promise I wouldn't be making fun if it was super serious."

He leans in to kiss me one more time before moving deeper into the house, but seems to catch sight of something in my face. It makes him cock his head to the side just a little, gray eyes searching mine.

"You okay?"

I nod. "I'm fine. I was just cleaning."

Cade looks around with a half-smile.

"Cleaning what? You keep this place spotless. I feel like I'm living in a museum half the time."

He laughs again, warm and real, coating my skin like raindrops. He doesn't really mean it, but we do have very fucking different views on the definition of 'clean'.

"Come on," he adds. "Let's eat."

"What did you get?"

I follow him into the kitchen, trying not to sound as wary as I feel. Nothing specific has happened today to make me feel any kind of way, but I also don't know if I have the emotional fortitude to fight with Cade about food.

"Sonic," he says as he throws the bag on the counter and my heart sinks into my stomach.

"Cade."

I don't like the whiny tone in my voice. I don't. I don't want to be this person. But not being this person makes everything in me feel frayed and disoriented, like I'm made of carpet that's so worn out the slightest touch will make it disintegrate underfoot.

He doesn't hear me, though, because he's busy rummaging in the brown paper bag and pulling out a chili-cheese Coney dog wrapped in foil. I already know it's not his first, because he would have eaten at least one on the ten-minute trip back from the drive-thru.

Once the wrapper's off, he unhinges his jaw to inhale about a third of the damn thing into his mouth, tearing it off with a smear of chili on his chin and chewing while he makes an audible, orgasmic little noise. He rummages in the bag again, grabbing something else wrapped in foil before turning around to thrust it into my hands.

"Here you go, baby," he mumbles around his mouthful of food. "Chicken sandwich."

My stomach tightens even more, and nausea begins to creep in. I turn the sandwich over in my hands a couple of times, trying to figure out what I want to do with it. There's a thin film of grease on the outside of the foil wrapper, and the texture of it on my fingers makes me want to gag a little, even though I immediately smash that thought down as an overreaction.

"Cade," I say again, my voice practically a sigh right now.

He must notice the down-turned expression on my face, because as soon as he does, his entire body sags. A frustrated, impotent kind of sadness settles over us, and I hate that it's becoming more and more familiar with every passing week.

Cade swallows his bite before putting down the remaining chili dog on the counter.

Directly on the counter, of course.

I ignore it, focusing on the weight of this stupid sandwich in my hands.

He sighs, like he knows what I'm going to say before I say it, because he probably does.

"You don't have to eat it if you don't want, Silas. I'll eat it if you want something else."

He reaches for it, which makes me flinch and pull the sandwich away from him on instinct. "No!"

I don't want to eat it. I know he likes this shit, but as much as I try to shift my mindset, and even though neither of us is a professional athlete anymore or ever will be, it still feels like putting poison in your body.

Cade holds up both hands then, wide and open, keeping himself still while I cycle through whatever conflicting thoughts are bombarding me.

"I'm not trying to make you do anything you don't want to, Silas. Sometimes you like these. If you want to eat something else, let me have the sandwich and I'll help you cook."

"I'm just going to throw it out," I say, moving towards the trash can, the twist in my stomach getting worse.

That's when Cade's expression shifts from patient to irritated.

"Why would you waste food? I'll eat it. I've been on my feet for over twelve hours, I'm tired and hungry and I need a fucking carbohydrate. Just give it to me and we can cook something else together that you want."

"I can cook for you, too."

I keep inching towards the trash can, but Cade sighs loudly, obviously not fooled.

"Silas, baby, I told you. I'm tired. I can't with the rabbit food today. I'm sorry I brought this home without telling you, I texted earlier but you didn't answer. I didn't think it would bother you this much. Can you please let it go before this turns into a giant thing for no reason? I will destroy the evidence of my poor judgment and we can both move on with our lives."

Now it's my turn to sigh. I know I'm being unreasonable. I hand him the sandwich, but turn around to disappear into the living room so I don't have to watch him. I can feel his gaze trail me as I leave.

As soon as I hit the living room, I drop onto the couch. I think I intended to sit on it, or maybe keep cleaning, but instead I end up lying across it curled up on my side, battling a sudden familiar sense of exhaustion.

This is probably something I should deal with. I should probably do some of my DBT skills, but I can't think of any right now.

I liked the DBT stuff I did–dialectical behavior therapy–way more than CBT–cognitive behavioral therapy. And not just because CBT apparently also stands for 'cock and ball torture', which Cade couldn't stop laughing at.

It's a shame it worked out that way, because the DBT was fucking expensive and not covered by insurance. But it was the only thing that seemed to help me when I started the whole meds-and-therapy monstrosity that Cade was so insistent on, so he busted his ass to make sure we could afford it. Barely. Once I was committed, and he'd thrown so much of himself into the process, I knew I couldn't let him down by not finishing.

And it really did help. I liked the group and talking to a bunch of other people with weird, fucked-up lives. I had group sessions online, and there was no one in there that was 'normal'. Not even 'normal' by mentally ill standards, like just a straight up-and-down depression diagnosis. No, it was all people who were truly fucked up, most of whom had some kind of unhinged childhood, just like I was coming to realize I'd had. A bunch of C-PTSD babies, each trailing a sack of various diagnoses and horror stories behind us.

It made me feel less alone, which isn't something that happens to me very often. And the whole thing centers around teaching you skills to deal with your emotions. They're supposed to be simple and easy to remember, so you build up your little mental tool box and then when shit goes sideways in real life, you whip them out.

There's a lot of acronyms. So. Many. Acronyms.

A lot of the time it helps. Especially for strong, overwhelming emotions. But this kind of sucking numbness is my greatest enemy, and my mind immediately locks down so hard, all of those thoughts and skills seem completely inaccessible.

It sucks. All that money, all that time and energy, and especially all the time I had to spend sitting around dwelling on things I definitely would have rather forgotten, and what did it get me?

Some days I think it just made me worse.

I'm still alive. That's what Cade always points out. But am I really alive on days like this, when I feel completely outside of myself, and a goddamn chicken sandwich was all it took to send me spiraling into the couch?

I hear more rustling in the kitchen, which is probably Cade inhaling the food like he said he would. I know he won't throw it away. He'll do a lot for me, but for whatever reason, throwing away "perfectly good food", even if it's just garbage, isn't one of them. I expect him to come in after I hear the trash can lid open and slam shut, but he doesn't.

I wonder if he's more angry at me than I thought. I would be. Having to tiptoe around me like this has to be annoying. But I've been living with Cade for a while now, and while he's far from perfect, he's reliable about that. Nothing ruffles him. Not me, at least.

His mom? Yes. They still fight like alley cats. But I also think that's how they bond, in some sick, twisted sort of way. Any mention of his dad will also set him off, and some of the other people in town, if they start acting like small-minded dicks. We haven't gotten a lot of shit from anyone, but on the few occasions when we have, it's taken all my energy to keep Cade from catching a felony charge.

But when it comes to me and the girls, he has the same kind of patience he manages to pull out of his ass for his patients at work. I don't know how he divides his personality like that, but I appreciate it.

It doesn't explain why he hasn't come in here yet, though. It's never taken him more than four and a half minutes to demolish a bag of Sonic.

I stare at the fabric of the couch, allowing my eyes to unfocus until the image blurs, and try not to think about it. I try not to think about anything at all, until I begin to drift.

"Sit up for me, baby."

Cade's voice snaps me out of my stupor for the second time tonight. I do as he says, rust falling from my limbs in brittle chunks as I force them to articulate and reassemble the pieces of myself into something vaguely human-shaped, sitting on the couch with my feet in front of me, feeling only slightly stiff.

"Here you go."

He puts a paper plate in front of me. I hate the paper plates—they make me feel like I'm still living out of motels instead of a home—but it's another habit that's so deeply ingrained in him, it doesn't feel like it's worth the argument.

Fighting with Cade is probably the most excruciating thing I've experienced, even if it doesn't happen very often. Because I spent a lifetime learning to rely only on myself. Then he eked open my walls just a little, just enough to squeeze himself inside and make me need him. Just enough so that whenever something bad happens, he's the first person I want to turn to.

And every time we fight, I feel the same way. But he's the one making me feel that way, so the whole thing makes me freeze, like a system error in human form. The thought of losing him after I never thought I'd find him terrifies me to my core, and I know I'll ultimately fold over any issue, contort myself into any shape he wants, just to keep him here.

I'm sure that's not healthy. My therapist says so, at least. But I also think it's pragmatic. And it's not like Cade demands a lot from me other than to... I don't know. Try to be a person?

The plate is piled high with a bunch of different food: apples slices, peanut butter, cold chicken breast in pieces, bread, cottage cheese, tomatoes cut into ragged chunks, and a very sad hard-boiled egg that he must have rescued from the back of the fridge. It's messy, because cooking will never be Cade's forte, but at least it's all food, and none of it is fried.

This time it's my heart that clenches, not my stomach. I'm still not hungry, but it gives me a swooping, weightless sensation to know he went to all this trouble.

"Thank you," I mutter, not really knowing how to express myself more meaningfully than that.

Cade doesn't say anything, his energy light. It's deliberate, I'm sure. He steals a piece of apple, swipes it in the peanut butter and then shoves it in his mouth as he nudges the plate closer to me.

"Eat," he says, leaning in to kiss me on the temple, holding my head with the heel of his hand so he doesn't touch me with his sticky fingers and making the world around me smell like peanut butter for a minute.

His tone is light as well, but I hear the undercurrent of warning in it. He doesn't stay to watch me, though, which I appreciate. I'm aware that I'm weird about food and it's not a challenge to guess where it came from. None of this is news to me. Someone staring me down like a criminal isn't going to help.

Once he's disappeared and I hear the shower turn on, I look at the plate. My stomach clenches again, but I try to ignore it this time.

It's already been a weird, pointless day. Don't make it worse, Silas.

CHAPTER TWO

CADE

I want to say it's not deliberate that I take the world's longest shower. It was a grueling shift, and my muscles are sore. I'm still not totally used to having the water pressure we have at Silas's house, as well as the amount of hot water that comes from only two people using it, not four, so it feels like a luxury on a daily basis.

The water pounds down on my back and chest as I move around, biting into my tight muscles and making me feel pure after a day of gross bodily fluids.

The fact that it gives Silas more time alone is just an added benefit. I'm not coddling him.

I'm not.

I'm frustrated with myself more than anything else. I don't know what else I can do. We contorted our brains to figure out insurance—which it's still kind of new to me to have—and all the rest of it so he could get actual care. He did six months of intensive therapy that was so time consuming, his life was basically that and work. He still has it twice a week. We talked, we learned, we grew; I've made it as clear as I can that I'll move the fucking Earth if I can to make him feel better.

His dad is 1,500 miles away and never setting foot near him again. Not unless he wants his nose to meet the inside of his brain.

I never expected him to be magically fixed. I've spent too much of my life around addiction and trauma and everything else to expect anyone's brain to ever bounce back. It doesn't work that way.

But I didn't expect it to still be this bad. It makes me worry I shouldn't leave him alone like this on his days off, but then that seems like a feral, possessive sort of thought that shouldn't be entering my consciousness.

He's still an adult. He's not hurting himself. He's truly loved, probably for the first time in his life.

He's just... lost. And in a way that seems so much more internal than before, not that objective touch-starved sadness that I could easily abate.

I don't know what to do. I need an adult, and none of the adults in my life are giving me anything more to work with than *be patient, keep doing therapy, keep taking the meds, it takes time.*

This doesn't feel right, though. He should be able to fucking eat.

I force myself to stop moving for a second. Deep breath in, hold, breathe out.

Silas has an app for breathing that's supposed to help him if he has a panic attack, and it's ended up helping me out more than I expected. I do a few more, not because I'm panicking, but because it helps me level myself out internally whenever things start to feel chaotic.

I can't control how Silas feels. I can only try to help.

It's become my fucking mantra, even if it's as useless as I am most of the time.

Exhaustion dogs at my heels as I get out of the shower and towel off. I pause for a second, staring at the floor. This has been happening more and more recently, and I don't know why. When I moved in, it seemed like a rational choice to switch to the master bedroom. It was bigger, it had the attached bathroom, and the whole plan was for us to chase out all the old, dark memories that were dragging Silas into the past.

I've been doing my best to fill this house with light and some kind of normal life for him. At least one to look forward to. He says it helps a lot. He says with so much conviction that he thinks about his shitty childhood stuff less and less, even if the psychological after-effects are still dragging him down.

If anything, I'm the one who's thinking about it more. When Silas came back to me after almost absconding to fucking Canada with the shitheel who spawned him, he walked me around this house and spilled all its secrets. The truth about his mom and how sick she was, and how his dad basically left her to spiral out of control, and baby Silas along with her.

"This is where Dad found me the time he thought I was dead. I was cold when he touched me. 'Like meat.'"

That's what Silas had told me when he showed me this spot, the words clawing their way into my chest and making themselves a fetid, rotting home.

I've touched and carried the bodies of people who were dead or almost-dead. The feeling is not something you can truly understand until you experience it. It's not just the cold, or the literal dead weight of them. There's a weight to their presence as well. Like a stiff, unnatural feeling that seems out of kilter with the living world around them, and your body pulls away from it on some instinctual level.

You get used to it quickly, and it doesn't bother me anymore when I'm at work. But it does mean that I have this completely realistic hypothetical sensation that my mind has attached to the memory of Silas's words, and whenever my eyes catch on that one spot on the floor, I can't help but think about it.

Like I can feel his skin—baby-soft but stiff; turgid, as the blood pools underneath because no one found him in time and he's really gone—stretched tight over his infant frame.

My stomach lurches at the thought. Maybe I ate too much, after all. I wasn't expecting to eat Silas' sandwich as well. He likes that one. Sometimes when I get it for him, everything's fine. He had the day off today and I was hoping he would be feeling relaxed.

Instead, he seemed more tense and spaced out than I've seen him in a while. He didn't have any appointments. I wonder what he did all day?

Tearing my eyes away from the bathroom tile is a struggle, but it's not the first time I've had to do it and it won't be the last. I wander into the bedroom, slipping on a pair of ratty sweats and my NOFX hoody with all the holes. It's comforting for some reason. So fucking destroyed it looks like it's about to fall apart, but keeps me warm anyway.

There's a parable there. Or a metaphor, or something. Whatever the fuck it's called.

I let myself sigh once, and then forcibly drag a sunny-fucking disposition over my face. If I have my way, I'll spend tonight wrapped up in Silas so deep that neither of us want to come up for air. I wasn't lying when I told him that work was fine, but it was also kind of grating. We had more than one call out that we wouldn't be seeing if they had more money or if the healthcare system in this country wasn't so fucking diabolical, and that shit always puts me in a foul mood.

Tristan always tells me to chill. You can't save everyone, but you can kill yourself trying, and dead men don't save lives.

It fucking sucks, though. The people who make all the decisions don't have to be elbow deep in fentanyl overdoses and dying grandmothers they could have saved. I do.

I need Silas tonight. I can feel this chasm of *need* and *want* opening up inside me, and I can already tell that it's ultimately going to be the source of my destruction.

Please, please, please dear Christ let him have eaten something.

When I wander back, I find him in the kitchen. The plate is already in the trash, so I can't see what was left. I'm immediately suspicious, but I do my best to knock that thought out of my head. If we turn into a household where I'm

14

combing through the trash to see what he ate and if he's lying about it, we really are fucked. Nobody needs that.

"Better?" he asks, although I was about to ask him the same thing.

"Mmhmm."

I slip behind him, wrapping my arms around his stomach and layering myself down his back like a second skin, taking a deep breath of the scent at the base of his neck and relishing in the overwhelming warmth of his body finally being close to mine.

He stiffens as soon as I touch him. It's happening more and more recently, depending on where I touch him. I hate it. I can't help the shiver of offense that hits me in return every time, even if I know that's selfish.

It's me. It's me touching him. How could that ever make him feel anything other than wanted and loved?

It's not like I don't still think he's the most mouth-wateringly delicious piece of ass placed on this planet, most likely just for me.

He was always handsome. Cut, classic features. That ridiculous Ken-doll body with all the abs and the other muscles I forget the names of, that we now know came from his dad's goddamn overtraining and underfeeding.

I got him away from Travis and he literally got hotter day by day. Thick, but without that dehydrated bodybuilder look anymore. Just flesh and muscle, with a healthier glow. And happy, too, so his face fucking shone. Big and bulky and warm and all. Fucking. Mine.

He's continued to work out obsessively since then, even though he doesn't have to. That's fine. Routine helps him feel in control, I get it. And working at the garage has made him pack on even more bulk on top of that, in opposition to how motocross needed him to be lean.

But as soon as he started the damn meds, it went from just muscle, to muscle and fat, and even though the meds made a very obvious difference in his mood, they also made a very obvious difference in his body. More soft over hard.

I, for one, want to drown in him. It's all just more Silas. He can sit on my face and choke me to death with those fucking thick, hairy thighs, I swear to god.

He hated it from the jump, though. I know it bothers him. I don't know exactly how much, because he won't fucking talk about it, but it's obvious. When he had to buy new clothes, that was a dark spell that took a while to get out of. For a while he worked out so much I knew he was going to hurt himself, but between me fucking begging him, and a few conversations with his therapist, he toned that down.

Still, nothing's been fixed. I know he feels... something. Something bad. It's written in how quickly he gets dressed after the shower or these constant tense moments when I touch him. And how much goddamn protein he takes, with very little food.

And I don't want to make it worse for him, but I also hate having to be careful all the time, and not being able to touch the person I fucking love. Especially when he's the only one who doesn't realize how goddamn sexy he is. I'm tempted to tell him, but I've tried that before, and I feel like it makes it worse, especially if he's already on edge.

Instead, I fist my hands so I'm not touching him in quite the same way, then squeeze him tightly so we're pressed inseparably close. My hips are pushed against his firm round ass—the one that I wish I could have in my hands basically all the time—and I let him feel that I'm already half-hard at the thought of what we could do next.

Silas lets out a slow, shuddery exhale while I lick and nibble my way up his neck to eventually suck his earlobe into my mouth.

"Bed?" I murmur into his ear.

He nods against me, relaxing bit by bit, but still not as much as I would like. I'm gripped by how much I want him, but his tension makes me tense, so there's an undercurrent to the whole interaction. I'm not sure what it is—fear, anxiety, resentment, something—but it's lurking there regardless, like an intruder in our home.

I focus on Silas in an attempt to chase the feeling away. I reach down, slipping my fingers under the waistband of his athletic shorts. He's not wearing any underwear, and I nearly groan at the feeling as my fingers drag through short, coarse hair on the way to his dick. He absolutely knows how to get me every time, and the exhaustion is quickly chased from my body.

I want him. I need him. I need my brain to stop making fucking noise.

"Fuck me, robot boy," I whisper as I fist his cock just a little too tight and begin to stroke. "Take me upstairs and fuck me until I can't even remember my own name."

Silas smirks a little, but turns his head to kiss me through the expression.

"Are you sure? After all that chili?"

There's a teasing tone to his words that I don't get to hear that often, so I don't have it in me to be embarrassed as I smile, getting out my words between short kisses.

"Yeah, that was maybe an oversight on my part. Whoops." I shrug. "How about 'suck me until I can't remember my own name, robot boy'. Does that work? Clearly someone doesn't want to have our *Brokeback Mountain* moment."

Now we're both laughing more than kissing, although still holding each other close, and the mood shifts into something lighter.

"That works, Cade."

I'm about to drop to my knees here in the kitchen to get the first turn, but I'm caught off-guard when Silas reaches underneath my ass and hoists me up with a grunt. My legs wrap around his waist as I cling to his shoulders.

He does this from time to time, and I can't deny how much I fucking love it. It's never going to be the dynamic it was the rare time I've done this to a petite girl, because I'm tall enough and heavy enough that we're structurally unsound, but that doesn't matter.

I'm not trying to feel dainty or feminine. I am trying to feel fucking overwhelmed, though, and this is a very good start.

Without complaining about my heavy ass, Silas marches us straight to the bedroom before tossing me onto the bed with enough force to make me bounce.

Before I get the chance to breathe, he goes after me like a man possessed. Hands push the hem of my hoody up and hook it over my head, so the fabric is bunched beneath me and my movement becomes limited. Then my sweats get heaved down, but left around my knees so I'm tangled up there, too. My chest, crotch and thighs are the only thing exposed to the room, and Silas runs his hands over all of it before leaning over to bite me right at the crease of my groin.

The pain sends a jolt of adrenaline through me, and I blow out a steady breath as I buzz with it. I was already getting hard, but that definitely doesn't hurt.

"Fuck yeah," I groan as Silas continues to bite me in the most sensitive places, worrying the skin beneath his teeth to make me shiver.

My baby knows I like a little pain with my lovemaking.

"Are you just gonna tease me all night, or are you gonna suck my dick at any point?"

My attempt to sound nonchalant fails so hard I can't help but laugh a little, and then even more as Silas reaches up to pinch one of my nipples way, way harder than is necessary. My laughing is abruptly cut off, though, when he fucking inhales my dick like that's his real dinner.

"Oh, fuck. Jesus. That fucking mouth."

The meaningless horny babble is already starting, whether I want it to or not, and I can't stop myself from also rocking my hips up into him as he sucks and slobbers all over me.

Silas doesn't say anything, but he hunkers his body even lower to the bed. I wish he was naked and that I could touch him, too, but I know he likes to take things at his own pace, so I'm rolling with it. Silas gets lower and lower, continuing to fit an impressive amount of my cock into his mouth, before sliding both his arms under my thighs until they wrap around so he can grab my waist.

He holds me like that—sweatpants dangling from one ankle now–my thighs spread open with his head between my legs. It feels like I'm even more open to him than before, and I shiver a little.

Silas breaks away my cock for a second to rub his stubbly skin all over the raw places that he was biting earlier, but he holds me completely still when I start to flinch away, so I stay pinned by the sensation. When his face dips down so he can tongue my balls, I can't help but cry out.

He licks and sucks at each one, working them over with grave attention before he goes back to sucking me. It's incredible, but I wish more and more he wasn't so far away.

Words are mostly beyond me at this point, so I reach down and tug at his shirt, hoping he gets what I mean.

"Up here," I breathe.

Silas bobs his head up and down a few more times. God, I'm already so close. But then his warm whiskey-colored eyes look up at me.

He seems to get what I mean without having to talk about it. Score.

Silas pops off my dick for just a few seconds, quickly rearranging himself until he's facing the other direction, his entire weight suspended over me and his hips straddling my face. He's still wearing soft shorts, but he's able to reach down and free his cock without much difficulty.

I'm not entirely sure there's anything more beautiful than this sight. His cock is rock-hard and flushed with arousal, thick and meaty and dangling overhead. His waistband is pushed down just far enough that his balls are out, but they're pulled up close to his body, and I can't wait to have them resting on me.

There's a little bit of shine to the head of his cock, and Silas shivers a little bit before a string of clear liquid drips from the tip to my lips.

I reach up, grabbing whatever part of him I can reach and pulling him down. Obviously, he doesn't want to crush me, but I can take it. Drown me right here and now.

It only takes a little coaxing to get him to lower his cock into my waiting mouth. He lets himself lean onto me bit by bit, and when I relax into the pressure, so does he.

Silas slides his mouth back down over me, hooking his arms around my legs again, but this time the other way around, and we both start to lose ourselves in the pleasure.

Almost all of my senses are obscured by Silas's body surrounding me, and I can barely breathe. It's perfect. I'm so hyperfocused on teasing him with my tongue everywhere I know he likes, that my own pleasure becomes more of a distant roar, and I don't feel so desperate to come.

Good. I want to taste his release before anything else.

"Fuck, Cade," his quiet voice echoes from somewhere near my crotch as he starts to thrust deeper and deeper into my mouth.

That's it, baby. Just let go.

I reach up to grab his ass, kneading my fingers into his flesh and holding him close.

Silas goes back to laving his tongue over me, but I can feel his attention start to break as his hips stutter and he fucks my face harder and harder.

I can't help but slide one of my hands up the curve of his lower back, under his shirt. Something about that spot is absolutely deadly to me. It should be illegal, it's so sexy. I'm doing it a second time when Silas finally gasps, stiffens and starts to unload into my mouth.

He's a little off-balance so his cock slips out as he's still pulsing out hot, salty cum, and the lower half of my face gets painted with it. His hips curl under as his orgasm finally ebbs, but I'm able to lean up enough to lick the seam of his balls and make him shudder.

Without pausing, Silas goes back to what he was doing before and fucking attacks me. He licks and sucks and presses his tongue into the slit of my cock until I'm coming as well, picturing the way his throat must be working as he swallows every drop.

It's clumsy when Silas drops to the side, but he manages to tuck his dick back in his pants and turn himself around until we're lying together without much difficulty.

I'm still half naked, pinned by my own clothes with all my soft, vulnerable parts on display. I'm pretty sure he likes it like that. And I really, really don't mind.

So, instead of pulling my hoody down, I just arch into his touch as he smooths one hand up my flank before pulling me close to him and kissing me more thoroughly than I thought was possible.

Neither of us says much. We kiss for a while, and it continues to ease the ache of whatever was dogging at me before. Then we slowly and peacefully move around our space together as we get ready for bed. Once we're under the covers, I wiggle around until I'm half on top of him with my ear pressed to his chest, letting myself be lulled by the steady rise and fall as well as the consistent lub-dub of his heart continuing to beat.

Once Silas's breathing is deep and even, I know he won't move again until morning. His meds may be imperfect, but at least they knock him the fuck out. Before he spent a lot of time looking like he was asleep, but I don't think he really was. It was more like he was powered down, but all those thoughts and anxieties continued to spark through him, exhausting him at a cellular level.

Personally, the amount of sleep I've been getting in a quiet house is also something that isn't as good as it should be. It's too damn quiet, if you ask me. The whole thing is unsettling.

How are you supposed to sleep if there's no ambient noise to cover whatever weird sounds creep out in the night? Because every time I hear so much as a creak in the darkness, my overactive imagination starts painting a picture of an intruder coming towards us. Or a ghost. Or a gremlin. Or maybe my fucking dad, methed up and looking for money under the mattress.

While part of it is my own unhinged personality, part of it is a finely honed survival instinct, and I don't think it's going away any time soon. I can already tell it's going to be one of those nights. My nerves are all still wound tight from work, ready to spark at a moment's notice, and while a good fuck definitely helps me relax, the intensity of what we did is contributing to my overall tension.

Without making more noise than I have to, I slip out from under the covers. Silas's hand was on my hip, and there's a specific moment where I feel the warmth of his fingertips disappear as I drag myself out of his reach. I regret my choice in that instant, but it's too late to turn back.

Once I'm on my feet, I pull on the same sweats-and-hoody combo from earlier and slip out of the room, closing the door behind me with a faint click. The heating works in this house thankfully, but it's still chilly at nighttime, so I also swipe a blanket from the back of the couch that was a housewarming present from my Aunt Jaz.

It has an old-fashioned pattern of horses galloping across the horizon, and it's so cheesy I should hate it, but I don't. The fabric is soft and worn, and the little imperfections in her stitching make it feel more human. Like a person is reaching through the material to touch me.

Which is crazy. I still let the concept comfort me as I wrap it around my shoulders and sneak into the kitchen.

There's a brief moment of panic where I wonder if we're out of booze. Not tonight. Please not tonight.

It's not technically too late to go out and buy beer, but I'd have to drive far to find a store that's open, and I don't want to risk the chances of Silas waking up to find me gone.

It's more than that, as well. I don't really want to be faced with how much time I'll spend arguing with myself about whether to go or not, weighing the pros and cons, instead of just accepting that we're out of booze like a normal person. That feels like something big and looming, pressing up against my mind too close for me to find the edges of it to get a grip. I'd much rather keep ignoring it for now.

Besides, it's not like I do this every night. Just some nights. Just when I can't sleep, and the deathly echoes of this fucking house are crawling into my brain one by one, keeping me awake.

Just to take the edge off.

Everything's fine, though, because there are still a few Bud Lites tossed in one of the vegetable drawers, as well as a few inches of very questionable whiskey left in the bottle on top of the fridge. Silas has basically stopped drinking altogether, because he wasn't really into it before and now it messes with his meds, so except for the rare occasions when my mom is both here and off the wagon, I'm the only one burning through it all.

I grab one can and crack it quietly while standing at the end of the kitchen, as far from the bedroom as I can be. Then I relocate to the sagging maroon couch in the living room, wrap the blanket tighter around my shoulders, and pull out my phone.

Silas won't wake up. I'm being paranoid by even being this quiet. But the thought of interrupting his sleep even once–especially if he's going to worry about why I'm not asleep–bugs me too much to risk it.

Once I'm settled, my mind immediately begins to float. I stare at my phone, thumbing between different social media accounts and getting caught up on all the creators I've started following whose content I'm really enjoying.

I never used to have time for social media. I thought it was shallow, and mostly about moms bitching each other out on Facebook or everyone I went to high school with posting cheesy engagement and baby announcements in between complaining about who got put on house arrest and who owes who child support.

Like a lot of things, it turns out I wasn't looking closely enough. Or maybe I was seeing what I wanted to see.

After me and Silas got settled, I got curious about LGBTQ+... stuff. I don't know. If I'm a part of this community, I should know about it, and I don't want to come across like an asshole that says the wrong thing all the time. I started out by asking Wish questions, even though it's not like I lived under a rock before and I'd always tried to be an ally.

Of course, it didn't take long for me to wear out Wish's patience. It turns out I had more questions than I thought. She told me to stop making her do all the work for me and go find information, so I went. And I discovered that the internet has more than just porn, if you look in the right places. And also that the right porn can be informative sometimes...

It took some trial and error, but now I follow a bunch of TikTokers who talk about queer rights issues and social issues in general, and the more I watch, the more it speaks to me.

I always knew I was poor. I always knew I had a raw deal in life and so did most of the people around me. And I was pissed about it. But I think I never realized just how deep all those injustices went in the world, or how deliberate most of them are.

Once I started listening, I couldn't stop. It's addictive. I just wanted to learn about Stonewall and shit so I didn't seem like a complete waste of space, but now it's like a switch in my head that I can't turn off. And the more I understand about the causes of it all, the more I see the effects of it everywhere.

Unfortunately, that also means I'm getting angrier and angrier with every fucking day that passes. But I can't do anything about that.

At least it gives me something to think about other than obsessing over the creaks in the house, or stopping myself from going through the trash to see if Silas really ate something, or waking him up to cry and scream and beg him to promise me that he's not silently slipping away from me, even after all the progress we've made.

I take a sip of my drink, tangle my fingers in the horse blanket, and thumb up to the next video. I'll keep doing this until I feel ready to go to sleep, and in the morning, things won't seem so bad.

CHAPTER THREE

SILAS

The only sounds in the shop are the constant metallic ones of the work I'm doing, and it's filling me with a deep sense of contentment. No TV on in the background, no constant chatter, nothing. I love the whole family I got when I ended up with Cade. I'd be nothing without them. But they're so fucking chatty, sometimes it's nice to go to work so I can let my mind breathe.

I can already feel all that malaise from yesterday drifting away. How I feel each day is unpredictable, which I hate. I think I used to have just all bad days, but they were constant, so it seemed normal. Now that I have more good days than bad, the bad ones seem that much worse. And I can see how it affects Cade, which breaks my fucking heart.

It's better. I'm a lot better. I ride out the bad days and then days like today, I feel like a normal person. But Cade doesn't seem to have that kind of patience, and wants to fix everything. Which makes me feel guilty, and the cycle continues. On and on and on.

We'll snap out of it, eventually. I'm sure. I just need to be patient, and focus on the shit I can do right, like fixing this fucking engine and basking in the peace and quiet.

Ford is in the office working on something owner-ey that I don't have to worry about. Not that he makes much noise when he's in here. We were always quiet together, because neither of us is naturally talkative and Ford only communicates by texting, writing, or sign. But I've been working hard on learning American Sign Language so he doesn't feel alone.

It's amazing that he found a partner who knows ASL in this tiny town, but that's still only one person. It seems fair for him to be able to communicate how he naturally wants to communicate, so I'm really trying not to be lazy about it. Which has turned into me signing to him half the time instead of speaking to him. I don't have to, because he's mute, not hearing-impaired, and I only need to be able to understand him signing for us to communicate, but still. It helps me learn.

The pall of silence that has fallen over this auto shop as a result wasn't the purpose of my plan, but it has been kind of a happy side effect. It's more peaceful than anywhere else I spend my time, and I want to cling to that with both hands.

I love Cade. He's my everything. But sometimes I worry that peaceful is the last word I'd use to describe what we have.

There's a loud tap of metal on metal, startling me out of my thoughts. I look up and see Ford standing a few feet away, putting down the wrench that he obviously used just to get my attention. It's not like I hate people touching me, but it still startles me sometimes if I'm not expecting it, and Ford gets that. He's the same way, although for very different reasons.

"You okay?" he signs, his brow furrowed.

"Yeah," I sign back. "Why?"

"You've been frowning at that thing for like ten minutes. Do you need help?"

I blink, because I really didn't realize I'd been lost in thought for that long.

"No, I'm fine." I figure out how to explain what I was thinking about and end up explaining my whole thing about how peaceful it is here, in a mixture of ASL and spoken English.

Ford nods, obviously understanding what I mean. He values silence as much as I do, I think.

"But everything's okay at home?"

A little smile tugs at the corner of my mouth. I spent the majority of my life with very few people caring if I lived or died, and the ones that did focused mainly on my ability to generate money for them. I'm not sure how I ended up surrounded by a bunch of misfit guys—all of them weighed down by a bunch of their own issues—who genuinely care about me now. Even if they act like it's no big deal.

It's a really big deal.

"Cade seemed stressed last night," I end up saying. The thought bursts out of me unexpectedly, so suddenly I forget to sign. When Ford doesn't reply, I continue. "I don't know why I think that. On paper he was acting like normal. There was something off about him, though. I feel like it's happening more and more. Or maybe I'm being paranoid."

I sigh, because how anyone is supposed to tell the difference between those things is a fucking mystery to me.

"Did you ask him?"

I shake my head. "No. He always says he's fine. I think he thinks he needs to be happy all the time or I'll get upset or something."

Ford's eyebrows raise, and he takes a few seconds to chew over the thought.

"That sounds like something you should talk about, then. Don't let him bottle that shit up. We all know where that leads."

The thought is a dark one. I'd been aware Cade was maybe putting on a happy face; not telling me when he had a shitty day at work, that kind of thing. Not that he was actually bottling up real terrible feelings. It's a concept that hits my gut like buckshot, ricocheting through my body and then dragging me towards the floor.

I'm searching for the right response when my phone rings. I keep it on *do not disturb* at work, with only Cade, the girls and their school set to break through in case of emergencies. It's a Saturday so it can't be school, but the girls could still be having an emergency and Cade is on shift, so he probably can't even look at his phone right now. I fish it out immediately and look at the screen.

Maddi

Without hesitating, I swipe to answer.

"Are you okay? I'm at work. What's wrong?"

There's a chance she just forgot I work on Saturdays, but it's unlikely. Maddi almost always texts instead of calling, like everyone else under fifty. So I'm not surprised to hear some kind of chaos in the background of the call and a tremble in her voice when she speaks, even if she's trying to hide it.

"Silas, can you please come to the trailer?" she asks.

I hear the distant sound of Kris—their mom—yelling, but it doesn't sound like she's yelling at the girls. I'd be surprised if she was. She's been doing so well lately keeping her drinking and narcotics in check, we thought she'd really turned over a new leaf.

Well, I had. Cade still isn't convinced, but he's tougher to crack.

As soon as I hear a deeper voice in the background as well, the pieces fall into place.

Maddi, are you calling the goddamn cops?

He's far away, but I can tell he's bellowing the words.

"Hurry, please, Silas," she whispers into the phone before pulling her mouth away to yell at the voice. "Yes! So you can get out of here before they show up."

"I'm on my way. If he lays a finger on any of you, call the cops for real. I don't care what Cade says. I'll be there in ten minutes."

I'm already running to grab my keys from behind the counter, so I barely catch it when she'd cut off halfway through saying 'hurry' again.

Fuck.

For a millisecond, I debate just calling 911 myself. But Cade would kill me.

It has to be their dad. He hasn't shown up since that one time Cade and I kicked him out almost a year ago, back before we were even together, but I know it used to happen a lot more. He still owns the property on paper and Kris never bothered with a protective order—or maybe she didn't have grounds for one, I'm not sure about the details—so it's hard to kick him out if he's not getting physical with them.

And Cade is convinced that any attention from social services, even if it's not their fault, is only pushing the girls closer to getting put in foster care. I would argue that they're in a very different situation now than last year, especially since Kris started working through the action steps or whatever the social worker gave her after the last incident, but I know he'd still lose his shit.

I can't make him feel that kind of fear if I don't have to. The trailer isn't far, I can at least see what's happening first. Last time, Cade was the only one the man seemed willing to get physical with, content to just yell at and intimidate the girls.

I'm jogging to my truck when I feel a hand on my shoulder and flinch away. Ford is behind me, holding his hands up.

"Do you want me to come?" he signs.

For a second, I consider saying yes. He's fucking huge and scary-looking, and could definitely take Cade's dad in a fight. But I can't be responsible for the shop getting robbed because we both bailed, and I can't wait for him to lock up.

I'm an adult. They're my family, too.

I can protect them.

"It's okay. I'll call the cops if he's really on a tear. Can you text Cade—no, wait, don't. Let me see what's going on and then I'll call him. Or I'll call you if I need help. I'll... fuck. I'll figure it out."

I don't wait for him to reply before jumping in the truck and turning the engine.

I can protect them. I'll figure it out.

When I pull up to the trailer, I don't think I even turn the engine off. I just throw it in park with the handbrake on and run for the door. There's still yelling, but not crashing and screaming, so my heart rate eases up just an iota.

The noise that the door makes when I yank it open makes me wince, because I think that might have been the final death knell in us needing to replace the damn thing, but I can worry about that later. Inside, I find kind of what I was expecting, kind of not.

"Silas!"

Sky runs for me as soon as she sees me. She looks like she's been crying, but she isn't right now, and seems content to throw herself into my arms. I hoist her up until she's balanced on one hip with her arms looped around my neck, even though she's getting a little too big for it at ten years old, and keep my eyes on everyone else.

Maddi is moving towards me slowly. Her phone is in her hand, but I think the screen is broken. Her face is set in anger, gray eyes flashing precipitously, just the way Cade's do, and it makes her look more like him than ever. She's fourteen now, and every day she looks more and more like her brother, somehow.

She keeps moving steadily until she's standing next to me, and I take a step forward to put her behind me, feeling her fingers tangle in the back of my shirt for comfort once I do.

Of course, the person here who looks the most like Cade is Kyle.

The one and only time I met him, I was amazed how similar they seem. The same lean but muscular build, the exact same perma-tanned skin tone and dark, perpetually messy hair. The same slate-gray eyes and high cheekbones.

But where Cade's all combine to make him look like a model who got lost in the discount section of a Dollar Tree, Kyle looks gaunt. Still strong enough to be intimidating, but with that thin-skin-stretched-over-bone thing that you get from too much meth and not enough decent food. His eyes have a hint of crazy to them, of course, and his fingers are twitchy with uncontrollable anxious energy.

He was pacing the living room and smoking a cigarette when I walked in, but now he's frozen in place, taking in the sight of me, the intruder, with his daughters in hand.

"Who the fuck are you?" he asks, his voice hoarse.

"Go get in my truck and lock the doors."

Sky makes a sound of protest when I put her back on her feet, but Maddi grabs her hand and hauls her through the door. I plant myself in front in case Kyle makes a run for them, but he stays still, continuing to focus on me.

At least that probably means he didn't come for them. I know an abrupt custody battle for some perceived value has always been one of Cade's biggest fears.

"Kris?"

I don't know what I'm asking her. I guess I'm trying to figure out what's going on.

Cade's mom is standing in the corner, also smoking a cigarette. She looks upset and a little mussed, but not visibly bruised and about as sober as she always is, as far as I can tell. That seems like a good sign.

She sighs like she's trying to expel so much breath from her lungs that they'll never refill themselves again.

"Get out, Kyle. We don't want you here. See?"

Kyle scoffs. "Is this your new boy toy or something?"

I wrinkle my nose without thinking, because no thank you, and Kris lets out a humorless laugh.

"Just get out. You know what Cade'll do when he sees you. I don't know what you thought was gonna happen. You fuck off all these times and then when you need a place to squat, we're what? Just supposed to roll the red carpet out for you and your skank?"

What?

"Watch who you're calling skank, lady. I didn't come here to start a fight but I'll rip that hair out of your head if I have to."

It takes me a second to figure out where the new voice is coming from. I take a step slightly deeper inside, and realize the person was tucked away in a corner so I couldn't see her.

She's rail thin, just like Kyle, but clearly closer to my age than his. Yikes. She has light blonde hair and pale skin showing under a lot of bronzey makeup, and I can't quite figure out if her short but willowy stature—highlighted by super-skinny jeans and a fleece-lined bomber jacket—makes her look delicate or tough.

Tough, I decide. Like battered steel: thin but durable. The bored expression on her face tells me this isn't her first time in a weird, conflict-heavy situation as well. Which is understandable, I guess. This is no one's first time. I'd also be bored if I weren't so invested in the outcome.

"What's going on?" I ask again, still confused about why Kyle's here.

"I'm still waiting to hear who the fuck you are, that's what."

Kyle stalks up to me as he says it, emanating aggressive energy, his movements loose and his hands out, making his implicit threat as obvious as possible.

I'm not a fighter. Not like Cade. I don't have that inherent anger in me that he constantly struggles to control.

But I do know a lot about men like this, considering I was also raised by one. My dad was less physical and more of a drunk, if that's possible, but still. I know right now that if I let him think he has intimidated me, he'll run with it.

And even if I still feel young and small most of the time, I don't look it. Not to people who don't know me.

I take a firm step forward into his space until we're eye to eye. I don't reach for him, but I hold myself strong, close enough to him that my nostrils burn with the acrid scent of his cigarette. He stares at me defiantly for a few seconds, trying to decide if he's going to fight me, I assume, and then it seems to click.

He remembers me. He was more fucked up last time he was here, but it looks like he remembers me tackling him into that counter hard enough to crack it before dragging his ass out of here with Cade's help.

"This is still my house. You don't belong here," he says with a growl.

We're going in fucking circles.

"It's my house, you asshole, where I live while raising your goddamn children!"

Kris stalks over to both of us as she yells in a hoarse voice, grabbing Kyle by the t-shirt and hauling him away from me with a surprising amount of strength. She starts pushing him and hitting his chest in frustration. Not hard enough to do any real damage, but still escalating the situation to a violent place that I don't want it to go.

"Whoa, whoa, whoa," I say, grabbing at Kris and pulling her off him.

She fights my grip on her and curses at me, but doesn't hit me, so that's something, at least. Kyle is staring at her with a predatory expression that I don't fucking care for, and his girl is still leaning against the corner, watching the whole thing go down with a half-smile.

At least she has no interest in defending Kyle. That helps. She pulls a vape out of her pocket and takes a drag, filling the trailer with the sticky-sweet artificial smell of cotton candy, which is gross as hell, but it's better than a brawl.

The tension running through Kyle seems to break abruptly.

"Why you gotta be like this? Why can't you act fucking regular instead of being a crazy bitch all the time? I told you, Kris–" he leans towards her, raising his voice to yell the last part slow and loud like she can't understand him, "I. Just. Need. A. Place. To. Crash."

The patronizing aura pisses me off and it's not even directed at me, so I'm not shocked when she lunges for him again and I have to snag her around the waist.

"Stop. Stop." I pull her back. "He's just trying to get a rise out of you."

Kyle laughs. "We were together for twelve years and that woman was terrible at getting a rise out of me," he says as he grabs his crotch.

I have officially been transported back in time and space into an episode of Jerry Springer. Just... no. No thank you. I decline.

Kris is yelling insults back at him, something involving him cheating on her with prostitutes and STDs that I'm so glad Cade isn't hearing—although he probably heard it the first time it happened, which makes me sad about his childhood all over again. They holler shit over each other, back and forth until I can't make out what either of them is saying, and the other girl seems content to watch them and keep filling the room with cotton-candy-scented vapor.

"Look!" I interrupt. "Kris, do you want to call the cops?"

"No!" All three of them yell it at me in unison like it was scripted, and I take a step back.

"Jeez." I hold my hands up.

I know I could defend them if Kyle was being violent. But apart from his need to square off with me, he's had a manic energy but only really seemed interested in yelling. Kris is the only person getting physical, and he didn't respond with anything but more insults, so maybe that's promising?

Either way, I can't just beat the shit out of the man for no reason. I know I don't have that in me. If he's refusing to leave and Kris won't let me call the cops, I don't know what else I can do.

"Look, it's fine, Silas. Can you just take the girls home with you? I'll deal with this syphilitic piece of shit," Kris says, her hands on her waist.

Kyle snorts like he's laughing and flicks his crushed cigarette butt at her feet, adding yet another burn scar to the threadbare carpet, but doesn't respond otherwise.

"Why don't you come with me? I don't want to leave you here alone."

"Fuck no. It's my goddamn house. I'm not letting him lay around here unsupervised so he can sell anything that's not bolted to the floor."

Not sure she can talk, given her history with pawn shops, but still.

"It's not safe, Kris," I look at her, pleading.

"The Smith & Wesson under my bed would beg to differ." She tosses her hair over her shoulder and arches an eyebrow at her ex-husband. There's a confidence to her stance now, like she's found some sort of equilibrium here.

I know she's lying about the gun. She better be, at least, or Cade will have one more thing to lose his mind over.

Kris turns to look at me, and for a second she lets the false bravado fall and sighs.

"Really, Silas. He's an asshole but he's not here to murder me with a skanky accomplice. This is my mess, let me take care of it. You can help me by getting the girls out of here. They shouldn't have to add more fights witnessed to their shitty childhoods."

I hesitate again. I don't want to go, but I also don't feel like I have the authority to tell Kris what to do in her house. And the girls are probably crying all alone in my truck right now, wondering what's going on.

"Fine," I say, terrified that I'm making the wrong choice. "I'll take them home, but Cade is on his way."

Shit. Actually, I still haven't called him.

"Okay. Go."

She waves me away, and Kyle looks at me with no interest, now that it's clear I'm not going to fight him. Unease sits heavy in my gut as I let myself out, but at least the whole situation felt significantly less like a powder keg.

As soon as I'm outside, I see that I was right and the girls are crying in the truck. Shit. I quickly text Cade 911 asking him to call me as soon as he can and then head for the driver's seat. He probably can't leave shift, but as soon as he's not in the middle of saving someone's life, he should be able to call me and tell me what to do. Because I have no idea what just happened, or if any of what I did even helped.

CHAPTER FOUR

CADE

It was difficult to understand what Silas was saying when I called him back. Which was right away, because while he'd been running around dealing with whatever clusterfuck of drama my family dealt him, I haven't had a goddamn call in hours. The rig is clean, the station is clean, and I've spent the last hour trying to convince Tristan to start a queer EMS workers TikTok account with me, when I could have been fucking helping.

My dad showed up. Silas is taking the girls to our house, and Mom refused to go with him. There was also a random other woman there, but no one knows who she is.

Fuck, fuck, fuck.

I feel dumb as hell for letting myself get complacent. I got wrapped up in doing normal-people shit, and for just a fraction of a second, I forgot that I was trash, and this is what happens when you're trash.

"Whatever it is, we'll take care of it."

Tristan's rational approach to this situation is a lot more comforting than blind optimism would be, at least. He's realistic. He knows there's no instant fix for it and he hates cops almost as much as I do, so I'm glad he offered to come with me. In the past couple of months he's also grown a mustache, which either makes him look like a hot West Hollywood OnlyFans model or a violent beat cop from the seventies, depending on the day. Hopefully, my dad's brain will go the cop route, not the gay route, and be intimidated into leaving.

The duty manager on shift today is chill, thankfully, and she unofficially gave us permission to go check on my mom as long as we stay within our service area and dropped everything like normal if a call came through. It's not technically within the rules, of course, but that's one of the benefits to working someplace small where everyone lives in each other's pockets. It's easier for things to slip through the cracks sometimes.

I really hope we don't get a call until this is resolved, but of course the EMS gods are not going to let me get away with this shit for long.

The cab of the ambulance bounces as we ease up the long gravel path that passes for my driveway. Well, it's not my driveway anymore, I guess, but still. We pull up in front, and I can't see any immediate signs of property damage or destruction. Not like last time, when Dad spent at least half an hour outside yelling shit and throwing anything that wasn't frozen to the ground.

That's a good sign, but I don't get my hopes up. I keep having brief flashes of possibilities run through the foreground of my awareness, and they're all so bad, I can't tease apart which ones are realistic or not anymore.

Maybe he attacked her, and inside there's some horrific, gory nightmare scene that's going to haunt me forever.

Maybe they're getting back together, and they're both going to spiral back into drug abuse until they both OD and I have to fight for custody of Maddi and Sky.

Maybe Silas mistook someone else for my dad, and it's really some fucking debt collector or something here to kidnap my mom and turn her out because she owes money she hasn't told me about.

They're all equally ridiculous and not, at the same time.

My breath is coming in quick, shallow puffs as Tristan and I pile out of the rig and jog toward the door. I can feel his eyes on me, but he doesn't say anything. He puts his hand on my shoulder when I open the door, though, and I try to mentally hang on to that feeling of solidity.

I've never relied on an adult for shit. And Tristan barely qualifies, despite being almost a decade older than me. But right now, the squealing, grasping part of me that doesn't want to face whatever's inside needs that reassurance to lean into.

Inside, it doesn't look like anything I was expecting. The quiet manages to set my nerves on edge even more somehow. I was amped up and thrumming, ready for a fight, and this unsettling level of calm only makes me feel more paranoid that something is deeply wrong.

Mom is in the kitchen, tapping out something on her cell with a cigarette pinched between her first two fingers—the skin there yellow-tinged and leathery from constantly being in this position—and a pile of ash crumbling on the Formica beneath her.

So much for no more smoking in the house.

She doesn't look bruised or anything, which is good, but I still feel like this whole thing is unnatural.

When I look at the worn-out old La-Z-Boy in the corner, I find Dad. He's fully reclined with the footrest out, his ratty boots kicked up on it, a fucking PBR in his hand that he must have brought with him, and—of all things—a girl perched half on the arm, half on his lap.

She looks bored as hell, also holding a PBR and scrolling on her phone. She can't be much older than me, although she looks like life might have dealt her even rougher cards.

In the time it takes him to notice Tristan and I bursting in the door, everyone looking up at us, I also clock his fingers curled around her hip, the pad of his thumb teasing at the hem of her shirt absently. It's an exact mirror of a position I end up in with Silas a lot of the time. We're almost the same size, of course, but Silas still likes to pull me into his lap and fold me up smaller, and I love the sensation of his rough fingertips tracing over the sensitive skin of my hip, dipping lower and lower like a constant tease. The physical feeling of being small and caged just does something to me.

I don't know why, but this weird parallel makes the kindled anger inside of me erupt into a blind rage.

Those are hands that have hurt me, hurt Mom, torn this place apart, and done more drugs and other shit than I can remember, and now he's sitting here with some fucking stranger, doing a sick parody of me and Silas and our actual, healthy fucking relationship.

I want to kill him.

"Get. Out."

I bite the words out but don't wait for a reply before crossing the room toward him and reaching for his shirt. He looks shocked, although I don't know why, considering how many rooms he's been kicked out of in his life. It's easy to get two fistfuls of his shirt and start pulling him up. His beer goes flying in the process. The girl scrambles to get out of the way but ends up on her ass on the floor, which I didn't intend to happen but can't process right now.

All I see is his stupid fucking face. It takes a lot of strength to yank him to his feet, but not as much as I'd expected. EMS work has really strengthened my people-lifting muscles instead of my motocross muscles, and I've been bulking out in ways I didn't expect. I'm not tall enough to get him dangling, but I have caught him off-guard, and that makes satisfaction take up residence at the base of my spine, continuing to fan the flame of my rage.

He doesn't deserve to exist.

Everyone else in the room is squawking behind me, but I'm doing my best to tune them out. I'm here to get rid of the problem, and that's what I'm doing. Dad starts to fight me, pushing against me and cursing. He's tearing at my shirt, but not actually throwing punches, so it's not enough to dislodge my grip.

41

"Cade!" Mom yells behind me, before I feel her deceptively strong hands tugging at my arms.

He's already twisted her back to his side again, I see. Just like the other times.

I take a few steps back towards the door, getting ready to push him through and send him tumbling down the couple of steps onto his ass, but there's something solid in my way.

The thing my back hits must be a person, because thick arms wrap around me from behind and start to squeeze. Not tight enough that I can't breathe, but tight enough to make more adrenaline buzz through me.

"Stop." I hear Tristan's voice, low and steady in my ear. "Stop. Stop. Let him go and take a breath. Stop, Cade."

It doesn't make any sense. He's squeezing me still, while Mom and the woman are both pawing at me, trying to get me to let go of Kyle. I had his ratty old Harley Davidson t-shirt fisted so tightly it must have been choking him out, because his face is beet red now and he's gasping for air.

They pry him out of my hands, both women pulling him away from me with expressions of horror that I don't fully process, but I know will hit me later and it won't be good. Meanwhile, Tristan is still holding me tight, dragging me backwards to increase the distance between me and Kyle. I realize distantly that I'm struggling against Tristan's hold, although I wasn't conscious of it, and another surge of anger takes over my body.

The idea of stopping and letting it all go exists. It almost seems like a physical thing sitting just outside my grasp, small and slippery. I'm reaching for it, but the anger is pulling me under like a riptide so my fingertips can only graze the surface of the thing but never get a grip.

I want to stop. I just... can't.

Plus, I can already feel the prick of shame for my actions waiting for me as soon as I let the anger slip away, and I'm not ready to deal with that yet. Stoking my rage keeps a wall between me and the consequences of my actions, even if it's only the consequence of shame, for another few minutes. It's not a conscious decision, but I'm dimly aware that some part of my mind has made this series of calculations, with or without my input.

I keep pulling against Tristan's grip, but his feet are planted and he's got height, weight and raw strength on me. There's a brief crushing moment where more than one reality layers on top of each other, and I think for a second it's Dad's hands crushing me, not Tristan's. It makes me feel a clench of deep, visceral fear that I haven't experienced since I was much younger, before I try to shake the irrational thought away. It's Tristan, not Dad. And he's helping me, not hurting me.

My skin is prickling hot, and I think I might be crying.

Tristan's still whispering in my ear though, in that same level tone.

"It's okay. I've got you. Just take a breath. Stop. You can stop. You need to breathe."

It doesn't make sense, because I am breathing, but it makes me realize that I'm taking gasping, ragged breaths for no reason. I concentrate on that, because the rest of the world seems hazy and more confusing than it did a minute ago. There's a flicker of an image in my mind of that stupid app. The breathing one, where it has a shape that sort of crumples and re-expands like a paper bag while it counts your respirations.

Slowly, the blinding, overwhelming need to get to Kyle and break his fucking face recedes. It slips out of my body like water, leaving my insides feeling damp and heavy, void of anything of substance, already beginning to rot. I can breathe normally again, and the feeling of Tristan pressing in on me from every angle is helping me keep the last few flickers of anger caged until they extinguish.

Tristan eases his grip on me a little, and for a second I wish he wouldn't. I can already see the torrent of things I have to deal with on the other side of this moment and I don't want to, but there's nothing I can do to stop it. Instead, I try to make myself feel numb and focus on the situation at hand, instead of whatever fucking emotional bukkake situation just happened in my brain.

When I'm finally standing on my own, Tristan watching me with careful eyes, I have an overwhelming urge to sit down. He puts a hand on my chest to steady me, which doesn't actually fucking help. Everyone is staring at me now, with some mixture of concern and annoyance, and the embarrassment and confusion is bubbling through me quickly, leaving an acid-trail of agony in its wake.

"You good?" Tristan asks me, still the only true calm one in the room.

Before I can answer though, my mom stalks back across the room.

"What the hell are you doing?"

Mom and I yell at each other a lot. We never throw hands, we just communicate via yelling. This isn't any different. She's a few feet away from me, hands on her hips, cigarette long-abandoned, her voice raised and her temper up but nothing out of the ordinary for a heated moment or just... a random Tuesday.

So, I don't know why it makes me want to fold in on myself until I no longer exist. Maybe it's because Kyle is standing behind her, staring at me with a mixture of irritation and smugness that I'm intimately familiar with, and I feel like the biggest fool in the world for ever assuming I was past the point in my life where my parents would gang up on me.

I swallow down the sudden urge to throw up and fish around for the tail end of that anger I just worked so hard to get rid of before I completely melt down in front of everybody.

"What am I doing? What are you doing? Why is he here and why am I and Silas the only people who seem fucking concerned about this?"

I spit the words at her, half expecting Tristan to pull me back again but faintly relieved when he doesn't. At least he trusts me that much.

"I knew you were going to come in here hissing and cussing, I didn't think you'd start fighting the second you walked inside. This is why I told Silas to let me deal with it myself. The last thing this place needs is more fucking testosterone."

I turn around and throw my hands up in the air, unable to look at her for a second.

"I can't believe Silas left you. You've been alone with Kyle for what? Forty minutes? And all of a sudden it's a decade ago and we're all supposed to pretend like he's not a piece of shit who's only here to squeeze you for something."

It's impossible not to point at him as I say it, which makes Dad bristle and take a step towards me. Mom throws her hand back up, though, planting herself firmly in between us.

She looks so different, all of a sudden. Confident and sure. It's not like she's ever stood in between him and me before when it mattered, so the fact that she finally finds a backbone now and he's the one she chooses to stand up for is so goddamn infuriating I want to tear myself open, spraying blood and viscera all over the room until everyone else is just as disgusted as I am.

"You're pathetic."

They're not the words I want to say. Those words are a lot more complex and make me sound a lot more pitiful, but I couldn't even begin to squeeze them out of my chest, so I settle for lashing out instead. Mom looks startled, hurt flashing in her eyes even though it's far from the worst thing I've ever called her.

Maybe it hits different when you're sober. When we've been getting along so well lately. I said it specifically to hurt her, so I don't know why I feel worse as soon as I see it hits my target.

"Cade, I think we should go."

Tristan crowds me again, pushing me towards the door, but I refuse to move.

"Not until someone tells me what's happening. Why is he here?"

"Oh, so now you're gonna let me talk? I thought you only wanted to come in here like a big swinging dick, showing everyone what a man you are."

Even the sound of his voice is like sandpaper on the inside of my skull, but I force myself to stay quiet while he speaks.

"There's a bench warrant out for me in Arkansas. It's total bullshit, obviously. The woman I was seeing found out I was cheating on her and ran to the cops with some fucked-up story saying I've been beating on her."

My heart clenches, because of course this is what's happening.

He looks me in the eye and points at me as he continues. "I ain't. She's a fucking liar. I've been cleaning up my act, like I told Kris. I didn't lay a fucking finger on that bitch."

I close my eyes, shaking my head because this cannot be my life right now.

"It's true," Mom says, interrupting my thoughts. "I called your cousin, and River says the girl already admitted she made it up. She just wanted to run him out of town. She's bragging to everybody who'll listen about it, apparently."

I can't help but sigh again. "Okay, so? How is this my problem?"

"I just need a place to stay out of state for a while, until I get my shit together. I got some money coming my way and a line on a couple other things. I'm just looking to crash and this is still my home. You can't turn me out."

"Watch me," I say, my anger rising again until Mom interrupts.

"We were in the middle of making a deal when you crashed in here like the lone ranger. If I help let him stay here while he gets this taken care of, he'll work on paying the child support he owes me. It's not like the state's been able to squeeze anything out of him all these years, he's too good at hiding and immediately spending whatever he makes. I'd rather deal with the devil myself if they're going to fuck around like this. Besides, he thinks he can get the whole thing thrown out because she's already bragging about it being a lie, and he just wants to wait it out. It won't take long."

"This is insane, you realize that," I say, but everyone's staring at me like I'm the crazy one. Except Tristan, who's giving me that grim expression of sympathy he saves for occasions like this.

"Yeah well, I could use the child support." Mom looks at me, her whole demeanor still set, like this is something she thought through. "It'll be a week, tops. Then he'll go back. Maddi and Sky can stay with you, can't they?"

"What, so you're just going to stay here with him and his... I'm sorry, who the fuck are you?" I ask the other woman, who's been watching this whole thing impassively, still scrolling on her phone and occasionally taking drags of a sickly-sweet scented vape.

"Krystal," she says. "With a K."

Awesome.

Dad steps in front of her like he's being protective, which is so ridiculous I almost laugh out loud.

"She's a friend of mine. I needed some help with gas money, because I left on the fly. That's all."

"And how long have you two known each other? If you're close enough to be road-trip buddies?"

Krystal glances at Dad for a second, but I can immediately tell that she doesn't care enough to lie for him. Instead, she shrugs as she looks back at me.

"A day or two."

Perfect. Absolutely perfect. I have absolutely no doubt that he drove around town without two nickels to rub together, convinced this poor fucking sex worker to fund his getaway, and promised her nothing but cash and cocaine as soon as they arrived.

"Kris and Krystal. I love that for you. You're friends with a lot of hookers, are you, Dad?"

"Hey!" Krystal's gaze snaps up to meet mine, her eyes narrowing.

I immediately feel guilty again, because I actually have a lot of respect for hookers. But apparently today is the day I turn into the worst possible version of myself.

With a fucking phenomenal amount of effort, I try to release the tension running through me. My success is limited.

"And what if I call the cops right now?"

"You wouldn't," Mom says. "You wouldn't risk the girls like that."

"Me? I'm not the one putting them in harm's way. Maybe social services should know who you think is fit to be around them."

Dad steps forward again, and then tension shoots straight back up towards maximum.

"I'm their goddamn father. No court ever told me I couldn't see them. I stayed away out of respect for your mother's wishes—" I snort, because that's a fucking lie, but whatever. "—but if I want to come back here I can, and the fact that you've turned into a goddamn narc since I left tells me maybe they do need their father's influence around. Your great-great-granddaddy didn't make the best moonshine around for half his life just so you could grow up to run to social services every time you get your tender fucking feelings hurt. I always knew you were a weak kid, but jeez. Grow some balls."

That's it. I move towards him again, but I'd forgotten that Tristan is still next to me, and he easily reaches out and snags me back.

"Okay, this has officially become unproductive. Cade, we're leaving. We're going to deal with this later in some sort of controlled setting when we're not both technically on shift."

I want to fight him, but at this point, the thought of not being here is also really fucking appealing. I soften just enough to let Tristan drag me toward the door.

He pauses before pushing me through, looking at Krystal and my mom.

"I know I'm a stranger here, and I'm not trying to butt in, but are you two sure you're comfortable being here with him? Even if this one warrant really is bullshit, from everything I've heard, there are plenty of other times that weren't. And there are a lot of ways he could have been abusing her that didn't involve a physical beating." He looks at my mom for a second. "It's not too late to change your mind." She shakes her head, still looking sure of herself, so Tristan shifts his gaze to Krystal. "If you want a ride, we can take you to a bus station now and get you the fare back to Arkansas. Not a problem."

Krystal shrugs, still perfecting her air of nonchalance.

"I'm fine."

"Suit yourself. Offer's still on the table if you rethink it later. Right, kid. We're leaving."

I open my mouth, because I feel like I should be objecting, although I'm not sure why.

"Is that the sound of our tones? Shit, we gotta go."

There's absolute silence and I definitely would have noticed if we got a call, but he says it anyway as he opens the door and somewhat indelicately shoves me through it. Not hard enough for me to stumble, but hard enough to make a point.

We trudge toward the ambulance in silence. Tristan pats me on the back one more time before I climb in, which makes me realize I was subconsciously worried he was mad at me and now I'm relieved he's not, as pathetic as that is.

Once he turns on the engine, I expect him to say something. To berate me about my behavior or give me a lecture or something. He loves to give me lectures. Instead, he just drives.

He drives slower than usual back to the station. The cab is silent apart from the sound of our breathing—Tristan's deep and even, while mine is still erratic and shallow.

It's all over, and I should feel better. Instead, I manage to feel worse and more stressed out by the second. I'm not sure why. I try to wrap my head around what just happened and why it's bothering me so much more than all the other shitfest incidents that have gone down in that trailer, but I can't.

It doesn't make any sense. Especially considering this is one of the first ones I've had any help for.

By the time we pull into the station, there still hasn't been a call. The EMS gods have blessed my meltdown, apparently. I feel scattered and useless, and I'm still waiting for Tristan to speak. To scold me, I assume. He turns off the engine and drums his fingers on the wheel for a minute, but still doesn't say anything or make a move to get out.

I start speaking without meaning to, with no conscious idea of what I'm saying, and my voice is already coming out croaky and raw.

"Mom changed a lot after Maddi and then Sky were born. I don't know if it was because three kids makes it feel more like a family, or because she cared more about protecting girls, or what. But it definitely pissed Dad off more, while she tried a little harder to do Mom shit, when she could. Still got fucked up a lot, but she tried. Fewer week-long benders, no more parties at the trailer with her creepy fucking friends."

I clear my throat, but it doesn't help. I lean forward, looking at my hands slung between my knees instead of at Tristan.

"When it was just me, I think it was easier for them. One kid was more like a pet than a family. It was easier to leave me somewhere when they wanted to go party, or drag me along with them, or just have people over whenever. I was always talkative and I'd do normal kid stuff, which would make them laugh, so they'd have me hang out with them and their friends a lot like some kind of entertainment.

"One time we were at their friends' house in the afternoon. They were fucked up but not like... Not terrible. I was playing with some shitty toy Nana had bought me that was a policeman kit or something. It had a plastic badge and a fake orange gun and some little handcuffs with a plastic key. I don't know how, but I managed to handcuff myself to the staircase. To one of the wooden bannister things. I got upset, because I was eight or something and I was stuck. Mom came over acting like she was going to help me.

"She was all caring and it made me feel better, then out of nowhere, she pulled out a goddamn butter knife. It was literally just a butter knife, it might have even been made out of plastic, I don't remember. But she tells me that there's no key and the only way to free me is to cut off my hand, and immediately starts pretending to saw at my wrist with this stupid knife. I start bawling because I think she's telling the truth, she's holding my hand still and pretending to saw while cackling like it's the funniest thing she's ever seen, everybody else in the room is laughing, my dad is dancing around behind her making fun of me for crying."

There's a long pause. I don't really know where I was going with the story. I was so worked up before, but right now I don't feel much of anything and apart from the rawness in my voice, the words come out evenly.

When I do look up, Tristan is looking at me and nodding. Not with pity, thank god, although I don't know if he really contains pity. But like he gets it. I nod back.

"It's not fair," he says.

I keep nodding. "I'm sorry. I was all geared up to have to get him off her or something like normal, when they were suddenly on the same side again, I think it threw me a little. I didn't mean to lose it."

"Don't worry about it now. We can talk about it later once things have settled. Unfortunately, we still have the rest of a shift to get through, and there'll be plenty of time for psychoanalyzing."

He opens his door and hops out, moving around to my side and opening the passenger door for me when I don't do it myself. I unbuckle myself slowly and climb out of the cab like it's ten-thousand feet off the ground and my body is made of cotton wool, everything about me clumsy and thick.

When I'm on the ground, there's another pause while I don't know what to do with myself.

"You need a hug?" Tristan asks, so I know I must really look like shit.

"No," I lie.

He sees through it and hugs me anyway, halfway in between a bro hug and something more familial. It's not the same as Silas, which is who I really want to be near right now, but it makes me feel less overwhelmed for a few seconds. When he lets me go, he slaps me on the back hard enough to get me moving back toward the door of the station.

"Come on. You can take a minute to check in on Silas and the girls, and then I'm sure I have plenty of tedious cleaning you can do until the shift is over that will keep you occupied. No need to think about anything at all until the day is over. Got it?"

"Sure."

We walk inside together, and I can already feel my brain shutting off all the memories from today that it can.

CHAPTER FIVE

SILAS

"When's Cade coming home?" Sky asks, trying and mostly failing to keep the worry out of her voice.

"He can't come back until his shift is over. He's not still at the trailer, he's just working. I promise."

Sky seems to relax, but Maddi is staring at her plate, pretending to pick at the food. I'm already apprehensive about the point when Sky gets old enough that she isn't easily reassured, either.

Guilt creeps in, all over again. These moments I feel like I should be helping to raise them, and raising other people just isn't something I'm equipped to do. I tried to raise myself and it was a disaster, I don't have any business trying to help living children build their own brains correctly. I can keep them safe. I can keep them fed and refrain from the kind of emotionally unstable behavior that their real parents are so prone to. But that's as far as it goes.

"Do you want something else to eat?" I ask Maddi, because the very boring chicken and vegetables that I made from shit in the freezer doesn't seem to be doing it for her.

It's a subject change. I'm not proud of it, but I'm flailing a little here.

"No. I'm gonna go watch TV."

No eye contact, her hand already reaching for her phone.

"Come on, Maddi. You have to eat something. And not just Cheez-Its. What about a baked potato?"

Carbs are the way to Cade's heart, it's worth trying with his sisters once in a while.

She raises an eyebrow but finally looks me in the eye.

"You're going to get in the kitchen and bake me a potato?"

I pause. "Well, I was going to microwave you a potato. And then put some shit on it. It tastes just as good."

Now they both snort.

"We don't trust what you say tastes good, Silas. You love vegetables too much. It's weird as fuck," Sky says.

Her over-aged potty mouth is as active as usual, but I'm used to it now. I think she just likes to copy Cade, and I get it.

A sigh slips out of me, because Sky's food is mostly untouched as well, now that I'm looking. She's fidgeting in her chair, shifting her weight from side to side as she looks around the room more than she needs to.

I swear, their entire family is chronically over- and under-stimulated at the same time, all the time.

I huff a little, and then remind myself I'm supposed to be making them feel better, not more stressed. Sitting at the table in the quiet is apparently too much for them.

"Okay, how about you guys go pick something to watch, and I'll make you some better food. But it will still have vegetables on it, and you have to at least pretend to eat them. We can eat in front of the TV. Deal?"

Sky nods imperiously, and Maddi even smiles a little. They both slip out of their chairs before I was even finished talking.

Cooking distracts me from worrying about Cade, at least. Well, mostly.

I know he went to the trailer and then left, and Kris is still choosing to stay there. I know he was planning to finish out the rest of the shift, even though I asked him not to. He's going to be a walking disaster-human. Of course, he won't admit it. I just hope the rest of the shift goes smoothly.

Eventually, I manage to focus enough to finish the food. I cut up all that chicken and veg, threw it on the microwaved potatoes and then added a bunch of cheese and melted it. Seems like a reasonable compromise, right?

Sky and Maddi both accept their plates when I head back into the living room and join them on the couch. They have *Heartstopper* on, which I only recognize because Wish got them a Netflix subscription for Christmas last year, so they've made me watch it more than once. I think they just have limited things to watch, but they insist it's part of some critical cultural development that I missed out on.

Both of them, like Cade, refuse to accept that I'm not really a TV person.

When the front door opens, all three of us tense in unison. A matching gut reaction, forged in pretty similar experiences.

"Yo!" Cade yells to us, and I can see Maddi and Sky both unclench. Maddi stays on the couch, staring at her phone and trying to school the tension out of her face, while Sky bounds up to meet him when he walks in the room.

His boots are off but his uniform is still on, including his coat, when he appears in the doorway. He has a big smile that I immediately recognize as fake, and he makes a big show of scooping Sky up into his arms when she runs to him.

"You took forever to get home, asshole," she says, and her voice is haughty but she's clinging to him with the mannerisms of a much younger child.

"Charming," he says. "What a welcome."

He strokes her hair before kissing the top of her head, but then puts her down with a muffled groan.

"I was out saving lives and doing very important things. You should be calling me a hero, instead of lying around here eating all my food."

He says it as he leads Sky back to the couch and collapses in between his sisters, and he's clearly joking, but that doesn't stop Maddi from tensing again. There's an unspoken fear that maybe he means it, I think, and the mood in the room sours a little further.

"You okay, squirt?" Cade asks Maddi in a softer voice. Sky is already snuggling down into the crook of his arm, but he still leans over to kiss her on the top of the head, as well.

"How was it?" she asks, not acknowledging his question.

"The trailer?" There's a flash of emotion in Cade's eyes before he shoves it back down again, and I worry more than before. He's too cheerful, it's too forced. "It was fine. Normal. They're gonna do whatever the fuck they're gonna do, and we are all going to hang out here and have nothing to do with it until he leaves. Cool?"

She sighs. "I need my school stuff. So does Sky."

"We can get it in the morning. My shift doesn't start until later. I'll drive you both to school, and we can swing by the trailer on the way. You can stay in the car while I grab your stuff. Does that work?"

"You're just going to fight with him and get hurt if you do that."

Maddi won't look at him, but she does glance at me for a second. Probably because she knows I'm thinking the same thing.

"Can you go instead?" she asks me.

"I can—" I start, before Cade immediately cuts me off.

"You start work at 6 a.m., dude. You'd have to do all this driving to get there and back and still get to work on time, it doesn't make sense."

"I can ask Ford to be late, it's not a big deal."

Cade rolls his eyes at me, which I find way more annoying than I should.

"Dude, it's fine. Don't miss work over it. I will go. Dad will be passed out on the couch, if he's home at all, and I will just slip in and grab their stuff. It's no big deal."

"Yeah but you shouldn't have to—"

"I said no!" He doesn't quite shout when he cuts me off for a second time, but he's getting there. Anger is roiling underneath the surface, trying it's best to peek out, and I can see this getting worse the more I push. "I don't want you in there alone with him. It's not worth it."

It's not safe, is the unspoken implication here.

I can't stop that a little warmth spreads through me, knowing how much he cares about me. But the rest of me is settling into annoyance.

"I'm bigger than both of you, and I'm the only one who isn't going to start a fight for no reason."

"Silas," he says, tilting his head and looking at me with wide eyes and a down-turned mouth. "Please. Just don't."

Sky is silent, still clinging to her brother's side but looking increasingly upset. Maddi is frozen, trapped between Cade and I as we talk and doing her best impression of a statue. I want to blow all this intensity out of the room, for all of our sakes, but I don't know how. The TV has kept playing along in the background, all that wholesome earnestness seeming like a ridiculous contrast to our shitty fucking lives.

I blow out a long, slow breath and work my fingers over the material of my jeans, trying to ground myself.

"Fine. Okay. How about you guys go to your room, though? Cade needs to shower and eat."

Sky shakes her head sharply, fisting his jacket like a toddler. Maddi looks at me disparagingly.

"But the show!" she says, pointing.

"Yeah, the show!" Cade joins in, raising his eyebrows at me. "I'm fine. I'm not going anywhere, we can chill."

I turn back to look at the screen, not saying anything.

"You can also chill," he tells me. Not in a mean way, though. Like he means it. "Come here, though. I didn't get the chance to say hello before I got tackled by the monster that lives under my bed."

"Hey!" Sky protests, but she's trying not to laugh.

He sticks his tongue out at her, and it makes me laugh a little as well.

I stand up, moving to his knees and then bending over. He lifts his chin to kiss me, but I catch it in my hand, holding him still for a moment while I look him in the eye.

"Hello," I say. I don't know what I mean by it, but I mean something.

"Hi." He's already breathy, like he always gets when I manhandle him a little. Then he smiles at me–all goofy and shit, as he would say–before I close the distance between us for a very PG kiss.

"Gross. Can't you do that somewhere else?"

Cade gasps dramatically.

"Selective homophobia! We're literally all sitting here together watching boys kiss on TV!" he says, turning to laugh at his sister as she glowers at him.

"TV kissing and real-life kissing are two very different things. One's cute, the other has saliva. I don't need to ever see either of you with spit on your mouths again, thank you. It's nasty."

I can't help but laugh quietly as Cade looks a little shocked.

"Well, I gotta say I'm a little happy you're so anti-saliva. It's very hard for someone to get knocked up without exchanging any fluids, so you can keep this attitude as long as you want, as far as I'm concerned." He nudges her elbow with his, smiling. "I'm not going to stop kissing Silas, though. You can learn to live with it. At least we let you put on something other than Home Shopping or the fucking Real Wives of Sheboygan."

Maddi snorts. "Yeah, you're a real prince. I'll be sure to mention you in my prayers for your great sacrifice."

She's dry and prickly about it, shifting away from Cade. I swear she gets funnier every day, even though I'm not exactly an expert on comedy. It makes me worried, though. I can tell that she's upset about shit. Maybe all the time. And cracking dark jokes is about all she's willing to do to let it out.

58

It's not my place to say anything, I always thought. But maybe I should. Cade is amazing with them, but I can't keep relying on him to take care of everyone all the time.

"Did you eat?" I ask Cade, always the master of the subject change.

"No, I came straight home. Don't worry though, I'll get something."

He starts to get up, but I can see how pale and exhausted he looks.

"Sit, Cade. You just finished your shift, I've been home all afternoon. I'll get you some food."

I turn and move toward the kitchen, before Cade shouts after me, "Something with carbs, right?"

"Vegetables are a carb, Cade."

"Aw man, don't try to trick me, robot boy," he shouts loud enough that I can hear him from the kitchen.

I smile, but don't answer, pulling another potato out of the bag to put in the microwave.

"Do you think Maddi's doing okay?" I ask Cade later as we're crawling into bed.

He stills, crinkling his eyebrows for a minute before turning to look at me.

"Yeah? I mean, why wouldn't she be? She seems normal to me."

The words I want to use aren't really coming, so it takes a second to piece together what I want to say. Cade takes advantage of the moment to burrow down further under the comforter and press his face directly into my armpit like a brat.

"She seems sad."

It's all I can come up with, in the end. Cade also takes a long time to think before he answers.

"We're all sad, man. It's sad. She'll be okay, though. She's tough."

"I don't know if that's a good thing. Sometimes people can get too tough. Take on everything themselves, always pretend that they're fine until they eventually break down."

I've wrapped my arm around the back of his head so I can tease at the hair falling over his face while I talk. He was leaning into it, but as soon as he gets the picture of what I'm saying, he freezes.

"Are we still just talking about Maddi?" he asks, his body stiff.

"We're just talking, Cade. Sometimes I worry."

He huffs a little, his breath warm on my skin, and shakes his head against me.

"That's the point, Silas. You shouldn't have to worry about this stuff. I have everything taken care of. Everything's fine. All you need to do is focus on yourself."

Irritation prickles through me, but I don't move. If I sit up and try to look at him, I have a suspicion this conversation will pretty much immediately turn into a fight.

"It's not all on you though, Cade, that's what I'm saying. I'm okay, I don't need you to spend all your time tiptoeing around me and protecting me from thinking about anything. I care about Maddi, I'm allowed to worry about her. I can handle like... experiencing emotions other than numbness. I'm fine."

Cade snorts, muttering his words into my skin so I can barely make them out.

"Yeah, like you were fine yesterday?"

I know he doesn't want me to respond, otherwise he would have said it louder, But I can't stop myself from tensing before letting out a long, frustrated sigh.

"I'm fine now. I get weird sometimes but it passes. I'm still a fucking person."

Cade doesn't say anything, instead tipping his head up to look at me, the edges of his cheekbones shining nearly blue in the moonlight. He looks ethereally beautiful, as always. Like a Rembrandt or something.

"You're *my* person, robot boy. Don't forget it."

My heart quivers, and all that quiet anger that was building in me dissipates. I lean down to press my lips against his, and his expression quickly smoothes out into something relaxed.

No one says anything after that. We continue to hold each other, content to be close in the dark until we drift off.

It isn't until sleep is pulling me under that I realize he never really answered any of my questions, and we still had a conversation without anything real being said.

CHAPTER SIX

CADE

S ilas was right, I should have called out. This shift is a dumpster fire.

I would hate to have left Tristan alone, though. I mean, they would have replaced me, but it's not the same as someone you work with all the time. You need to be able to work without speaking sometimes, and predict each other's moves.

I could be at home right now. I could be sulking in the darkness of my own miserable bedroom, contemplating its history of attempted infanticide and possibly day drinking until these things mattered less. Instead, here I am, less than six hours into a twenty-four hour goddamn shift—because mandatory overtime is a thing, and I have foolishly said before that I like the long shifts and the pay bonuses they include—and I'm already fucking exhausted.

At least it's a Friday, and Jaz agreed to take the girls for the weekend so they're not stuck at the house while me and Silas are working. I'll be here until noon tomorrow at least, and he does a stupid early and stupid long shift at the garage on Saturdays, so they'd be unattended and bored for most of the day.

We've had four—*FOUR*—overdoses already, which means there's probably a bad batch of fentanyl doing the rounds. We've also been called to a bar fight at 11 a.m., and seen multiple frequent flyers. They've all been short runs so far, but that just means the mountain of paperwork for the shift is getting higher and higher and I'm already losing track of how many patients we've seen.

Just when we were thinking about eating, we got another call, so I'm going into it cranky and hungry. Which isn't ideal.

I'm aware of it, though, so that's better than nothing. Although once we pull up at the address, I realize it's not even close to enough. My irritation is already bristling right beneath the surface, begging to be unleashed in the most unprofessional way possible, and I haven't even seen what's happening yet.

"You alright there, killer?" Tristan says as we're getting out of the ambulance and unloading our shit.

His tone is half-mocking, half-real concern, so I must be giving off some terrible fucking vibes already. I pause for a second, taking a breath and attempting to let my muscles unclench.

"Yeah," I say with a shake of my head. "Just... Y'know. This."

Tossing my head in the direction of the house as I say it, Tristan nods back. He gets it. This is an incredibly frustrating family that we've been called out to again and again. Their son Jaden is eleven years old and has a history of mysterious neurological symptoms, including seizures. Probably childhood epilepsy that will resolve on its own, but possibly not. The worst part of cases like this is that there are different kinds of seizures, and that throws people sometimes when it doesn't look like what they've always been told what a "seizure" looks like.

Which means he could be having seizures a lot more frequently than his parents—and therefore his doctors—are aware of.

His parents are trying. Kind of. Mom cares; Dad seems unconvinced because he's not having full-on grand mals all the time. They do take him to the doctor, but money is tight. Et cetera, et cetera, et cetera. We all know the story. Hell, I've lived the story.

Which should probably make me more empathetic, but instead it just makes me fucking pissed. Every time his dad shrugs at me like I'm making too big a deal over something because *he* can't see what's going on, or every time we have a conversation about follow up that I know they can't afford to do, or just won't, it chips away at another little piece of my patience.

Apparently I'm not doing a good enough job of relaxing, because Tristan walks past me, taking over as lead into the house, and manages to smack me unnecessarily hard with his jump bag in the process.

Point taken.

The scene inside is the same as usual. Jaden is on the couch, lying flat. His mom is next to him; Dad hovering nearby. Everyone looks sort of gray and drained, and it's something I feel acutely as well. Tristan immediately takes over, which I'm grateful for, because his voice is a blur of sound.

The scene seems to run into all the other ones we've had here. I do my part; taking vitals and following directions, but apart from that, I'm checked out. I also do everything I can to avoid looking at Jaden's dad, because whenever I do, the level of fury that rises up to choke me is completely disproportionate to the situation.

Jaden has dark hair and pale skin, making him look even more washed out when he's not feeling well. He accepts all our poking and prodding with a practiced kind of stoicism. His brown eyes and set expression is serious, even while his parents seem more focused on bickering with us and each other than actually giving him any support. The sound of their voices is a constant nagging hum in the background that I can't get rid of, so I focus my attention on the child, trying to make him as comfortable as possible.

My heart squeezes, and I'm overcome by a wave of empathy. That doesn't happen a lot while I'm working. I'm generally good at staying detached, even on the really sad cases like little kids, especially with Tristan's experience and support behind me. But this one just fucking gets to me every time.

He reminds me a little of Maddi, so serious and calm. Like a little adult in a tiny body. Except I can't really picture her or Sky in his place, because no matter how little money we had, they always, always had some fucking emotional support and affection. I made sure of it. If one of them were here, I would be sitting with them and comforting them, not arguing about it.

I'm lucky I was a healthy kid at that age, despite everything. Things could have been a lot different for me.

Time passes, and it's when Tristan is explaining his recommendations to the parents—trying to get them to come in just to be safe, while we all know there's just no way they can afford it and the money would probably be better spent on other things—I realize what it is that's getting to me.

He doesn't remind me of Maddi. He reminds me of Silas. I don't have that many memories of him at this age, because off the track he was pretty much a ghost anywhere he went, and I was already friends with all the other burnouts back in junior high. But I do remember this aspect of him. He was quiet and soft, gravely serious and totally alone, always with this air of impermanence. Like he was made out of paper and a strong wind could take him out.

I never really cared then. I guess I was too busy trying to survive, because that's when my own wrecking ball of a father was still here, but the guilt eats at me on a daily basis.

How much better would his life have been if I'd become his friend back then, instead of waiting until it was almost too late? He probably never would have ended up at that quarry in the first place.

Now that question makes me angry, and I'm pushing it down when a deep, masculine voice breaks through my thoughts and startles me back to reality.

A flush of adrenaline hits me, and it takes a few seconds to remember that it's not my dad getting angry, and I'm a mostly functioning adult at work right now. He's not even mad at me, he's getting into it with Tristan. Still, the bile at the back of my throat just from the sound of it is a weakness I don't want to admit.

Why the fuck is everything hitting every button I have today? I'm not normally weak like this.

Get it together, Waters. Dad isn't even here.

"Sir, you don't need to raise your voice at me," Tristan's rumble breaks through my mental fog. "I'm just here to tell you what I see. I recommend that you go to the ER for an EEG and monitoring. I'm not forcing you to do anything. Jaden's stable and not currently seizing. If you want to save yourself the ambulance bill, I get that, but please consider going yourself, or at least following up with your primary tomorrow for a check up. Do you have a neurologist yet? We talked about this."

It's his even-toned talking-to-irrational-patients voice, and it seems to be making things worse.

"This is why I tell you not to fucking call them all the time," Mr. Halloran snarls at his wife. "All we get is attitude. He's fine. Look at him. He's not hurt. There's no goddamn need to do any of this."

I'm waiting for Tristan to jump in, but instead he holds up his hands and starts to back away, packing up our equipment and nudging me to follow along. I do the same thing, picking up gear mechanically and tapping in the last few notes in the iPad while my fingers have a death grip on the industrial rubber case, for some reason.

Why the fuck are we leaving? Why are we not having this fight?

"Your choice. Let me just get your signature here," Tristan continues, thrusting his own iPad under the man's nose as if he can't sense the anger rolling off him.

Mr. Halloran signs, Tristan says the rest of his legally mandated spiel, and Jaden continues to stay silent, looking spaced out. His mom is just as bristled as her husband, but I get the feeling she's waiting for us to leave so they can fight about it.

Exactly what their child needs. Another fucking fight to overhear and feel like he's responsible for.

I'm still trying to find the words to stop all of this and make them see how neglectful they're being when Tristan grabs my arm and drags me outside with him, all our gear in tow.

"Thank you for your time," he calls back, like he's a fucking waiter, or something.

"What the fuck are you doing?"

I'm trying to get his attention, but he's busy bee-lining for the ambulance like our shift is over. He doesn't say a word as he hustles me inside, practically throwing me into the back and then following me before closing the doors behind us.

I stow my bag before sitting on the cot, looking at him with a *what-the-hell* expression.

"What was that about?"

His eyes are narrow and his gaze is sharp, like he's daring me to lie to him. Which I couldn't even try to do, because I don't know what the fuck he's talking about.

"What was what? I don't think I said a single word."

"You didn't have to, your face said enough."

Tristan arches an eyebrow at me. I feel like he's trying to make a point here, but I still don't know what he's talking about.

"What?" I ask, my voice not as indignant as I was hoping for. "I went in. I took vitals. I took notes. What could I possibly have done wrong?"

There's a beat of silence between us where he's probably trying to figure out if I'm bullshitting him, but when I continue to stare right back at him, waiting for the big reveal, he lets out a long, heavy sigh. Tristan brings both hands up to rub his face, like a sudden wave of exhaustion just hit him, before eventually looking at me again.

"What?"

I need him to spit it out.

"Your attitude in there was so fucking toxic, you didn't need to say anything. Everyone knew you were pissed. The parents did, I did, that little fucking boy did. You're dropping shit and moving around like you wanted to hit something. And you really expect me to believe you had no idea you were acting like you were a cat's whisker from turning that call into a fist fight over god-knows-what?"

I jerk back, initially just trying to process what he's accusing me of. I wasn't like that, was I?

Normally when I'm pissed, I know it. I feel it everywhere. Down to my toes, like a cleansing burn. The whole time I was in there, I only felt numb.

"You're exaggerating. Maybe I was a little annoyed. That guy's an asshole. He's obviously neglecting his child. You're the one who hustled us out of there giving him all that 'yes, sir' bullshit. We should be in there forcing him to take Jaden back to the doctor, and reporting him to child services for neglect if he doesn't. You've seen how he is, he obviously doesn't think anything is wrong."

Tristan stays very still, continuing to stare at me for long enough to be completely unnerving. When he does speak, his voice is soft, which is somehow worse than if he was yelling at me.

"I agree he seems like an asshole, but we both know how expensive this shit is. The system is fucked. They can't afford specialists. The fact that they're trying not to go into massive debt isn't neglect. They call the ambulance when he seizes. They go to their pediatrician. It's not perfect, but they seem like they're trying. And it's probably really confusing for them that the seizures are so hard to catch, you know how difficult it is to see absence seizures like that. What's confusing for me is seeing you talking about calling DSS on someone. In a million years, I never thought I'd hear you say it. Not for something that isn't cut and dry."

That trips me up for a second. Why was calling child services on this family the first thing on my mind?

I ignore the thought, because I don't have an answer.

The important thing here is that I'm right. He doesn't deserve to have a kid like this if all he's going to do is stare at him like he's an alien and fail to take care of him. Jaden's sweet and smart and kind and he deserves better.

"Cade?" Tristan's voice breaks into my thoughts.

"Look, whatever. We're mandated reporters, right? Don't we have an obligation to do something?"

"Yeah," he says slowly, like I'm a child. "If there's evidence of abuse. He's being taken care of, though. Maybe not in the way that you would, or the way they would if they were richer, but last I checked being poor isn't a fucking crime. Technically."

I roll my eyes at him and don't bother to hide it, because he's not getting it.

"So, what? We're just supposed to walk away like a couple of assholes? You see what he's like. He's not right. He doesn't act like someone who loves him. There has to be stuff we don't see. How do we know he's not abusing him in another way?"

Tristan cocks his head to the side, brow creased and all of his concern and incredulity written clearly on his face.

"What exactly do you want me to do, Cade? Have him arrested on vibes? Walk in there and say I'm sorry, but it feels off in here, you seem like an asshole, I'm taking your kid. And then what? Drop Jaden off at emergency care? Or do you want me to call DSS and yell at them when they ask me if I have a shred of evidence other than your gut feeling? I'm not gonna lie to you kid, I'm getting very fucking concerned here, and he's not the one I'm concerned about right now."

I exhale sharply, my irritation fighting to take over. We need to do *something*. We can't let things happen to him just because he's a stranger.

I get up, my head bowed under the ceiling of the ambulance as I try to move past Tristan and get through the doors. He grabs me though, pushing me back to the cot with a firm hand on my chest and holding me in place while he keeps talking.

"Look, I understand that you're upset. I really do. And I promise, I don't disagree with you that something's off here. I'll do every screening I can any time we get called here. But there's a reason our powers are fucking limited. If you and Silas had a kid and called an ambulance in ten years, and the paramedic looked at two men living together and said *'oof, vibes are off here homos, I'm taking your kid'*, would that be okay? It's an imperfect system but I'm very much pro us not being allowed to be fucking baby snatchers based on our personal whims and feelings. You hear me? I just want to know why you're so worked up about this in the first place."

I can't do this right now. I.... I can't. I don't feel right. Everything inside me is clicking and pitching slightly off-center, and it's making my skin crawl for no reason.

Distantly, I wonder if this is what Silas feels like when he gets overwhelmed by situations.

But that wouldn't make any sense, because I've had a lot of problems, but social anxiety isn't one of them. I'm fine.

"Fine. Can we go?"

He looks at me for another minute, but then nods. Reluctantly. I hustle past him, desperate to be out of this sweat box and back into the driver's seat with some semblance of control.

"We're not done talking about this, though," he mutters as I walk past.

Great.

CHAPTER SEVEN

SILAS

I know exactly the moment that Cade gets home, because he slams the door so hard the house shudders and rattles, like a bone-chattering skeleton in an episode of Scooby-Doo.

Interesting. He's never been great at restraining his emotions, but this is probably a first for us.

"Cade?"

Silence. I can feel him, though. I know he's standing in the entryway, his shoes still on as he clutches whatever anger or misery is fueling him, trying to let it go before he gets any closer to me. Again, I feel a twinge of guilt, because even his worst days still seem to revolve around managing me.

Instead of waiting, I go to him. He's standing exactly where I expected; one hand on the worn bannister, his shoulders slumped but every muscle in his body tense. Even the air around him feels tense. It's the kind of sensation my brain is hard-wired to avoid—either by leaving the room or desperately appeasing the source of the tension—but forcing myself to stare at Cade's features rolls back that initial instinct.

I never want to avoid him. I want to help; even if I feel too useless to, most of the time. Asking him what's wrong is not my next step. I've learned at least that much after spending the better part of a year living together.

"Hey."

The word slips out of my mouth before I can think of something meaningful to say. It's a start, at least.

When Cade's eyes flick up to mine, I expect to see anger there. Rage or frustration because of whatever happened to set him off into this mood. Instead, I see grief. It's a hollow expression, like a dark, empty room with waves crashing against the outer walls, trying to get in. I know it well.

But it's not an expression I've seen Cade wear before. I'm briefly grateful that Cade agreed to have the girls stay with their aunt for the weekend, so he doesn't feel the need to put on a brave face for them more than he already does for me.

"Did something happen?" I ask.

Cade shrugs, before letting out a deep sigh. I see his eyes flick from side to side—like he's trying to reset himself—but it doesn't really work.

"No," he shrugs, affecting nonchalance. "I'm just tired."

I nod. I don't believe him for a second. "Okay."

There's no point in pushing him.

"Do you want me to make you something to eat?" I ask, prompting Cade to rub both hands over his face, looking paler than usual.

"Like what?"

He doesn't say it in a bitchy way, but it stings nonetheless. The food thing is still a sticking point between us, even if neither of us is willing to explicitly acknowledge it out loud.

When I don't respond, Cade does a weird, aborted sort of flinch before casting his gaze to the floor.

"I'm sorry, I'm..." he trails off, still not looking me in the eye and not seeming to really know what he's trying to say. "I'm gonna go for a ride."

My heart thumps too hard when the words drop into the space between us. This time he does look up, catching my eye and holding me pinned there.

Yet another thing we've stopped fighting about, without really getting to the bottom of. Jesus, maybe our relationship is a lot more precarious than I realized. Maybe we're just getting really good at avoiding acknowledging anything that causes conflict between us.

Or maybe Cade just keeps changing himself to appease me. The thought makes my pulse race from guilt and shame more than the anxiety that normally comes from anything to do with motocross.

I never asked him to stop riding. I never would. It's not his fault that as soon as I was able to free myself from something I'd come to fundamentally hate, all the anxieties I'd suppressed about it suddenly spiraled out of control. I'd always had shuddering flashes of getting injured during a race. I think a part of me thought about it so much because I secretly wanted it. I wanted to be crushed and broken so badly I wouldn't be able to perform as my father's prize cash cow anymore, and we'd both be forced to find out whether he'd even tolerate me if I didn't bring anything productive into his life.

If the only thing that tied him to me was the fact that he was supposed to love me anyway.

But when Cade and I got together, those images were suddenly replaced with him. Cade hurt; Cade broken; Cade taken away from me. And the more he rode, the worse it got. I tried to hide it, but he's always been able to read me better than anyone else.

It got to the point where I was having a panic attack every time he went out, especially if it was for a competition, but even if he was just riding by himself. So, he stopped. And I never thanked him for it, because that meant acknowledging that he did it for me. Because I couldn't control my emotions enough to not take something away from him that he loves.

Instead, neither of us ever discussed it. Just like everything else new and painful that's slowly filling this house around us. I'm worried that this mountain of unsaid will ultimately smother us. Or is it only going to keep pushing us together, until we're bound more by the threat of mutual destruction than any real desire?

"I'll come with you."

My voice breaks the silence before I'd really formulated the thought. Cade's eyes widen, just as shocked as I am at the suggestion.

There were a couple of months between when my dad left me—taking my bike with him as his consolation prize—but before I'd let myself acknowledge I never wanted to ride again. I'd gotten a beater dirt bike on the cheap, just to have, and fixed it up as part of my training at the shop. It's nothing fancy, but it runs.

And when I gradually stopped using it altogether, the idea of getting rid of it felt too much like a final admission of weakness. So I held on to it, sitting next to Cade's bike he's had for years, both of them now gathering dust I have to shake off every time I do routine maintenance. I know how much Cade's bike means to him, which keeps me doing the bare minimum to make sure the engine doesn't seize up from disuse, even if I secretly hope he never rides it again.

Until this moment, at least. This moment where it feels like he needs it.

Cade and I are still looking at each other. I'm wondering how much needs to be said right now, and if I had to guess, I'd say he's wondering the same thing. Maybe he'll tell me no. Maybe he wants to be alone.

I don't know if I can really help him. But I know that watching him suffer like this hurts too much not to try.

"Okay," he says, finally, his voice oddly flat. "Let's go."

It's getting into the early grip of winter, before the earth gets hard-packed and semi-frozen, instead being wet enough that it's more like riding on sludge.

The mud out by Cade's family's trailer is so bad we had to let some air out of the tires before we left. We keep the bikes there because there's plenty of space, and all the trails he used to practice on are snaking around his neighbor's property. No one was home when we parked, thankfully, so we didn't have to have any awkward conversation. We just pulled out the bikes and our gear and got ready to go.

It all happened in a silence that was a mixture of companionable and tense. I love the quiet, but when it's coming from Cade, I find it unsettling. He fills my life in a lot of ways, but one of them is definitely a constant stream of conversational chatter. As much as I would never have expected to enjoy it, I do when it's coming from him. I love how animated he gets when he tells me about something cool that his sisters did, or some new medical thing he just learned that I won't even pretend to understand.

This stillness from him is so out of character, it has me more worried than the door slamming. I'd almost prefer it if he picked something random to fight with me about, just so he could get this dark energy out of him.

Hopefully, this will help.

I focus on that to get myself out of my head once we head out on the trail. On one hand, every sensation is familiar in this bone-deep way, which is kind of soothing. Even if I immediately start feeling aches and pains in the riding-specific muscles I haven't used in so long. It's easy to let myself think about that, and keep my eyes trained on Cade a dozen or so feet in front of me.

Once we pick up speed, I see him whip away a tear off from his goggles to clear his vision, the plastic already spattered in mud, and throw a look back over his shoulder as he shoves it in a pocket. I can't see his expression, but it's like I can feel it. It's written in every line of his body, and the way he's so alert, body ready to respond to every single bump or twist in the trail.

It's joyful.

He looks so happy. Don't ask me how I know that from staring at his back, I just do. I struggle to read people a lot of the time, but I've dedicated the last year of my life to learning every expression and gesture Cade produces and interpreting what they mean, and the Cade in front of me is happier than a Golden Retriever launching itself into a lake over and over.

Cade speeds up, and I match his pace. I try to lose myself in the jolting movement, the vibration of the bike underneath me, and the satisfying constant micro-adjustments of my body. It starts to feel like I'm in sync with the bike, and we're both in sync with the earth underneath us.

We wind through the trees, me following Cade's lead until we're so deep it barely feels like we're on a trail anymore. It's more like a deer trail, weeds whipping at my legs as we blow past. My abs and thighs ache, and my wrists are already exhausted, but it doesn't matter. My eye is on my love, and I'm going to chase him down.

Cade's bright gear is all brown by the time we dismount, and I'm sure I look the same. I don't think I've ever flung that much mud in my life. I'm already dying for a shower, but I can't fight the budding elation I feel looking at the smile on Cade's face.

There's a red imprint from where his goggles were sitting, and the rest of his face is flushed with adrenaline beneath the mud spatter. He's smiling, though. A real smile, that I'm only now realizing I haven't seen in a while.

I suddenly don't care how dirty we both are. All I care about is drinking him in. He's swaying slightly as he gets his equilibrium on the non-moving ground, looking long and lean in that way that always makes me want to run my hands over him. I can picture the jut and curve of his hipbones under his pants, and the perfect way my hands wrap around them just to shove him into the wall.

We're in the shed that passes for an extra garage that we put up next to the trailer. It's enough to protect our bikes from the worst of the elements, but it's not exactly sturdy. It's mostly particle board with a little waterproofing slapped on top, and the whole thing shudders with the force of Cade's body hitting the wall.

I absolutely cannot bring myself to care right now, though. Let the whole damn thing collapse. I'll build another one. And another. As many as I need to fuck him senseless in.

"I see someone has their motor running," Cade purrs directly into my mouth, all while he grinds his hips into mine, happy to be pinned between my weight and the wall.

"I will fuck the puns right out of your mouth if that's what you need, boy."

I can feel his breath catch, and his body is melting into my arms like hot butter.

"Yes, please."

The words are muffled, because Cade's mouth is already on mine again. I push him harder into the wall and bring one hand up to pin his forehead back, holding him still as I push his mouth open wider to explore. It's a slow, lascivious kiss, and I get so lost in it I almost forget that we need to do anything else.

Cade lets out a whine, though, which snaps my attention back to the present. I can feel how hard he is, needy and grinding against me, and I know he's close to losing it just from this.

Watching him fall apart whenever I truly dominate him is something I don't think I'll ever get tired of.

"You've been hard this entire time, haven't you?"

As soon as the words are out of my mouth in a growl, I yank at the collar of his jersey to suck bruising kisses into the skin beneath. He smells like mud and clean sweat, and the salt and musk is an incredible assault on my senses. All I can feel is CadeCadeCade and it's making my rational brain flatline.

I grind the heel of my hand just a little too hard into his erection, and watch the flush that climbs up his neck as he inhales sharply.

"Have you always been this much of a slut for getting an engine between your legs? Or are you feeling neglected?"

Cade honest-to-god whimpers, and I don't give him the chance to answer before I'm forcing my tongue into his wet, waiting mouth.

I don't know if I'll ever understand why I get like this with him sometimes. It feels like nothing's enough. I want to crawl inside him and wear his skin like a suit of armor, but I can't, and I don't know how to put that into any words that make sense. So all I'm left with is pawing at him and marking him and turning him inside out and doing anything it takes to make him scream.

And Cade, for whatever reason, seems to be hardwired to turn to jello for someone willing to rough him up and put him in his place. I don't want to know why, actually. At least if I'm the one doing it, I know it's because I love him so fucking much there's too much emotion to get out of me any normal, not-kinky way.

So, we don't talk about it. We just feel.

I scrabble at Cade's clothes as he pants at me, yanking his jersey up and hooking it over his head so it's still tight across his shoulders, looking like he's about to burst out of the seams. Then I pin both of his wrists over his head, his body squirming beneath mine, as I use my free hand to yank open his pants and drag them down to his thighs.

When I take a second to look at my handiwork, it already takes my breath away. He's filthy everywhere the clothes didn't cover, mud arcing over every line of his body. There are red indents from everywhere his clothes have been strangling him, and his entire chest is heaving with every breath he takes. At the center of it all, his cock strains toward me, as if it knows only I can give him what he needs, already pink-tinged and wet at the tip.

"You didn't answer me," I say, my voice low as I hold my face close to his.

"Uh," is the sound that escapes him, breathy and formless, his brain already struggling to keep up with whatever endorphins he's bathing his internal organs in right now.

"'Uh' is not an answer," I say, reaching out to flick the swollen tip of his cock with my finger, pulling a strangled sound out of Cade and making the whole length of his penis flex for me, like some kind of magic trick. "Have you always been such a slutty rider, or is this just for me?"

"You," he manages to get out, his voice choked and pitched too high. "All for you."

I reward him by palming his length, and the way the hot skin pulses under my touch tells me he's already close. I'm torn between wanting to drag this out, or make him come early and then fuck him boneless through the oversensitivity.

Either way, it needs to be quick. I'm too fucking turned on to let this drag on forever. Cade's not the only one whose motor is running after this little throwback afternoon.

"Where's the lube?" I ask, trying not to smile at the face he makes while he's attempting to concentrate.

"Wha-?"

"I know you brought some, because you can't resist the chance to get dicked down over a motorcycle. Don't tell me you don't have any, because I'll call you a liar."

"Pants. Back pocket."

He grits the word out as I stroke his length, my grip tight enough to border on painful, and he squeezes his eyes shut for a second, like he's trying not to come.

"None of that, slut. I want you to come for me as soon as you can," I say, but let go of his cock as soon as I do, leaving him panting and sagging behind me.

I snag his jeans and sift through the pockets until I find the small tube he shoved in there, slathering my hand with some before I turn back to him. He's still in the same position, hands up against the wall even though I'm not holding them, dick out and desperate for my touch.

Slick sounds fill the air as I coat his needy cock in lube, stroking him a few more times than is strictly necessary, but needing to feel him shudder beneath me again.

"Silas," he moans, his voice thin and reedy.

"What is it, slut? Isn't this what you need?"

Cade doesn't say anything, just exhales loudly, trying to get his hips closer to me even as I take his wrists back into my hand to continue pinning him. I drop his cock, reaching beneath him to palm his balls, rolling them in my hand for a few seconds while he whines before moving even further. His thighs are still trapped together by his pants, so I have to push to get my slick fingers in between his cheeks and find his hole.

Once I do, I don't hold back. I start with two fingers, not being rough, but unrelenting as I push inside him. He lets out an inhuman whine as soon as I find his prostate, and I work over it intently, determined to make him come as quickly as possible.

"Silas. Silas. Silas," he moans over and over, probably not even conscious of what he's saying anymore. He's flushed and wanton, and I need to see him explode before I lose my mind altogether.

I drop his wrists, and this time he doesn't keep holding them up, instead letting them fall until he's clinging to the back of my head as he rides my fingers. His fingernails scrape over my scalp, making me shudder, and the need to be inside him soon consumes me. I almost forget about making him come first, until his face starts to pinch and his noises get that little bit higher, and I know he's right on the edge.

"Come on, baby. Show me how desperate you are," I'm murmuring in his ear, pulling us close enough together that he can rub his erection against my hip, letting my jersey ride up as he leaves a trail of precum over my superheated skin.

"That's it," I say. "I want to feel you clench as you come all over yourself, like a needy little thing. Go on, baby. Show me what you need."

Cade's movements are smaller and more controlled than before, but he's grinding down into my hand with determination, and I can feel his muscles tremble as he reaches the edge. The tip of his cock drags slowly over my skin as he pulls us closer together, then his hips jerk a few times before he finally paints me with his release. It's hot, slicking my skin, and I love the way he trembles as he holds me close.

My fingers are still inside of him as he clenches and then relaxes, but I can't give him enough time to truly relax. Before the last few drops of cum have spilled from him, I pull my fingers out, spin him around to face the wall and then plunge them back in to the hilt, adding a third in the process. My fingering becomes less precise now, rougher, trying to open him up wide and overwhelm him at the same time.

I forget all about his cock as I get him ready for me, the noises he's making—half desperate, half pained—falling around me like raindrops. As soon as I think we're there, I pull out of him and press my hands on his shoulders. His jersey is still bunched and stretched across them, confining him as I bend him over at the waist and shove his face into the wall. I'm trembling with desire as I pull my own desperate, stiff cock out of my pants, slick myself with more of the lube, and as soon as I press against his entrance, I push myself in as hard as I can.

Cade makes a garbled, harsh sound of surprise, but I still don't give him the chance to adjust. He's still relaxed from his orgasm, welcoming me into his tight heat, and it's easy to set up a brutal rhythm that has his face knocking against the cheap particle board and his breath coming in raspy shouts in time with every fuck.

"What are you?" I ask, leaning forward to drape myself over his back and reaching up to pinch one of his nipples until he squirms.

"Yours," he groans. "Your slut."

I can see his hand, trembling hard, move down to start fisting his cock before his erection even flags.

After that, we fall into a sort of lull. I keep fucking him hard and fast, rumbling in his ear about how desperate he is and how pretty he looks split open for me. I call him my whore, and listen to him moan. I listen to the wet, sucking sounds of my body invading his and feel the rumble in his chest as I pinch and squeeze every part of him I can reach.

When I finally come, it's with a groan, my fingers digging into Cade's hips to hold him close to me. His hand speeds up, desperate to drag another orgasm out of himself. Even once I've filled him with my cum, I keep moving, grinding into him steadily, working him even further open with the base of my cock, telling him how much he needs it until he finally gasps and spurts more cum onto the dirty floor, his ass gripping my dick in the process and a raspy noise of desperation coming out of him.

Eventually it's just the two of us, panting and leaning against the wall, clinging to each other.

Guilt begins to creep in. Only a little, but still. I don't like how out of control I feel when I get that way. I'm calling him a desperate slut, but I'm the desperate one when it happens. And even though Cade assures me with a smitten, starry-eyed expression that he loves it, I never know if there's going to be a day that I take it too far.

We're both quiet as we clean up—as much as it's possible—and put our gear away before slipping out of the shed. Thank god no one was home, or was conscious enough to come out and notice us. I don't have it in me to talk to anyone who isn't Cade right now.

CHAPTER Eight

CADE

My body fucking hurts when I wake up. Every inch of it. I try not to think of it as a sign I'm getting old, because I'm extremely aware that I haven't been as kind to my body as I should for the last twenty-three years.

It's been a long time since I actually went out and rode, and even longer since I went that hard. It felt amazing in the moment. Pure. Just wind and dirt and Silas next to me, so I wasn't distracted by worrying about him having a panic attack like I had been before I kinda-sorta quit. My muscles are screaming at me now, though, especially considering I didn't come close to anything like warming up beforehand. Stupid.

Worth it, but stupid.

And then to get dicked down like that after... bliss. I think the universe melted away there for a minute, with Silas's dirty talk wrapping around my spine and squeezing it as tight as he was squeezing the rest of me.

I caught him watching me after, though. The familiar expression of quiet concern crept onto his face, and I did everything I could to ignore it.

He doesn't need to worry about me. He's supposed to be focusing on himself for the first time in his life.

I'm chill.

I decide to prove this to him by convincing him to go out with me tonight. Despite the ache in my ass and everything else, I could stand to do something other than work followed by sitting around, vacillating between over-analyzing everything Silas does and staring out the window like a blank-faced war widow, waiting for some kind of solution to my problems that will never show up.

The girls are still with Jaz, neither of us works tomorrow, and it's technically still the weekend.

Just to drive my point home, I try to wear a vintage t-shirt I got for a fucking steal online recently that reads 'YOUNG, DUMB, AND FULL OF CUM' in block letters, but Silas side-eyes me until I give in and change.

I know he's right. Possum Hollow isn't some cartoon version of a rural town where fundamentalist Christians are lurking around every corner, stones in hand, waiting for any queer person they come across, but I don't need to push my luck, either. When Silas and I first moved in together, I was determined to defend us from all the shitty comments, even if it meant getting physical with every red-hat asshole we came across.

I wanted Silas to know that I wasn't ashamed of him. Or regretting my choice, or something. He would never say it out loud, but I was always hyperaware that he might feel like an experiment or a phase or something, and the thought freaked me out. Maybe that's why I threw myself into my whole bisexual identity so hard. Or maybe because it felt nice to belong to something for once, even something as nebulous as a sexual orientation.

Instead of reassuring him though, it made everything worse. He was terrified I'd push someone too far and get myself fucked up, which made him retreat even further inside himself, as if we could both act straight enough in public to avoid getting any bullshit comments, even though it's a small town and everyone in it is aware that we're fucking.

So, I try to rein it in any way I can. That doesn't stop me from feeling this ineffable urge to be as queer as possible as loudly as possible most of the time. Especially now, when the shadow of my dad and whatever shitty judgmental things he's probably thinking is lurking around every corner.

So instead, I settle on a t-shirt that says 'ALL PANIC, NO DISCO' with a possum underneath, because it seems fitting, as well as tongue-kissing Silas in the parking lot of the Feral Possum long enough that we're both walking in with a more-than-socially-acceptable amount of wood.

It'll go down. I don't really care, though, letting my fingers graze Silas's ass as he shuffles past me to slide inside.

Even here, the action feels dangerous. But I think that's more a me thing than a reality thing. I know Gunnar would never tolerate open bigotry in his bar. That's the whole point of this place. For people like us to have someplace safe to go.

Which is the reason I blame for being here probably more than I should be. It's one of Tristan's favorite haunts as well, and even though he's significantly more domesticated now that he lives with Ford, he's still a feral cat at heart and in need of someplace to hang out beyond work and his house. We've stopped here after a shift more weeks than not recently, and it's a simple thing that always seems to release the pressure valve inside me just a little.

I'm not surprised to see Tristan here tonight, tucked into a round booth at the back. I am surprised to see his boyfriend, who is even more introverted than Silas when it comes to public activities. But with the goofy, love-struck look on his normally impassive face—goofy by his standards, at least—as he watches Tristan animatedly tell some story, I can guess how he got sucked in.

I'm glad, anyway. As much as I would have been happy to just hang out with Silas, some company will help ease any lingering tension. You can't talk about real shit in front of your friends. It's just not what you do.

"What's up, motherfuckers," I say with an energy I don't feel, collapsing into the booth next to Tristan hard enough to interrupt him mid-sentence.

"You know you're allowed to stop talking like a teenage boy who just discovered cursing whenever you want. Consider me officially declaring you enough of an adult for that."

Tristan stares at me with one eyebrow raised as he speaks.

"Bitch, please. Every other fucking word out of your mouth is 'fuck'. And you're fucking ancient. As if you have a leg to stand on."

"That's different, you tool. I'm from the East Coast. We increase swearing exponentially as a sign of maturity. Like how the cartilage in your ears never stops growing as you get old. You're supposed to be one of those good old-fashioned country boys I keep hearing about. Not a Jesse Pinkman wannabe."

I can't help but snort.

"Don't talk shit about *Breaking Bad*. That show basically raised me."

I make sure to make eye contact with Ford and up-nod him in between the banter, because it must be easy for him to get overlooked a lot when he's always next to Tristan running his mouth. I'm waiting for the next retort in our little back and forth, but Tristan doesn't say anything for long enough to get me looking at him.

His eyes are crinkled at the edge, like the start of a smile, and he's looking at me all fond and shit. It's unnerving.

"What?" I ask, suddenly self-conscious.

"It looks good," Tristan says, quiet and serious as he reaches up and cups my cheek roughly with his palm. He does it sometimes and it always feels sort of paternal in a way that makes me freeze up and not know how to hold my body anymore.

This time his thumb is resting by my eye, and I realize what he's talking about.

"Oh. Uh, thanks. It's not a big deal, I just follow this guy on TikTok that's always doing it and I thought it looked cool."

In reality, it kind of is a big deal, because not only was learning how to put on fucking eyeliner about a thousand times more difficult than I expected, leaving the house with it still makes me feel more vulnerable than I'd like to admit. But I wasn't lying when I said it looked cool. I'd always thought of makeup on guys to be specifically drag-related. Which is fucking dope, I've discovered, but also not something I think I'm built for. I think.

But there's this queer guy who constantly rocks a smokey eye and does these little tutorials I got hooked on. He somehow manages to make it look super masculine and feminine at the same time, and I couldn't get it out of my head. It's stupid, because I've never really thought that much about my appearance before.

Okay, that might be a lie. I fucking love my tattoos. And I think about my hair sometimes.

A lot. Whatever.

Either way, it's not something I expected to ever do, but it feels good. It feels like I'm connected to something outside of all my normal day-to-day bullshit. Like if I ran into the TikTok dude in the street he would see me and recognize that we have something in common, instead of writing me off as just another dumb redneck straight guy. I have this urge to feel seen that I can't really explain, and this kind of thing satisfies it. I don't know if that makes me attention-seeking, or asking for trouble or something.

I'm probably overthinking it. But I'm not overthinking the way I saw Silas's pupils dilate the first time he saw me all kohl'd up, even if it was fucking messy, and I thought tonight might be a good night to try it out in the real world. Or the slightly safer version of the real world that the Feral Possum is. Without meaning to, I curl my hands into fists, suddenly feeling exposed and not wanting anyone to notice that I also painted my nails black. It's messy and my nails are super short, but I think it looks cool. Kind of goth-pretty. I'm sure they have noticed already, but it's suddenly too much attention on something that I should feel comfortable with, but keeps catching me by surprise with these weird feelings of shyness. It's not like me.

Tristan must sense me getting self-conscious, because he lets go of my face, but doesn't stop looking at me with that weird proud expression that's making me squirm. As if I actually did anything worth noticing.

"Right, Cujo? The kid looks good. Like an influencer, or someone else who gets paid to be pretty."

"Right," Ford signs to me in ASL, always careful to go slow so I can understand. "I like it."

I roll my eyes, but it's kind of nice that they think it's cool. I don't embarrass easy, but I felt a little weird leaving the house, and somehow the fact that two very fucking masculine, blue-collar dudes like it is helping me feel comfortable. Even if they're queer dudes. It still counts. I wish I didn't need that kind of validation, but baby steps. I'm working on it.

"Yeah, yeah, yeah," I say, affecting indifference. "You're just jealous no one will ever pay you to be pretty."

"Technically, I live rent-free at Ford's house. So he's paying for me to look pretty. Among other things."

Tristan flinches hard as Ford elbows him in the ribs, but it only makes him cackle like an idiot. Ford immediately reaches for a sip of his beer, a look of chronic exasperation on his face, but I can see him smiling behind it.

"So, I know where my mechanic is, where's yours?" Tristan asks, about twelve seconds before Silas makes it over to the booth.

"Are we having a party or something?" he asks, putting one beer down in front of me and what I'm sure is a seltzer with lime and no alcohol in front of himself.

"Yes, Silas," Tristan deadpans. "Four people in the back of a bar who will all be home by midnight definitely counts as a party."

"Sorry, have we disappointed you since you moved here?" I ask, side-eying Tristan. "I didn't realize you were expecting a town called Possum Hollow to have its own branch of *Hedonism*."

Tristan whistles low. "Someone's been doing research for vacation plans, I see. I didn't realize you two were swingers."

Silas rolls his eyes again, but there's no heat behind it as he takes a sip of his seltzer. Tristan doesn't know any way to have a relationship with people other than endless snark interspersed with super-serious, soul-baring talking to's.

We're saved from more of Tristan's rambling when Tobias pops up out of nowhere, a feral grin on his face.

"Hey! Look who's here. Can I sit with you? Gunnar kicked me out from behind the bar because he hates me. He's intimidated by my natural charisma and he's worried it'll raise the bar for all the other guys."

He doesn't wait to get an answer before sliding in next to Silas. He's a little out of breath, like he ran over here, but in a playful way, and there's a dark flush crawling up his cheeks.

Gunnar walks over from the bar to stand next to him, having clearly heard everything that was said, despite the ambient noise. He puts a mostly empty tumbler in front of Tobias, a sad piece of lime floating at the bottom.

"Uh, I believe I said, 'I love you, but you can't stand behind the bar when you're drinking.' Oh, and also, you don't fucking work here."

"That's a technicality," Tobias replies, still grinning.

"I'm pretty sure the state liquor board has quite the hard-on for technicalities," Tristan says, inserting himself into the conversation.

I gasp, lifting my hand up to Tristan's forehead like I'm checking his temperature.

"T, did you just encourage rule-following? Are you well? Is he well?"

I turn to Ford, but he shrugs, still pretending he's not amused by the conversation.

"Tristan just realizes that if I lose this bar, all y'all will have to start hanging out in your own homes at night. If he has to experience that much silence, he'll end up spending time with his mom voluntarily just so he has someone to fight with."

"I'd rather suck Lucifer's nutsack, but whatever." Tristan takes a swig of his beer, Ford now completely failing to fight back his smile.

Gunnar lets it drop, looking down at Tobias with that love-sick-puppy expression. I get it. Right now, Tobias is full of energy, red-cheeked from the alcohol, shifting in his seat as he finishes his drink and gets ready to continue the Tristan trash talk.

It was not that long ago that he was sitting right here, getting checked out by me and T after nearly being beaten to death by his abuser, convinced he had no future. This version—full of life and enthusiasm for everything—is still new enough that we all get a little emotional to see it. I can't imagine how Gunnar must feel, watching him heal like this.

I know how I felt watching Silas recover from his dad, and it was like mainlining joy. I might have gotten addicted. Maybe that's why I'll do anything I can to keep him smiling.

A thread of something bittersweet hits my brain, but I ignore it. It's a nice night. Now's not the time for thinking through shit.

"You need another drink?" Gunnar asks Tobias, leaning down so he can murmur it close to his head.

"Nah, I'm good." Tobias looks back over his shoulder, grinning up at him for a second before hitting him with a quick kiss on the lips. "Go do work. Be responsible. Someone has to be the sugar daddy in this relationship, and it ain't going to be me."

Gunnar exhales through his nose like a sexy dragon, but he doesn't address it. He knows it would only invite more teasing.

"Anyone else? Drink?"

"Oh! Me, please!" I shake my mostly empty beer glass before chugging the rest of it. That hit the fucking spot.

"Coming right up," he says before grabbing the empties and heading back to the bar.

I force myself to relax as I settle back into the booth and wait for my drink.

The warmth of is it spreading through me like a fucking hug, and I think that all I want to do tonight is lean back, relax, and stare at Silas while thinking about how much of a fucking smokeshow he is.

When I lean over and whisper that in his ear, he blushes, and it completes the whole picture. Yeah, I could do this all night. No fucking problem.

CHAPTER NINE

SILAS

I know it takes more than three beers to get Cade drunk, but he's riding on a wave of elation I rarely see from him. Maybe it's just getting out of the house and hanging out with other people who don't treat him like shit. Or being around people where we can act like ourselves without having to censor everything.

Maybe it's the eyeliner. I really don't know. Even situations like this where I'm genuinely happy to be here with my friends are still... draining. To a certain extent. But Cade's not like me in that way, and it's making me realize how much time he spends cooped up at home, slowly wilting like an unattended houseplant.

Tonight was a good idea. Going for the ride was a good idea. Doing things that aren't wrapped up in me and my broken brain seems to be good for both of us. My bad days are well and truly outnumbered by my good ones, and I'm sick of both of us seeming to revolve around them, regardless.

Everyone—in fact—is having such a good time, I don't think the others even notice when Cade grabs me by the hand and leads me toward one of the single-occupancy bathrooms. Normally, I would discourage him from getting too horny in public because Gunnar tries to keep this place relatively upstanding, and I don't want to do anything to ruin that for him. But maybe I'm high on the tone of the evening, too, because I don't object.

All I can think about is how fucking diabolically hot he looked yesterday while we fucked over the bikes. I'm not an expert on relationships, but I know people talk a lot about the sex aspect getting worse. Or less interesting, maybe.

Cade and I definitely have some problems, but that is not one of them. If anything, it seems like the more the world is falling apart around us, the more desperate I am to cling on to him in any way I can.

That's probably not good, either. But I'm not going to worry about it now.

Cade drags us both into the stall, closes and locks the door with a click, and then shoves me against it. I bounce off the surface a little, raising my eyebrows at him.

"That's how it's going to be?" I ask.

Cade doesn't reply. Instead, he makes a show of looking me up and down, licking his lip before biting it and giving me a slow, sensual nod.

"I could hear you guys while I was waiting at the bar. Tristan was right, you know," I say, reaching out to touch his cheek like Tristan did before, but with a very, very different purpose. "You look fucking phenomenal. I want to make you cry it all off. Does that make me sick?"

I'm mostly teasing, but there may be a slight undercurrent of concern there. I'm aware that we go hard, sometimes. A part of me worries it's too hard. But we're both into it, and I know Cade would always tell me if he wasn't into something, so fuck it. I guess we keep going until something happens to change either my desire to make this boy fucking wrecked, or his desire to get it.

"Maybe it makes us both sick," Cade says, voicing exactly what I was just thinking.

There's no time to reply, though, because he falls to his knees with an eager smile and absolutely attacks my fly. I'm half-hard already from the proximity to him when he's like this. He has no difficulty finding my cock, pulling me out and then immediately inhaling it like he's been waiting all night for this moment.

It's overwhelming. The soft, wet heat of him. I let my head loll back until it thunks against the door, taking a deep breath as Cade ravages me.

But like always, it's not enough. My fingers wind through his hair, tugging and pulling sweet little noises out of him that garble around my cock. I tug harder and harder, rolling my hips until I'm pushing deeper into his mouth.

Cade goes a little slack; still sitting up and working over my cock, but softer for me.

An image pops into my head, and I can't resist.

With a single fluid movement, I pull myself out of Cade's mouth and spin us around, until he's on his knees but pinned between me and the door. When I sink back in this time, his head is leaning back into the surface.

I crowd over him, slowly pumping myself in and out of his mouth, letting him acclimate to the new position and how restricted he is. The only things he can really move are his hands, which he brings to the back of my thighs at first, before his fingertips crawl up and grab the edge of my back pockets as something to cling to.

Heat curls in my stomach, and I reach down to grab him gently by the throat. If I drop my shoulder, I can reach him from the side, and while my fingers don't wrap all the way around, it's enough to hold him still and put pressure if I want to.

Slowly, inch by inch, I push into his mouth until he starts to choke. I stroke my thumb over the tender flesh it's covering, and then I squeeze, choking him there, too. A few seconds pass as Cade's muscles tighten, his eyes start to water and his skin turns red, then I release.

I pull myself all the way out of his mouth and look down, checking how he's responding. Cade is gazing up at me through wet eyelashes, eyeliner smudging and his face going blotchy.

The expression on his face is making me feel drunk. I don't even know what it is. Devotion?

Whatever it is, it fills something deep inside of me that's always felt catastrophically empty.

I continue this pattern: push in, squeeze, retreat so he can breathe. Again and again, while the tension between us builds to a fever pitch.

"Touch yourself for me," I whisper, and Cade hurries to obey. He's uncoordinated, swimming in endorphins, but he manages to get himself in hand and start frantically stroking.

"Oh, fuck, Cade," I mutter, letting my forehead thunk against the door as I fuck his face. "I'm gonna come."

Cade speeds up as he jerks himself. The door vibrates against my face, and I'm so lost in the moment, it takes me a minute to recognize that someone is knocking. Fuck. Well, we're almost done.

It doesn't take more than a few seconds and another look at Cade's messy face to get my orgasm to hit, filling Cade's mouth as I grind against him.

Cade follows not long after, making a mess but managing to catch most of it in his hand. I let him go, leaning back so he can finally breathe, and hand him some toilet paper to clean up before I situate myself and zip my pants back up.

Once we're both semi-presentable, I pull Cade up to his feet. He sways a little, happily pressing against my chest. As soon as we're only inches away, I have to take the opportunity to kiss his swollen lips.

He tastes like cum and beer, and I don't care. It's perfect.

Leaning our foreheads together, I only break away from the kiss for a second to tell him the truth.

"I love you more than anything, Cade. I'll never stop. I don't think I could if I tried."

Cade's eyes are still a wet, bloodshot mess from before, but I think for a second I might see him tearing up.

The moment is interrupted by another knock on the door—this one louder and much more insistent—which puts us both in motion. I cup Cade's face in my hands, swiping under his eyes with my thumbs in an ineffective attempt to clean him up as we both laugh softly. Between the watery panda eyes he's got going on and the swollen lips, plus a faint red outline of where my fingers were pressed against his throat a minute ago, it's pretty damn obvious what we've been doing in here.

Which isn't the end of the world, but it's built into me to be as discreet as possible in all things. Go unnoticed. So, when Cade wraps one long-fingered hand around my wrist and tells me to stop fussing, it's kind of insane that I just do it.

"Let everybody here know how crazy I get for you. Fuck 'em," he says, his voice a hoarse rasp that completes the just-got-facefucked aesthetic.

I can't help but lean into his space when he says it. Since the day I met Cade, it's felt like we were tethered together by something I couldn't see. But in these little moments, the tether is so tight, any space between us seems to burn. My body sways in his direction, like we can push out all the oxygen in the room and fill it with our combined presence instead.

My hand turns the tiny lock and pushes down on the handle, pulling the door inward as Cade wraps one arm around my waist from behind, tied to me as well, prepared to walk of shame our way back to the booth.

I don't know what I expected. I think I didn't expect anything—I wasn't thinking about anything but Cade.

But if I had, even in my right mind I wouldn't have expected Kyle Waters to be standing there, staring at us.

It's a toss up who here looks more shocked. Kyle freezes, raising an eyebrow as he takes in the sight before him. 'Disheveled' is not a strong enough word for how Cade and I look right now. And while we agreed a long time ago that we weren't hiding our relationship from anyone anymore, I think the concept of being out to his dad and the abrupt, unintentional experience of it are two very different things

The air around me becomes tense as Cade stiffens behind me. His fingers stay on my hip, but the touch is so light I can barely feel it, and I know without looking that his spine is straightening and his shoulders are pushed back as he contorts himself into the specific version of himself he normally allows his father to see.

Kyle makes a show of looking Cade up and down, and while the silence is better than the explosive homophobia-laced rage I was halfway expecting, it's still not great. There's a tremor in the air, and it takes me a second to realize that it's Cade.

"What are you doing here?" Cade snaps, breaking the silence. His voice is deep and filled with barely-contained anger.

"Drinking," Kyle drawls, looking entirely unintimidated, his fingers loose around the longneck he's holding. "Krystal wanted to go someplace nice, and I've never been here before. Although maybe I misread what kind of place this is."

There's a teasing lilt to his voice, and the mechanism inside me that decodes social intent is whirring and humming, frantically trying to decode if the tone is violent in its intent, or just giving us shit.

I'm not sure. I don't have the danger-alarms going off that I normally get with the truly violent, but I don't trust Kyle for a second, based on his history.

Cade is frozen behind me—still trembling, although hopefully not severely enough for Kyle to notice—and the need to diffuse the tension is overwhelming.

"We should go," I murmur back to Cade, using the same easy, non-confrontational tone I perfected over a lifetime spent with my own explosive father.

I can practically feel Cade doing a record scratch behind me, before he swells up again.

"Fuck that," he says. "If anyone should leave it's him. The bar, the state, the plane of existence. Why can't you just leave us alone?"

Kyle holds his hands up in mock-innocence, but there's no tension in his body. He really doesn't seem like he's about to snap.

"I didn't mean to interrupt," he says, his tone still teasing but light. "By all means, as you were. You might wanna check your makeup, though," Kyle gestures toward his own eye. "You look a little... mussed. Krystal might have something in her purse—"

He doesn't get the chance to finish his unfunny joke, because that was all it took to push Cade over the line. One second he's standing behind me, his body at war between frightened child and fronting man, the next he's on his dad and they're both tumbling to the floor in an explosion of violence.

CHAPTER TEN

CADE

A ll these years, my father has existed inside of me like a demon that couldn't be exorcised. The demon operates me like a puppet, moving my arms and legs, talking through my mouth sometimes. It's the part of me that can't control my anger. The part of me that clings so tightly to all the little hurts and scars that people have inflicted on me over the years, and uses that hurt to keep me warm at night.

Anger feeds the demon. Liquor, too. I know I should stop. I know I should starve it out, the way you deprive a fire of oxygen to extinguish it, but the demon's in control too often. I let it take control, because both it and I secretly love to fan the flames. It makes me feel alive.

I don't mean any of this in a dissociative or hallucinatory way. I'm fully aware that I'm responsible for my actions. All of them. Especially the worst ones.

But it feels like the me that is responsible was birthed from conflict and neglect, and the strength that this version of me developed by learning to survive is the only thing carrying the whole of me forward. So, if I want to keep going and letting the better parts of myself exist, I need the demon to keep its residence inside me before my body crumbles like a rotten rooftop.

I feed the demon just enough to keep going. Just enough to keep the rest of me alive. Cutting it out would make me collapse from the inside out.

Or maybe I'm too scared to confront that part of myself, because I don't know how much good there really is in me outside of it. Does the 'good' really count if it's only there to make up for all the shit? Forcing myself to act good isn't the same as holding it within myself the way someone like Silas does, so do I really get credit for faking it?

I mean, I'm the only one keeping track, so nothing really counts.

Either way, I cling to the one thing I know without a damn question.

Without Kyle and the chaos he created me from, this side of me wouldn't exist. I wouldn't need it to. It seems only fair that I unleash it on him once in a while, and that's the only fragile logic I need to move forward in that moment.

The arc of my fist is a thing of beauty, and I'd trade my beloved bike to see the look of shock on his face again. It's such a perfect punch that he crumples immediately, conscious but on the ground, and I don't hesitate to climb on top of him and swing again as he tries to react and get in a hit of his own, grabbing at me anywhere he can reach. He and I are interchangeable. We're extensions of each other, a snake eating its own tail if the snake were made out of rage, and the rest of the world falls away as I search for nothing but the purity of flesh on flesh, destroying everything I can reach.

"Motherfucker!" I vaguely hear Dad growl, garbled around what I hope is blood in his mouth.

We're on the ground, his body underneath mine, and I can't even focus enough to think about where I'm hitting him, I'm just lashing out. His hands flail, pushing me back even though it's futile, until he seems to get over the shock of it and find a grip on me. Silas is also pulling at me from behind, but it's not enough.

One of my father's hands is wrapped around my throat—not squeezing, but using it to push me away—while the other pushes on my chest. It makes my mind jump the rails for a second. He used to do this when I was little. He never choked me—that I remember—but he'd use that gut-punch, instinctive pain that comes from pressure on your throat to push me away from him if he was pissed.

Nowadays, Silas is the only one who puts his hand there, and it's in a very different fucking way. I hadn't connected the two things until now, and I'm distantly aware of how fucked up it is.

It's not news that I have daddy issues, I guess.

The whole cascade of thoughts is enough to break my concentration, so Kyle gets the advantage and keeps pushing. He knocks me on my ass in the end, sending Silas careening into the wall in the process. As soon as my back hits the tile I panic, but like father like son, because Kyle doesn't let up. He climbs on top of me, straddling my hips while I get so panicked I'm doing more scratching at him like a frightened creature than throwing punches. He tries to grab my wrists, his weight still pinning me down, but he can't. I've sense-memoried my way right back into being a toddler—flailing and thrashing with the unrestrained fear that comes from operating on instinct before your brain is even fully formed.

There are a lot of different ways to fight. Even if it looks the same from the outside, the vibe can be different. In retrospect, I could pick out a lot of fights from my past that were charged with a heady, sexual energy I wasn't able to name at the time. Fighting other guys my age in high school, especially, had a much different motive than I was consciously aware of in that moment.

This is not like that. This is rough and painful and feels like I'm a fractious calf being wrangled and tied up by the rancher that secretly can't wait to slit my throat.

"Stop. Cade. Knock it the fuck off," Dad's saying over and over, still trying to get my arms under control as I lash out. It feels like I've heard that word a lot lately—*stop*—but that doesn't help it land.

Eventually he gives up, changing strategy to smack me across the face. Open-handed, like some people—abusive assholes, obviously—do to a "rebellious" child. The sensation shocks me still, and he takes the opportunity to grab my face with one rough hand, the other finally getting a hold of my wrists.

I feel small. The anger that was fueling me before drains right into the floor, and it's all I can do not to cower beneath him. I have a split-second to truly feel scared—and scared for Silas, who is still pushing himself up from being knocked to the ground and is definitely about to fucking murder Kyle—before the bathroom door pushes all the way open.

Then chaos takes over again, but this time I'm shrinking away from it instead of letting it devour me. Someone drags my dad off me, and the sudden space triggers a coughing fit as my throat spasms where he pushed me before. I hear men and women yelling, then someone is grabbing my shoulders and pulling me. I flinch at first, until the unmistakable scent of Silas hits me and I force myself to relax.

"Cade! Cade, look at me? Are you okay?"

His voice sounds more distant than it should, but I force myself to focus on him in the blur.

"Silas," I croak, even though I'm not really saying anything.

"Jesus fucking Christ, you scared me," he says, pulling me into his lap and wrapping his arms around me awkwardly.

There's no heat behind his words though, instead he sounds sort of desperate and raw. I can still hear other people yelling, but Silas is filling up my vision.

"You really fucking scared me, you asshole. Let me see your hand," he says, reaching for it with one hand while the other comes up to cup my face. But over his shoulder I can see Kyle being dragged away by Ford and Gunnar, red-faced and trying to buck off their grip.

His expression sets in rage. His eyes meet mine in between cries of, "Let me go, motherfucker," and he pauses for a split-second. When he does, I become acutely aware of Silas's hand on my face, and feel my cheeks flushing even more with adrenaline and something too close to shame for comfort.

No. I will not be this person. I will not care what he thinks of me, or deny how important Silas is in my life.

I can't.

Dad looks grim as he yells over the guys to me, "Jesus Christ, you interrupt one fucking blowjob and suddenly the gay gestapo shows up to get you. I didn't know you were so sensitive, boy."

Flooded with adrenaline, all I can think of is getting him away from me and away from Silas. I lurch toward him, tearing Silas's hands from me and reaching out like I'm going to restart the fight all over again.

The rage feels better than fear, but it makes my mind white-out.

"You fucking cocksucker, don't make me kill you," I yell, balling my fist to throw another punch just as someone snags my body and pulls me backward again.

A small, buried part of me winces. *Cocksucker* was my favorite curse word for so long. I never meant it as a slur or used it against queer people, it was just something you said. Eventually, I realized that it was a shitty, garbage-person thing to do, and how meaningless all my excuses were, and broke the habit. It hasn't come out of my mouth in years.

Apparently, I'm reverting to all the worst parts of myself I've buried. I can't think about that now, though. Not when Kyle is almost within reach.

He looks taken aback by the insult though, which I don't think I've ever called him before. Of course he would take extra offense. He's just that asshole.

"Boy, I will wash your goddamn mouth out with soap if you keep talking to me like this."

It's a ridiculous thing to say. I'm not a little kid anymore, surely beating on him is worse than insulting him, and we're both being held apart by bigger, stronger men who are shouting to each other over our conversation.

But the threat hits me hard. Again, I feel like a toddler, about to be dangled upside down over a sink in a public restroom by my dad while mom shoves cheap pink hand soap in my mouth, getting waterboarded as foam streams from my lips and I scream to passing strangers who don't care, because for some reason, this is normal.

The surge of adrenaline is enough for me to pull one arm out of someone's—maybe Tristan's?—grasp and land my own open-handed hit on Kyle's face, before we're both wrenched painfully apart.

"That's it, outside!"

I think it's Gunnar shouting. It's all too much of a blur.

I stumble over my feet until I'm practically picked up and carried out to the gravel parking lot. The rush of cold night air slaps a little sense into me, and the world around me comes more into focus.

Kyle has blood running from his nose and mouth, and he's making unintelligible growled threats to everyone around him, all while still looking me in the eye. Ford is pinning him to the ground with his arms behind him now, but it looks like more effort than you would expect. Kyle must really be putting up a fight.

Something in me withers and dies, right in that moment. All of this over what—a blowjob? Because he hated me so much even before he knew I was queer, and this is what pushed him over the edge into true, boundless violence?

If they let him go, would he try to kill me? Maybe that's what he's always secretly wanted. Freeing himself from the burden of my existence.

"Christ, Cade, will you give it a rest?" Tristan's strained voice is right in my ear, and he has both of my arms pinned behind my back pretty successfully now, holding me in place. At least I'm not getting shoved to the ground.

Well, fuck him. And fuck Kyle. I need to... I need to fight for Silas. Show him I'm not ashamed.

"Fuck you, bitch!" I yell at my dad, summoning some kind of bravado while I feel blood pooling in my own mouth as well. "You wanna interrupt us again? Maybe you'll see me taking it up the ass. I'll bend over for him every day and still beat you to the fucking ground. We know exactly who the real man is here. You can't even take care of your own fucking family, you have to run away and make me do it. Touch me again, and I'll fucking kill you. Don't even look at Silas. Our gay assess are done with your fucking shit."

Technically, I'm bi. And Silas is... Silas. Probably demi, but we haven't talked about it. But none of that sounds as punchy.

I swell with pride at my little takedown, and Kyle finally seems to have given up fighting against Ford. He's not even looking at me anymore because his face is in the gravel.

My pride comes crashing down when Silas gets in my face again, grabbing me with both hands and holding my face still.

I think there are tears on his cheeks.

"Cade, fucking stop," he says, sounding angrier than I ever would have expected. "Shut the fuck and stop. You're going to hurt someone."

My breath catches.

I... What?

I'm standing up for myself.

My expression must have given me away, because his face gentles but when he speaks again, it's still just as stern.

"Stop, okay? This is done. We need to leave before the cops show up."

"I just... I was protecting us."

Silas takes a deep breath and sighs, some unspeakable kind of heartbreak in his eyes.

"I know you think that. Just—stop. Okay? Breathe. Can Tristan let you go now?"

Not knowing what to say, I nod. My limbs are still tense, muscles straining where my shoulders have been jerked backwards, and trying to soften them feels like unrolling cardboard that sat in the sun until it baked itself stiff.

I nod again, taking a conscious breath, and finally the hands on me relax. My muscles scream in protest as my hands fall down to my side, limp because I don't know what I'm supposed to do with myself. The pain and exhaustion are starting to set in, and I can feel it when my hands begin to shake.

"Fuck me, kid, you really went for it, didn't you?" Tristan's voice moves from behind me to in front as he comes into view, stepping between me and Silas to start peering at my face. He's already in medical mode, I can tell, but I'm distracted by the fact that he's also covered in blood, and his nose is swollen and bruised.

I reach toward him without thinking, but he flinches away and then bats my hand down.

"Wha—?" I start, but Silas interrupts me.

"You did that."

His voice is hard, and he's standing farther away than I want him to.

"Fuck, I'm sorry T, I just—"

"Not now," he says. "We can rehash all the questionable choices you just made and their consequences when you're sober. I'll be fine. Now look at me so I can make sure you don't have a concussion."

I've only had three fucking beers, and I'm pretty sure this whole ordeal has burned any alcohol right out of my system, but I get the feeling defending myself will not go down well right now.

I focus on being compliant, following Tristan's directions without question while my brain retreats into itself in an attempt to beat back the tide of shame that's threatening to drown me.

Silas's hard gaze is on me the whole time, and I can't bear it. Tristan uses the flashlight on his phone to do a quick exam, checking my pupils and reactions, before he moves his hands to my throat. I wince, because it's definitely bruised, but it's difficult to know how much of that was from what me and Silas were doing, and how much is from Dad hitting me there.

I'm so fucked up is the only concrete thought I can hold onto.

Tristan sighs, finally, apparently satisfied that I'm not about to die.

"I think you should go to the ER just in case, but I already know you won't. Silas, will you watch him? Rest but don't go to sleep for a couple hours, make sure he doesn't start acting weird or having trouble breathing. And call a fucking ambulance if he does."

"I'm fine," I say, but my throat is raw and it comes out embarrassingly raspy, I suddenly notice. "I'm sorry."

My gaze flits between both of them, but I see hard expressions looking back at me. Behind them, I see Krystal walking my dad toward the other side of the parking lot, hopefully to get in his car and fucking leave.

God, he's going home to my mom. I hope he doesn't tell her how bad it was.

I hope he doesn't take it out on her.

"Shit, Mom, we should—"

"No," Silas and Tristan say in unison.

Silas sighs again. "I'll call your mom and let her know what happened, and make sure she's alright. But I don't think he's going to feel like fighting any more by the time he gets home. You're not going anywhere other than the hospital or our home."

I don't know why he stresses 'our' like that, but my brain isn't really firing on all cylinders right now.

"You good?" Tristan asks Silas, his eyeline already sliding over to Ford and the others, probably anxious to make sure they're alright. Silas makes a noise of confirmation and nods.

Most of the crowd has dispersed, either leaving to avoid the drama or heading back inside. But Ford is watching Kyle, presumably to make sure he stays gone, and Gunnar is standing there with his arms around Tobias. And is that... Shit, does Tobias have a black eye?

107

Guilt cripples me, hard and fast, as I wonder if it was me or Dad that accidentally clipped him while we were too wrapped up in trying to get to each other.

It doesn't matter, I guess. It's still my fault.

Fuck.

"I'm sorry," I say to Tristan one more time as he starts walking away, but he only shakes his head.

"Go home, Cade."

It's all he says. It feels like a gut punch.

Silas reaches for my shoulder, the air around us heavy, and turns me in the direction of where we're parked. I let him. I'll let him do anything he wants, because I'm only here to fuck shit up, apparently.

CHAPTER ELEVEN

SILAS

C ade is quiet the whole drive home. Which is good, because it lets me silently wrestle with my own torrent of overwhelming emotion for a little while. Once I made a quick call to Kris to give her a head's up about what's coming back to the trailer right now.

That was terrifying. I've seen Cade fight before. I've seen him get into it with his dad once, I've seen him argue with his mom a million times, and I remember all the scrappy teenage fistfights he used to get into back in school.

I've seen the way his temper can operate on a hairtrigger, easily snapped when he feels like someone's being disrespectful to me, or homophobic toward us.

I know it's important to him to make sure people know he's not ashamed. It seems to be for my benefit a lot of the time, but I'm not sure that's all there is to it. I know how he feels about me. I've seen it, as he's gone to the mat for me bleeding time and time again. I see it in all the little things he does to take care of me and love me the way no one else ever has.

People are always going to be assholes, and a lot of them are going to be homophobic assholes. Why should I care what they think about who Cade is or how he feels?

Cade cares a lot, apparently.

I'm pretty sure he still thinks this was all something that got out of hand, but that he was fundamentally justified, because he was protecting me from his dad and standing up for our relationship.

All I saw was him lashing out, over and over and over, with no thought of holding himself back. No restraint, no hesitation, just unbridled violence at some provocation that I still don't totally understand.

Kyle had looked surprised, more than anything. I hate to defend that piece of shit, but it's not like he was dropping f-slurs and threatening to disown Cade, or something. He seemed like a regular insensitive asshole, not a hateful one.

I have to talk to him about this. I have to make him see how it looks to everyone who isn't him.

Unfortunately, I have no idea how.

He spends the drive silently staring out the window, occasionally looking down to pick the flakes of dried blood off of his nails, intermittently using his good hand to hold a wad of napkins to his forehead where the skin is split open and bleeding.

I keep glancing down, because I can see how swollen his hand is getting and it's worrying me more every time I glance at it. It's red, dark and getting darker by the minute, with scrapes over the knuckles like he was punching drywall instead of his father's face.

It all happened so fast. It felt like an eternity that would never come to an end, but it was also too abrupt to really understand what was happening. At one point, I was ready to jump in and attack Kyle myself, because seeing Cade under him, bloody and wide-eyed with fear, woke up something instinctive in me. Plus, I just fucking hate Kyle. But once I got that urge under control, I realized just how out of hand the whole thing had gotten.

Thank god the guys were there to help break it up. If it had just been me, I couldn't have managed it. And if the cops had come, we would have been fucked. Because despite what Cade probably thinks, he was the aggressor in any way anyone else would understand.

I hope they're all okay. I saw the moment Cade's elbow caught Tristan's nose, and it looked bad. I also saw Tobias end up with a black eye somehow, and Gunnar and Ford both got scratched to hell by trying to contain Tornado Kyle, once his temper was flaring as uncontrollably as Cade's.

Cade's hands are shaking badly, and I can see how hard he's trying to control it, holding them tightly in his lap.

I want to reach over and grab one. Normally, I wouldn't hesitate. Even if we were in the middle of a fight. But right now, I feel too lost.

Tonight scared me deeply, and I don't know how I'm supposed to claw my way out of that fear to give Cade what he needs so this can stop.

By the time we're inside the house, he still hasn't spoken and neither have I. He won't even really look at me. The shaking in his hands has taken over his entire body, and if I had to guess, I'd say his physical pain and adrenaline crash and shame spiral are all coming down on him at once.

The thought makes me hurt for him so hard it feels like I might crumble, but I can't. I need to focus. Time seems slow as I take a deep breath, tapping each fingertip against my thumb a few times, letting the repetitive sensation ground me in the moment and pull me out of my head.

After a long minute, I feel calmer. When I reach for Cade, gently grabbing his arms from behind, he jumps. But as soon as I pull him close, he relaxes into me. His back presses against my chest, letting me take some of his weight, as the shaking gets worse.

"Let's get you cleaned up."

My whisper sounds like a shout in the stillness of the empty house, but Cade nods anyway.

I walk him to the bathroom, taking over stripping him down when his swollen hand is useless and the other is shaking too hard to be helpful. There's eyeliner smeared over his face, mixed with the dark, dried blood, and his cheek and eye on the left are already swollen to hell. I pull off his shirt with one hand while reaching in to turn on the shower with the other, making sure the water is as cool as it can be without freezing him.

Stepping into the tub is precarious. Cade is long: long limbs, long torso, muscular but rangy; and now that he's so unsteady it makes him look like he could topple over at the slightest breeze. I quickly shed my own clothes, also covered in blood and other fluids I don't want to think about, so I can step into the shower with him and make sure he doesn't fall.

I stand behind him, both of us facing the showerhead, so I can feel how he flinches when the water hits all his cuts and scrapes. I loop one arm around his stomach and press him close to me, leaning the other hand against the wall in front of him for support. He stiffens initially, like he's trying to hold himself upright, then seems to wilt all at once.

His good hand splays over the tile next to mine, and that hand combined with my entire body pressed up against his from behind seems like the only reason he's still upright. I can see how hard his muscles twitch and tremble, and he bows his head low, letting the water run down the back of his neck and looking like he's trying to crumble to the ground.

"Shh," I whisper in his ear, because I can't think of anything else to say. I spread my fingers wide over his abs and dig them into his flesh, reminding him that I'm here. I press my lips to the warm skin behind his ear, trying to project some sort of calm directly into his brain. "It'll be okay."

I didn't want to say that it is okay, because we both know it's far from it.

His eyebrow is bleeding again now that it's wet, running thin rivulets of red down the side of his neck that he doesn't seem to notice. His knees bend suddenly like they gave out, and together we stumble forward until we're closer to the wall. Cade's forehead hits the tile and the shaking gets worse, feeling more like how you move when you're sobbing, except no sound is coming out of him, just harsh, ragged breaths.

Oh, Cade.

Tears fill my eyes abruptly as I can practically feel the anxious pain running off of him.

I don't know what to do.

I need... I need help.

But there's no one here but us.

A stray tear spills out of me—not for the first time tonight—and I settle for squeezing him tightly, burying my face in the back of his neck and holding him as close to me as possible.

I press shapeless kisses into his skin, trying to pour all my unspoken love into him to help hold him up while he shudders and threatens to collapse. He's breathing more and more heavily, like a panic attack is attempting to open up inside him, but he's fighting it.

Sliding my hand up to sit over his heart, I take a deep breath, making his body move with mine. It's something he's done for me countless times before, and it's the only thing I can think of to help. I take a deep, slow breath, waiting for him to join me. Eventually, his body shudders and his chest moves beneath my hand.

We do it again and again, with Cade gradually feeling steadier beneath me, even though the shaking continues.

Eventually, I lean back. The water is cold and we've been in here too long. I need him to lie down before he collapses.

"Let me wash you up, baby," I say softly in his ear.

Out of the two of us, he's the one into using pet names. I always feel awkward about it, like I'm doing it wrong. But it feels natural right now. Cade doesn't stiffen when I move him, staying soft beneath my hands until I've got him facing me, leaning backward against the tile. He's out of the stream of water now, with most of it hitting me inconveniently close to my face, but I think he needs the support.

I focus on washing him up quickly, squirting soap into my hands and then moving over him with quick, gentle strokes. I wash the sweat and dirt from his chest, then his arms, skipping his swollen hand that I'll need to do something about in a minute.

I wash his legs and his groin, his cock soft and vulnerable in my hand. When I move up to his face, he winces again, but it needs to be done. The soap obviously stings, making him hiss and turn his face to the side. I sweep my thumbs over his cheeks a few times as gently as I can before I call it good. His eyes are still dark with makeup I'm not going to scrub off right now, but the worst of the blood and smudging is off his skin, revealing the true color of the bruising below.

When I've done as much as I can, I turn off the water and step out, getting a towel ready before pulling him after me. It's hard to get him dry without being too rough, so I do my best but focus on getting him out of the bathroom and into bed. I throw the towel on the dresser, too wrung out to care about the mess right now, and then peel back the covers so he can climb under.

He lies down obligingly, but looks tense again, instead of relaxed. After a second of leaning against the headboard, he arches his back awkwardly, an expression of pain crossing his face as he holds up his trembling hand between us.

"I, uh," he coughs, his voice even rougher now than it was before, making guilt bubble through me for a second as I think of how roughly I fucked his throat right before his dad ended up fucking hitting him in it. "I think I broke my hand."

The words make something inside me clench abruptly, my eyes filling with stupid, pointless tears and my stomach swooping like I might throw up. I have to swallow hard before I can speak.

"Should we go to the hospital after all? Get an x-ray?"

Cade looks at me with wide eyes, then shakes his head and slumps down into the bed.

"No. Please." His sentences are getting more and more fragmented as he succumbs to the exhaustion of the night. "Tomorrow, maybe."

I know it's wrong. I know we should go sooner rather than later, if he's really hurt himself, but I can't bring myself to force him. And the thought of doing all this under harsh, fluorescent lights, surrounded by people asking questions about what happened makes it so much worse.

I don't want to go, either. It makes me a shitty boyfriend, but it's true.

He needs to rest. We both need to breathe. We can be better in the morning.

Fuck, I'm supposed to pick the girls up in the afternoon. I'll have to call their aunt and tell her... something. It's not like she won't hear about it from Kris eventually, I guess.

All I can do is focus on right now. I'm still naked and dripping from the shower, the carpet wet under my feet, so I grab the towel I used on Cade and quickly dry myself off. I slip on some sweats and a t-shirt before running to the kitchen to get an ice pack out of the freezer. I convince Cade to rest it on his hand, and then hold still as I slap a bandaid on that cut on his eyebrow before it starts bleeding everywhere again. It looks nasty, swollen and gaping open more than I'd like.

As soon as I crawl under the covers next to him, he turns into me and presses his face against my chest. It must hurt, because there's so much swelling, but he does it anyway. His good hand rucks up my shirt and grasps my stomach. It makes me twinge immediately, desperate for him to not feel the softness there,

115

but then I feel guilty for being so superficial even when Cade's all fucked up and looking for comfort.

Instead, I lie there, stroking up and down his back as softly as I can and trying not to let myself tense up too much as he grabs at me.

At least there's no chance of me falling asleep anytime soon. Tristan said to watch for his throat swelling suddenly, which is a terrifying concept, so I'll be watching him sleep for at least the next few hours.

He doesn't fall asleep, though. He takes one long, shuddering breath after another, his eyes open and vacant and his fingers continuing to anxiously grip at my stomach. I stroke my fingers through his hair in an attempt to soothe him, but he stays stiff.

"Go to sleep, Cade," I say after over an hour of this. "I'll watch you and make sure you're still okay. I'm right here."

Cade shifts, looking up at me from an awkward angle, our faces too close to see each other properly but not close enough to kiss.

"I can't sleep," he says, his voice hollow.

"Do you want to go to the hospital after all? We can still go."

My fingers dig into his scalp a little harder as I pet him, my own anxieties mounting at the thought of dealing with the ER.

"Can you fuck me?"

He says it so quietly, and it seems so out of left field, that at first I don't register what he said. When I don't immediately respond, he shifts himself a little farther up my body, obviously holding back a groan at the effort.

Once his face is level with mine, he presses a soft kiss against my lips. I kiss him back, because I'll always kiss him back. But I'm gentle, because his lip is swollen and it has to hurt.

Cade shifts until his body is blanketing mine, and there isn't even a hint of hardness pressed into me—exactly like I'd expect at a time like this—but he's rolling his hips against mine a little as he clings to my side with his good hand and kisses me again.

"Cade—what?"

I'm stuttering, but I'm so confused right now.

"Fuck me," he whispers. I think he's trying to be seductive, but I can hear how raw his voice is, even through the quiet words.

He kisses me again, parting his lips this time and trying to push his tongue into my mouth. At the same time, he puts his hand between us to palm my also-soft cock, and the weird sensation makes me jump.

"Cade," I say, pulling back as far as I can despite the headboard behind me. "No. What? We can't—you're hurt."

"I'm always a mess. It's just a couple bruises. Come on, I was an asshole tonight. Don't you want to punish me? Show me what you think of me?"

My mouth is literally hanging open at this point. Cade comes out with a lot of random shit, but I don't think he's ever said anything that's thrown me sideways quite as much as this.

The sex we had was never vanilla. We started out weird, and got weirder from there. And recently he's been pushing the degradation stuff more. I noticed, but I just thought he was finding himself, or something. I have a weakness for dirty talk anyway, so what does it matter if I'm calling him a little bitch, as long as that's what he's into? I did a little googling, this is all stuff that healthy people in good relationships can do.

A part of me worried a little that it was coming from a bad place, but I'm a worrier. It didn't seem right to judge what he wanted.

I am now officially judging. This feels wrong. This feels deeply, deeply fucked up.

"Cade, I'm not doing that right now. Are you kidding? It's fucked up. Even the thought of having sex right now seems so wild, and even worse to do... that."

"What? You were into it before. This is just how we fuck. Come on, I know you're pissed at me. Let it out. I fucking deserve it, right?"

I sit up, all my internal alarms ringing at the line this conversation is taking.

"I'm not pissed at you. I'm fucking worried. You scared me. And even if I was pissed at you, I wouldn't literally want to take it out on you through sex. That's not right. I thought we were just doing that because it was hot. You know I don't actually mean that shit when I say it, right? The degradation shit? It just seemed like it turned you on, so I went with it."

"It does turn me on. I like seeing it all come out of you. And then after you're always so sweet when you take care of me after you fuck me up."

A feeling of horror sinks into me before I can fully process what he's saying. In my mind, we were doing something kinky. Something fictional but fun, and then I made sure to take really good care of him, because I know that shit can be hard on your hormones and your body. I learned enough about BDSM and kink to understand that, because I wanted to know what I was doing, and that just makes sense.

He's describing the exact same thing, but not in a way that sounds like kink and aftercare.

He makes it sound... gross. Manipulative.

My gut clenches and I wrench myself into a seated position, accidentally jostling him enough that he winces in the process.

"It's supposed to be a game, Cade. I'm not actually angry with you when we do it. I'm not getting out some secret, pushed down anger that I hold for you. I don't... I don't hold any anger for you. Where the fuck is this coming from? How long have you secretly thought I was hate-fucking you?"

Cade looks up at me, wide-eyed and clearly confused.

"Silas, I—"

He trails off, and the whole thing continues to sink deeper and deeper into my consciousness.

"Oh, god," I whisper to no one in particular, looking around in desperation like there's an answer on one of the bedroom walls. "This is so fucked up."

"Why are you upset? What's happening?"

Words cannot express all the things I feel at this question. I'm not good at articulating my feelings at the best of times. Therapy has helped a lot with that, but still. And this is the most unhinged conversation I've ever had with my boyfriend who I now know thinks I, what? Secretly hate him?

I was always so impressed with how well Cade came out of his fucked-up childhood. He was barely raised, he was abused—even if he won't call it that—he watched his mother trapped in an endless cycle of domestic violence, and he held it all together to do a damn good job of taking care of his sisters. He downplays how bad it was a lot, but I thought he was just trying to not make a big deal about it.

Now I think that maybe he never really accepted how bad it was, and absorbed more of his parents' shitty dynamic than I realized.

I scrub one hand down my face while Cade continues to stare at me, confused as ever. He looks so tired. I don't like that we've started this conversation when he's all beat up and dazed, but I can't exactly drop it now.

I sink to my knees at the side of the bed, because I hate towering over him like this, but I can't bring myself to crawl back under the covers with him yet.

Leaning forward on the mattress, I take hold of Cade's non-swollen hand, making his eyes widen even more.

"Cade, I need you to understand that that's fucked up. I only ever want to hurt you during sex or call you names or anything else because you want it. Because it turns you on. Not because I have some kind of negative feelings toward you that I need to work through. That's abuse. Hurting you because I'm angry at you would be abuse, even if it comes with an orgasm. That's the difference."

Cade shakes his head. "I don't understand. Everybody gets angry sometimes. It's intense when we fuck, because we love each other so much. There's nothing wrong with that."

"But I'm not angry with you. Do you get that? And I'm sweet to you after because you deserve it, because I love you. Not because you earned it by what

119

you took. You don't have to... bribe me with sex to get fucking cuddled as reward. I always want to take care of you, you just won't let me the rest of the time."

Cade's face scrunches up like he's glitching.

"Please tell me you understand," I say. "Tell me you know I'll never fuck you to punish you for something I'm genuinely angry about."

There's a long pause, where I don't feel like it's really sinking in. But he nods, eventually.

"Okay, robot boy. I understand. I'm sorry, I'm being weird."

The nickname makes me unclench a little. It makes Cade sound more like himself.

I blow out a breath, willing all the tension to flee the room so he can finally rest. I still feel very on edge in a way I can't really articulate, but at least I said what I needed to out loud.

"Can we please sleep?" I ask. "You need to rest. And in the morning, we're going to the fucking hospital, because your hand looks worse and worse."

Cade sighs and flops backward on the bed. His left hand lies on the mattress in front of me, even darker and more swollen than an hour ago.

"I don't think I can sleep. It's like I can feel my whole pulse in it, and it hurts every time I take a breath."

I shake my head, frustration brewing in me.

"And you thought I should be fucking you like that."

"It was a stupid thing to say, okay!" Cade's words come out angry all of a sudden, and he throws his other hand over his eyes. "I was being stupid. I do that a lot. Can we please drop it?"

I can see his chest moving with deep, pain-tense breaths, and I make up my mind.

"Fuck this, we're not waiting."

"What?" he looks at me, his eyes shadowed black by his hand over them, expression difficult to make out in the soft moonlight.

"Get up. We're going to the hospital." Cade doesn't move, so I stand up and hold out my hand. "Now."

I know how much he must be hurting when he doesn't argue with me, but starts to move.

CHAPTER TWELVE

CADE

"Do you need me to tell you why you're an idiot, or have you gotten that speech enough times already tonight?"

Micah is staring at me hard. Because of course he's working tonight, and of course as soon as he saw me he swapped cases with the nurse I'd been originally assigned to.

We're not like, good friends. But we've met a bunch of times now, and his ex-stepbrother/current boyfriend works at the Feral Possum where I hang out a lot, and I think he's possibly the only real friend Tristan has other than me—and by extension Silas—in this town. It's a small town, and when you have enough connections with someone you end up being friends by default.

Which means he feels entitled to skip even the pretense of a bedside manner. He did get me seen by the doctor pretty quickly, and then rushed me around pulling strings to get me through x-ray and everything else about as fast as this hospital ever can. But now everyone else has done their part, and he's the only one left to finish bandaging me up before I get turfed back to the world.

My hand isn't broken, but it is sprained. It's wrapped in a rigid brace with an ice pack on top. I got a stitch in my eyebrow, because it reopened after I got in the car with Silas and wouldn't stop bleeding, and I got a strangulation work up that made me burn with embarrassment, because there was no way for them to distinguish between the bruises from Silas and the bruises from my dad, and I sure as hell wasn't going to tell them the details.

They can think Dad strangled me if they want. It's not like I'm pressing charges.

It's not like I didn't start the fight.

"I've been lectured enough, thank you. I'm fine." My voice is almost completely gone at this point, sounding like air rushing through empty space, because I've been talking for hours and it wasn't in great shape even before the fight.

Silas snorts softly, but doesn't say anything. He hasn't said anything the whole time, just stood there like a sentry, watching me with careful eyes and exhaustion clear in his face.

I feel terrible for having put him through this whole shitfest. And for managing to make it worse at every turn, even though I still don't really understand why he was so upset before.

Was it stupid to try to exorcise my guilt by fucking? Sure. But my head was loud and busy and everything hurt in the bad way. I knew he was angry at me. I knew I deserved it.

I thought maybe we could hate fuck and get it all out of our systems.

Apparently, that's not something we do.

I don't have the brain-space to work out the implications of any of it right now. All I want to do is let the tramadol kick in, try not to puke, and go the fuck to sleep.

I will still be a walking disaster in the morning—well, now it's the morning, but later in the morning—and we can talk about it then.

Or never.

Never is an excellent option.

"You're so far from fine, boy," Micah says as he moves around me, cleaning up and bandaging the smaller cuts and scrapes that have been ignored until now.

I bristle, having to focus on tamping down my anger at the word. Micah doesn't say it like my dad says it. Micah almost said it like he was about to call me "girl" but pivoted at the last second, like I might get offended.

Which I don't, but like I said, we don't know each other that well.

The memory of my dad threatening to wash my mouth out with soap comes back to me and I have to suppress a shudder.

Micah takes a step back and stares at me, hands on hips and a critical eye checking out his own work.

After a minute, he clearly decides he's done, and then he softens with a sigh. When he sits down in the chair next to the bed I'm perched on, putting us eye to eye, I know I'm getting a lecture anyway.

"Nobody wins when you do that. You know that, right? No matter how much the other person deserved it. You both end up fucked up, and you're never going to change the part of them that made them deserve it in the first place. You can't beat someone into being something they're not. Trust me."

Yeah, but it feels hella good in the moment.

I don't say it out loud, because I know it wouldn't be well received. Instead, I stay silent.

Micah huffs after a minute and stands up again. He goes through my discharge instructions quickly, mostly for Silas's benefit, and hands him a plastic bag with my meds, before adding the part of the instructions that I'm sure most patients don't get.

"Do not think you're a fucking badass and know your limits, and start playing fast and loose with the tramadol dosages, or mixing it with booze or other painkillers. It's a weak opioid, but it's still an opioid. Your body is fucked up, whether you want to admit it or not. You can overdose. You can become dependent very fucking quickly, and ruin your life. And you can also give yourself a bleeding gastric ulcer. So take as fucking directed."

"Sir, yes, sir," I say, saluting lazily with my splinted hand, earning myself an eye roll.

"Your work note is also not optional. If you use that hand too soon, you could do more damage. Take this time to rest. Maybe take an anger management class with all this free time. Or get a therapist. And no, blowjobs do not count as therapy, no matter how transcendent it seems in the moment. Bitching to Tristan also doesn't count. Please unburden yourself to a professional. Self-reflection is strongly encouraged."

I stare at him, because that was a lot for the wee hours when I'm already starting to feel the effects of my painkillers.

There's a moment of tension between us, and I can almost feel the intensity of how much he cares. It's surprising, but makes me feel weird. Embarrassed, almost. I guess I'm not used to this kind of unabashed care, except from Silas. Who is less talkative about it, obviously.

"Therapy beats a jail sentence, I promise," he continues. "Plus, you're a good EMT. I'd hate to lose you if you got fired for catching a felony charge."

I push back on the urge to snark, and nod at him.

"Okay, Micah. Thank you."

He gives me a sharp nod back.

"Good. I don't want to see you in here until you're back at work. And I don't want to see you at that fucking bar for a while, either."

Silas saves me, walking over to help me stand up, taking most of my weight for the millionth time tonight.

I look at him, our faces too close together, and for a second I feel the overwhelming urge to start bawling like a little kid.

"Can we go?" I say instead, my voice tight.

"Yeah, baby," he says, kissing me softly on the side of my head, even though I'm sweaty and smudged with iodine. "Let's go."

I shiver, and allow myself the luxury of burrowing deeper into his arms. Let people see me leaning on him, I don't give a fuck. I'm too fucking tired to walk by myself.

I haven't done much but sleep since we got home. Silas woke me up after about eight hours to make sure I was alright and forced me to drink some water, but when I told him I was still tired he turned out all the lights and ran his fingers through my hair until I fell back asleep.

Now that I open my eyes again, I think it's late. I can't tell for sure, because a little while after I moved in, Silas rigged up an amazing blackout window situation to help when I'm working nights. It could technically still be light outside and I wouldn't know.

I just... feel it. It's probably like 10 p.m..

When I hear whispered voices ghosting through the closed bedroom door, I realized what woke me up. Maddi and Sky were supposed to come back tonight. Fuck, I totally forgot. I'm such a shitty brother sometimes.

I cut off that train of thought before it threatens to consume me. Everything inside me feels fragile right now, in a way I don't particularly fucking care for. And I don't even have a good excuse for it.

Dad's not the one who started the fight, I was. Even though he obviously deserved it. And it's not exactly the first time we've gotten rough with each other.

I'm an adult now, he's not wailing on a kid. It shouldn't feel any different than getting into a fight with some random guy at the bar.

Right?

I can't do this right now. I need the distraction, and I can tell from the tone of the voices that the girls are worried and Silas is trying to calm them down. They don't need to freak out over something that's already over with.

It takes more effort than I expect to throw off the covers and pull myself out of bed. God, I feel like one big bruise. I've put my body through a lot of punishment in my life—motocross is not a gentle sport, even when you only do it as an occasional thing—but this shit hurts. Everything throbs in a diffuse, numbing kind of pain, while specific points spark a bright hurt every time I move.

I'm in my underwear, and I decide it's worth the discomfort of pulling on clothes to make sure the girls see as little as possible of the bruising. I find a pair of Silas's grey sweats in the hamper that look realistically too clean to wash. I pull them on, where they hang low on my hips. They're actually not that loose, which makes me think they're probably way too tight on Silas and he's bearing the discomfort for the sake of not having to cave and buy new clothes. Again.

I get a clean black Possum Hollow EMS hoody out of the drawer, and putting my arms up to slip it on is the thing that hurt the most so far. Fuck, I think my ribs are bruised. Did they tell me that at the ER? I can't remember the details, it was all kind of a blur of shame and exhaustion.

As soon as I crack open the bedroom door, I can feel eyes turning toward me. Maddi and Sky are sitting on the old, sagging couch, both of them looking worried and small, like the couch is threatening to swallow them up. Taking one step out of the bedroom is enough to have Sky up and running for me, while Maddi holds her position, an inscrutable expression on her face.

Sky crashes into me, her little arms wrapped around my middle. It knocks the breath clean out of me, and behind her I can see Silas reaching out impotently with a tight expression on his face.

"Sky, careful—" he starts, but I don't let him finish.

"It's okay."

So I maybe get a little dizzy when I reach down to pick her up like she's a lot smaller than she is, but that's what the wall behind me is for. I end up leaning against it as Sky clings to me, shoving her snuffling face into my neck, clearly trying to hold back tears.

"Jeez, what a reaction. I'm fine. It was just a fight that got a little out of hand. No biggie."

My voice comes out just as hoarse as last night, though, and I can see Maddi's expression as she clocks it.

She looks pissed.

"What happened?" she asks, her voice flat.

I look at Silas, still holding Sky up and leaning against the wall, not totally sure what I'm supposed to say.

I never lied to them about this stuff before, but something tells me the truth will not go down well.

"I ran into Kyle. He was being an asshole, and we got in a fight. It's not a big deal."

Maddi's expression doesn't change, but for some reason, Silas is the one that's suddenly glowering at me from across the room.

"What did he do?" Maddi asks, but Silas sighs the second I open my mouth to answer.

"Nothing," he says, making my gut twist. "Your father didn't do anything. Cade lost his temper."

"Jesus, Silas," I say, my body getting tense with shock. "What the fuck? You were there, you saw what he did."

Silas rolls his eyes, huffing at me in a way I feel like he's been doing a lot lately.

"He was *maybe* a little snide. Maybe. Or maybe just drunk and not really realizing he was running his mouth. And you tried to fucking kill him. I think that qualifies as you losing your temper."

"Are you taking his side?" I forget for a second that we're not alone, as anger bubbles up inside me all over again. I also forget how sore my throat is as I

128

desperately try to push sound out of it. "I should just let him shit all over us like the homophobic asshole that he is?"

"He didn't even say anything homophobic!" Silas's arms are spread wide as he stares at me, and I realize with a jolt that this might be the most agitated I've ever seen him get around me. It doesn't feel right.

"Please don't fight," Sky wails, clinging tightly around my neck and pressing on all my bruises.

The sensation makes me lightheaded, but it also rolls back the mounting anger I was about to lean into. I bend over, trying to deposit her on the floor without looking like I'm about to pass out.

Her face is blotchy and tear-streaked, and Maddi has shifted from teenage surliness to wide-eyed apprehension, still sitting on the couch.

"We're not fighting," I say lamely.

Nobody speaks. Silas blows out a long breath before beckoning to Sky.

"Come on, let's sit down," he says. "You too, Cade."

Begrudgingly, I move over to the couch and sit down next to Maddi. She doesn't respond, but when I put my hand on her back I can feel her soften a little.

She's so tough. She wants to be so tough. I hate it, but I'm not doing a good enough job of making her feel safe that she's going to stop. Things like this probably don't help, I realize way, way too late to do anything about it.

Sky follows me and climbs into my lap instead of sitting next to me, even though she's getting too big to fit. The pressure of her makes it even harder to breathe, but also eases some of the tension in me. I look at Silas over her shoulder, trying to convey my gratitude to him through my eyes when it's not something I could ever put into words.

He looks calm now, watching over us, but he doesn't sit down. When he's about to turn away I reach for his hand.

"Sit with us," I say, but he doesn't look at me.

"You should eat something, you've been sleeping all day."

The sensation of his hand slipping out of mind echoes through me like an omen. My head throbs, my ribs ache with every breath, and the room seems like it's closing in on me for no reason.

Silas disappears into the kitchen, and I feel an ache where he's supposed to be. I tell myself I'm being dramatic, but it doesn't quite stick.

"Why do you let him get to you like this?" Maddi finally asks in a quiet voice. She pulls her legs up on the couch to rest her head on her knees, and it makes her look younger, even while her expression is the kind of weariness no child should have to feel. "He's never going to change. You're the one that told us that. So what's the point in fighting him?"

"Sometimes you have to stand up for yourself."

It sounds true. It sounds like something that should be impossible to argue against, but Maddi just huffs.

"Sure. Standing up for yourself against a drunk drug addict who probably won't even remember what you were fighting about tomorrow. Totally mean-ingful. Definitely worth getting fucked up over. I can't wait until you hurt yourself so bad you can't work anymore or ride your bike or do anything else, and all you'll be able to do is lie around taking oxy and telling everyone about how you're a real man because you 'stand up for yourself'."

I'm not shocked that Maddi managed to see into a situation with that kind of insight, because she's always been like that, even for her age. I am shocked that this is the situation she's drawing the line at in terms of supporting me.

She thinks I'm an asshole, obviously. Silas hasn't made it a secret how pissed he is at me. And Tristan and Micah both are just waiting to read me the riot act, I can feel it.

How the fuck is no one on my side?

CHAPTER THIRTEEN

SILAS

The house is unnaturally still and quiet, and for once, it's making me anxious. Normally, this would be a brief window of peace, followed by Cade coming home and filling the house with noise, which brings me an entirely different kind of peace.

Both of them are things I crave, and normally they're both things I get to have. But not right now.

Because Cade is home, and he's the source of all this silence. He's off work completely for at least the next five days, and then he'll be on limited duties at best. It makes sense that he'd want to rest while he's hurting, but I've never seen him like this before. Normally, when he's sick or injured, he's still a little ball of sunshine, trying to make me laugh with non-stop jokes and creative bitching about being bored.

I've never seen him quiet like this. I got him to eat and drink a little before we all went back to bed last night. I know the conversation with his sisters was... fraught. He still doesn't seem to fully grasp why he was so out of line, and we're not all falling over ourselves to praise him.

131

I wasn't worried when he slept through me getting the girls up and out the door for school, but when I came back in the bedroom to find him awake and just lying there, it was disconcerting.

He eats if I make him. He won't really talk to me, and says he's too tired.

And my house—my home—is starting to feel like a tomb all over again.

By the afternoon, I'm beginning to wonder if it's making it worse by my being here, and I shouldn't have taken the day off work after all. Is it me that he's upset about? Because I wasn't on his side?

When I wander back into the dark bedroom, I regret installing the black-out blinds. The darkness is making everything about this situation seem ominous, when it should be easy. If there's anything Cade and I have always been able to do, it's talk to each other.

Although, the more I think about the past year, the more I wonder if that's really true. We never seem to talk about anything real lately.

Without allowing myself the chance to hesitate, I pull off my t-shirt and toss it in the direction of the hamper, lift up the comforter and slide underneath. Cade's on his side, facing the middle of the bed, and I shift until I'm mirroring his position, our knees touching and our faces on the same pillow, inches away from each other. Cade's eyes are open, watching me closely as I get situated, but he stays silent. The bruising on his face is barely visible in the darkness, but it's almost as if I can feel it. Like his hurt is radiating from him in some way that's beyond sight.

"Hey," I say, my voice sounding too loud and jarring.

"Hey."

Cade looks at me, but doesn't say anything else. I think about all the other times we've been in a bed together, next to each other but kept apart by some kind of invisible, unspoken barrier.

"Do you wanna play video games and jerk each other off? Heterosexually, of course."

Cade is still for a moment, before gracing me with a small snort and a half smile.

"Oh, he's got jokes. Robot boy, world-renowned for his sense of humor, here to Patch Adams me back to health."

He's speaking softly, and still so dull compared to his usual self that I worry for a minute he's really making fun of me, but then I catch sight of that half smile again and relax.

"No homo," I murmur, which makes his lips tug up again. Cade went through a phase of ironic *no homo* jokes after we started living together that I thought were always a little on the nose, but made him laugh every goddamn time. I follow it up by taking gentle hold of his chin and planting a chaste kiss on his lips.

"Full homo," he sighs, the second half of his call and response bit. "Extra homo, if that's possible. With rainbow sprinkles on top."

He still sounds exhausted, but at least he sounds like Cade, deep down in there somewhere.

It takes me a minute to figure out what I want to say. How to keep it light.

"Yeah, well you won't let me baby you the way I want to. Jokes are about all I have left to offer. Which is pretty dire for both of us, I reckon."

I almost think his lip quivers, but it's gone before I can be sure. The thought breaks my heart, either way.

"You don't need to baby me, robot boy. I'm fine. I just need to sleep it off. It's not like I didn't bring this on myself."

It's nice to hear he's stopped putting 100% of the blame on his dad, but piling on himself until he's drowning in shame isn't helping anyone, either. I wiggle to shift a little closer to him, reaching up to smooth a stray dark curl off his forehead and then cupping his chin in my hand.

"You're always mine to baby. That was the deal, remember? Whether you think you deserve it or not."

"And what about you?" Cade asks, his voice thick.

I force myself to speak with a lightness I don't feel. "I let you baby me plenty. You're still my hero. You still saved me." My fingers tighten on his jaw. "We take turns saving each other, remember? It's not like either of us got a lot of babying when we were kids, I don't think it's weird to fill that void now. I'll cut the fucking crusts off peanut butter and jelly sandwiches for you every day, if you'd let me."

He doesn't say anything, and the tension continues to mount, until I break it by leaning across the space between us to kiss him, more deeply than before. Cade's lip is still swollen, so he winces, but kisses me back with more energy than he's shown since the fight. Hands find their way to me under the covers, grabbing at my torso with a sudden kind of desperation.

In an instant, the kiss deepens, and I grab his hip as we grind together the same way we have a million times before. I feel overwhelmed by the need to touch him—to taste him—to make him feel good, and don't let myself second-guess as I break off the kiss to move down in the bed. For just a few minutes, I want to forget about everything else, and it seems like he does, too.

Cade's only wearing sweats, and he's not hard yet, but I can still tell he's commando underneath. As soon as I tug down the waistband and gently slide them off his legs, I'm rewarded by the sight of him naked, the comforter thrown somewhere to the side. His bruises are fading, and he's starting to look enough like himself—minus the hand splint and the nasty eyebrow gash—that I don't immediately feel a throb of pain. Instead, I start sucking deep, bruising kisses into the skin at the crease of his groin, dragging my teeth over his inner thighs to make him shiver.

My eyes flick open, looking up at Cade for confirmation that we're on the same page. He's staring down at me with something other than lust. Desperation, maybe. But when he slides his fingers into my hair and sighs, his body relaxing incrementally, I know I chose the right path.

His cock is soft as I take it in my mouth, the skin tender and warm. He gasps when I suck him gently, and I run my hands up his ribs as tenderly as I can manage. The overwhelming need to be as close to him as possible has me burying my nose against his pelvis, hooking one of his legs over my shoulder until it feels like I'm a continuation of his body. I pull off him to lick at his sac for a minute before gently sucking one of his balls into my mouth, making him gasp again and again.

The noise is all I need to get hard, already aching for his touch, but it isn't about me right now. It's about me a lot, I realize. Cade loves to throw himself at me, opening himself up to me and begging me to fuck into his mouth or ass as hard as I can. I know he loves it. But right now I feel compelled by the urge to treat him tenderly, something he hardly ever allows.

I lick and suck a trail around his groin, finding every piece of sensitive skin I can find. It's easy to reach underneath him and tilt his hips up, moving my face lower until I drag my nose through his crease. Cade gasps a little, but relaxes into the contact as I gently lift his balls out of the way, split open his ass cheeks as much as I can and then run the flat of my tongue from the bottom to the top.

He shudders when my tongue hits his hole, and that's all the encouragement I need to go back down to it. I attack his hole with as much force as I think his body can handle right now. Already, all my plans of tenderness are drifting away, but the way Cade begins to groan and fist my short hair in his fingers makes me think it was the right choice.

There's so much sensitive skin to tease. I lick at his hole before eventually pushing my tongue inside, and when he relaxes even more into the contact, I join my tongue with a finger. I'm not trying to make him get off this way, I want him to just lie back and enjoy something for the sake of it.

I'm not sure how long I play with him for. Long enough to know his mind has drifted off on the pleasure, and he's finally unwinding a little of that tension he's been carrying around since the fight. He's noisy, like always, and constantly moves underneath my grasp in the way that makes me crazy for him. This time, when I take his cock in my hand, he's mostly hard, and makes a hissing noise as I start to jerk him off.

Moving up his body, I sink my mouth back over him, and he fucks up into me once, just a little. I barely want to move, instead rocking us gently together as I work my tongue up and down his length, feeling him stiffen bit by tiny bit.

It seems to go on forever. We move together, slowly building up friction but keeping his sweaty flesh pinned beneath me as tightly as I can. Cade isn't quite as loud or as active as he usually is, but he's still making choked, bitten-off noises that drive me crazy. He sounds raw and desperate, and by the time his fingers tighten in my hair and he pulses hot cum into my mouth, he's whispering the word "please" over and over into the quiet room.

I swallow most of his release, but there's still cum on my tongue as I climb back up his body and push it into his soft, open mouth.

Cade reaches for my cock with his busted hand, then reconsiders and reaches with the other, but I bat him away. I'm laying so much of my weight onto his body that I have to squeeze my own hand between us to fist my cock, but I'm so turned on from making him come that I'm almost there myself. I push the waistband of my sweats and boxers down, grinding down once to drag my erection through the dark hair trailing down from his belly button. Then I press us together—forehead to forehead, hips to hips—and jerk myself just a few times before spilling all over his stomach with a gasp.

We're both breathless as I collapse next to him, and he doesn't fuss when I drag him into my arms. I refuse to let him go, but it's cold in here, so I manage to only semi-awkwardly catch the edge of the comforter with my foot and drag it up until I can reach it, finally wrapping it around both of us until we're totally cocooned.

Cade still isn't saying anything, but his nose finds the underside of my jaw like a bloodhound, and he presses his hot, swollen face into me so hard that it has to hurt. I run my hand up and down his bare back, ignoring the cum that's getting transferred from his chest to mine.

I hear something mumbled, but his face is buried too deeply in my neck for me to make out the words. When I pull back he chases me, so I awkwardly tilt my chin down to try to see him better.

"What did you say?"

Cade coughs a little and lets a half-inch of space slip between his lips and my skin.

"I said I like it better when you're shirtless. You should be shirtless all the time. It should actually be illegal for you to wear a shirt. I'm going to start a petition. All the neighbors will sign, I know they all have the hots for you. Especially that biker dude at the end of the street."

I can't help but smile, as the little ramble sounds much more like my Cade than the silence I've been getting all day.

"I'll see what I can do," I say, because I don't want to get into this tense conversation about my body again. Not when it feels like his mood is finally lightening. "How do you feel?"

Cade stiffens, and for a second I think he's about to stonewall me, but then he relaxes into a stretch, loosely caged in by my arms. His spine curves like a cat's, and some more of the tension seems to slip away as he settles back against me, running his fingertips through my chest hair.

"I'm okay. Just sore. And embarrassed, I guess."

His voice is still raspy, which makes me instinctively want to worry, but I push the urge down. I thread my fingers through the hair at the back of his head, holding him so I can press a kiss against his forehead while I work out what to say next.

Saying the right thing isn't my greatest strength. But I know I have this overwhelming urge to keep him safe right now, even though the thing that seems to be threatening him the most is his own anger.

"Do you want to talk to your dad?"

Cade freezes, stiffening against me, and there's a long pause while he tries to find his answer.

"Why would I?"

It's hard to explain. I'm not even sure why I said it, but it feels necessary.

I buy myself time by shuffling down in the bed, turning on my side until we're nose to nose, just like we were before I derailed us with a blowjob. My hands twine around his waist so I'm still holding him against me, but I look him in the eye when I finally speak.

"I think all of this happened because of a misunderstanding. We could go talk to him. You could come out to him for real. See what he says. Even if he's a dick about it, at least you'll know where you stand. There won't be room for... interpretation. In the heat of the moment."

Cade's frowning at me, and I can see the fight already swelling up in him. He doesn't pull away from me, but there's tension in his raspy voice when he answers me.

"Maybe it was a misunderstanding. Maybe not. I get it, I overreacted. I shouldn't have gone that far. But he made me so fucking mad, and that was always going to happen. I just need to learn to control myself better when he pisses me off. I get it, I know."

My therapist is big on 'naming' emotions. She stares at me, flinty-eyed through the Zoom window, waiting with endless patience until I finally come up with whatever word she was waiting for to describe how I was feeling at a particular time. It's exhausting, and seems impossible to get right most of the time. But right now, as I look at Cade from the outside in, I start to see her point.

"Were you really angry? Or were you scared?"

He stiffens, staring at me, and I see it again. That fear. The same fear I'm pretty sure was driving him that night.

He barely starts to pull away from me before I hold him tighter.

"Don't," I say. "Don't run away from me. I'm not making you do anything, I'm just asking."

"What the fuck am I supposed to say to him?"

He's obviously pissy, but he's not trying to get away from me, which is as much as I can hope for, I guess.

"I don't know. Tell him you're bi. Tell him we're together. Tell him you're sorry you fucking attacked him but you were scared he'd disapprove."

Cade snorts. "I don't give a rat's ass what that man thinks. He barely has two brain cells to rub together and has treated everyone in his life like a punching bag. His opinion is worthless to me."

I try not to audibly sigh, but I'm not really successful. I push that same loose curl off his forehead again before I speak.

"I think we both know that's not true."

The silence that sits between us is heavy, and I stay very still, waiting to see how Cade's going to react. When the seconds pass and he still doesn't say anything, I panic and keep going.

"I'm not trying to be a dick. I spent my entire life trying to make my dad happy, and he didn't do a damn thing to deserve it. You know this. You've told me a million times that it's okay, and I shouldn't be mad at myself, because parents fuck you up and your brain is always still kind of a little kid when you deal with them. Why is it okay for me, but you have to be totally above it all? You're just what? Over it? Magically healed from all his abuse and what that does to you?"

"He didn't abuse me," he says, like a reflex. I ignore it, because we both know it's a lie but there's no point in fighting about it.

"Whatever you want to call it. He's a piece of shit. That doesn't mean you can't want him to approve of you. If anything, it probably makes you more desperate to please him. On some level. It's an instinct."

Cade is silent a little while longer, but at least he's not getting angry.

"I should never have let you go to therapy. You were already scary smart, now you're all insightful and shit as well. Unbelievable."

The better corner of his mouth tugs up in a smile, but the humor feels forced.

"Come on, Cade," I whisper. "Can you be honest about something, for once? I feel like all you ever do is run around telling everyone how fine you are."

For just a second, I think I have him. I think he might talk to me. It's becoming more and more glaringly obvious how overdue this conversation is. Instead, he locks up. I see him tense, and his expression shutters as he pulls away from me.

"Fine. If you want me to talk to him, I'll talk to him. Just talk. But afterwards, when he's still a piece of shit and it hasn't made a damn bit of difference except opening ourselves up to his cheap-ass ridicule, I'm going to say 'I told you so'."

He's pulling himself off the bed, his movements jerky with anger and obviously painful as he winces through getting dressed. I try to follow him, but he moves away from me, making a point of digging around in the drawer for some underwear and then putting it on without my help, even though it looks awkward.

"Cade, that's not what I meant. I'm not trying to force you to do anything, I just thought it might help."

"Sure. And I'm going to do it, to show you it won't. Let's go. We're burning daylight, and if we leave it any later he'll probably be unconscious, if he isn't already."

Cade has officially draped himself in a flinty resolve. I'm pretty sure this is all my fault for taking us down this path, but it's too late to go back now. As I quietly get dressed to follow him, all I can do is cross my fingers that his dad really is trying to be better, like he said.

CHAPTER FOURTEEN

CADE

I don't really talk to Silas on the drive over to the trailer. I hope Kyle is there, because I've been building momentum the whole way, and if I lose it now, I don't know if I can go through with this again.

I'm proving a point to Silas. That's it. I don't give a damn what Kyle thinks.

The amount of times I have to repeat it to myself makes me think it's not true, but I want it to be. If I keep pretending, eventually I'll have to feel it.

Right?

At some point in the swirl of thoughts coursing through me, I realize that there is no best-case scenario here. Even if he apologized for everything—which he won't—it won't help.

On the rare times that I end up dwelling in my memories, I put most of my mental energy into gaslighting myself that it wasn't that bad. My child's eye must have made the bad things bigger and the pain brighter. The people around me were adults doing their best, burdened by their own abundance of pain.

I'm sorry. I shouldn't have done it. I wish I'd been a better father. Everything you remember is true, and you have every right to be furious.

Even picturing him saying the words makes me shiver. It should feel good, right? The idea of acknowledgment and apology?

Instead, it makes the whole seething mass of memories creep closer. As if him acknowledging it makes it all so true that it will wrap its jaws around my soul and shake it, like wounded prey finally caught at the end of a long hunt.

And if he apologizes, then would I even have the right to be angry anymore? Or would I have to let that go, along with everything else. And try to be a whole person without that rage to shore up my personality. Without the doubt hampering me, providing a constant excuse for my failures.

I realize dimly that if he really did apologize, I would just consider it one more reason to be angry at him. Like he'd unburden himself and move on with his healthier, more responsible life, and I'd still be stuck here, mired in my own issues and unable to extricate myself from jack shit.

I'm aware that I look like a stompy, petulant child as I park sloppily and practically collapse out of the cab of Silas's truck. Especially considering how much I fought him to drive, even with my bad hand, like some worthless point of pride. But I'm tired, sore, and already gearing up for the inevitable fight that's about to happen, and petulant is about the best I can do right now.

I can't think about what I'm doing. I can't think about any of it. I'm just going to go in, have whatever conversation Silas wants me to have, and then flee the scene as soon as possible. And get the fuck back to my bed.

I'm about to yank open the door, when I realize I should take it down a notch. The last thing anyone needs is for my bubble of rage to ratchet all their own issues up a notch without warning. Instead, I knock. My entire body feels stiff and useless, and I can sense Silas hovering behind me like a shadow.

His silence is an indicator that he's regretting his suggestion, but it's too late now. We're in this shitfest together.

Anger feels like a physical growl trapped inside my throat, and the pressure of it is so sudden, it snaps me back to reality a little. I roll my shoulders back, forcing my muscles to unclench, before reaching behind me without looking to take Silas by the hand.

I'm not angry at him. I'm just angry. And if I keep letting that spill over like this, I'll turn into someone no better than Kyle, anyway.

Silas squeezes my hand and quietly blows out a breath, his other hand wrapping around my hip from behind. He continues to stand there like a wall between me and the rest of the world, and I have the strongest urge to collapse back into him, begging him to pick me up like a child and carry me all the way back home.

None of this is my finest moment.

When the door finally swings open, it's Kyle, and he does a double take. I stiffen on instinct, squaring my shoulders and looking him in the eye.

He looks worse than I do, which makes me feel a tiny bit of satisfaction. Two black eyes, a swollen nose with a laceration across the bridge, jaw on the right twice as big as the other side, and both hands obviously stiff with swelling. Despite the physical evidence of the beating he took, he still holds himself tall, though.

I've never understood how he does that. How he can do the shittiest, most chickenshit things possible and still walk around with his head high. Like he's never doubted himself or his actions a day in his life.

He's eyeing Silas warily when he finally breaks the silence.

"You're mother's not here right now," is all he says, voice flat, left hand tightening around the bottle of blue Gatorade he's holding. I'm honestly shocked it's not a beer. It's well past noon.

"I didn't come to see her."

I spit the words out with more venom than intended. I don't know exactly why I've had a short fuse for her as well the past week, but I definitely have.

Kyle's eyebrows raise while the rest of him stays completely still.

"Well," he says, not following the word with anything else.

We all stand together, suspended in this awkward moment, before he turns around and ambles back into the trailer. His gait is easy, with long, slow steps. The way a predator walks. The way someone does when they're not afraid to show you their back.

He doesn't invite us in, but he also doesn't close the door, so I take that as a hint. It'd piss me off if he invited me into my own home, anyway. Silas and I slip through the screen door and then close the main door behind us to keep out the early-winter chill.

Dad takes his time settling back into the armchair with a series of masculine grunts, swigging some more of his sad, room-temperature-looking drink and then fishing around on the side table to pull himself a Marlboro. He goes through all the motions to light it up, and blows a long stream of smoke in my direction before he finally looks me in the eye again and speaks.

He doesn't even have to say words to make me feel about two-feet tall, though. He just does. The familiar smells. The way he moves like we're waiting on him to get comfortable. It all tells the story of who's in charge here. I don't even know if it's deliberate, or if it's just how he is.

"Well," he repeats. "What do you want?"

I start to open my mouth, but before I get to the point of shaping the words, I realize I don't actually know what I'm trying to say. All the thoughts that tumbled through my head on the drive here, none of them involved the actual beginning part of the conversation.

What am I supposed to do?

Just... come out?

Even the thought makes me wince, like it's something that doesn't belong to me. Coming out is for kids who know themselves and are brave; I'm an adult. I wasn't repressed or dating women for show, I just figured out this part a little late. The idea of having some big coming-out storyline makes me feel like I'm appropriating something that isn't mine.

But as the thoughts bat around my head like rogue ping-pong balls, they always lead to something I know is not fucking cool.

I don't need to come out, I'm still normal.

Nope. Scratch the word 'normal'. That's a gross, intrusive thought that's not fucking cool. Bad brain.

I don't need to come out. Coming out is for gay people.

I'll take 'internalized biphobia' for a hundred, Alex.

I don't need to come out. I don't deserve it.

Ouch.

"Um," I start, but don't follow it with anything.

Dad's still staring at me expectantly; half-engaged, half-bored. Silas puts his hand at the small of my back, stroking his thumb a little in a way that makes me shiver. I want to press back into the touch, but I can't give in to the weakness right now.

It occurs to me all at once that I haven't done this before. I haven't consciously, deliberately come out to anyone. People just sort of found out one by one that me and Silas were together, and then once news spread around town, it was so well known I mostly didn't even need to address it.

And it was always in terms of me and Silas. Us. Together, being gay. Because even if neither of us is specifically gay—although Silas might be gay, I really should fucking ask sometime—we're in a gay relationship, and that's what people are responding to, whether their reaction is good or bad.

This feels like it's about me. Who *I* am.

I don't like this. I don't fucking like this at all.

"I'm sorry I hit you, sir."

The words slip out of me without my permission, making my stomach drop, and I can physically feel how startled Silas is behind me.

We didn't come here so I could apologize. That's not the point of this little venture. But it abruptly felt like what I was supposed to do. Even the fucking 'sir' tacked itself on the end without my permission, like I'm still the obedient little punching bag I used to be.

I take a few deep breaths, but they come quickly and more ragged than intended, so I force myself to stand up tall and look Kyle in the eye.

Mentally, I'm flailing, trying to grasp some kind of structure to this conversation that isn't fucking humiliating.

My expression gets hard, and I look at him like I normally do, injecting as much disdain into my voice as possible and burying the hint of fear that crawled up my throat a minute ago.

"I shouldn't have turned it into a fight. People got hurt, and we fucked with Gunnar's business, and it wasn't cool. I'm here to tell you that it's not going to happen again, if I can help it." I continue, my confidence growing with every word, because at least that stuff I actually mean. "But I'm not sorry I stood up for myself. If you want to be homophobic to me and Silas, it's just another reason I'll work to haul your ass out of town."

There. That was coming out.

Kind of.

Dad pauses, taking another long drag of his cigarette and looking me up and down in a way that's designed to make me feel small.

"This is Silas?" he says at last, pointing with the cigarette.

I nod. "This is Silas. My boyfriend."

I wince internally at how childish the word boyfriend sounds, but it's too late to take it back. Partner? Whatever. None of them could ever sum up exactly how monumentally important Silas is to me, so why try?

"Hello," Silas says; quiet behind me.

Silas and I are both braced for whatever he's going to say next, but he continues to look at us instead, relaxed as all get out, drinking his fucking Gatorade.

"Alright," he says, and I feel my jaw drop a little. "Is that all you came here to say?"

I freeze, losing the thread of what this is all supposed to be about.

Is that all I came here to say? He's not being a homophobic dick, which I guess is a plus. But internally, I'm screaming for something I can't really identify.

Say something, Dad.

Say anything.

Fucking care about me, even if it's just to be angry.

I sniff, even though it's a dry sound, and feel myself settle into a calm, uncaring facade.

"Yep, that's it. So if you have anything shitty to say, now's the chance to get it off your chest."

Dad shrugs. He's the picture of someone who couldn't give two shits and is bored by this whole conversation, and I feel my gut cramp in response.

"I don't care who you fuck," he adds, flicking ash toward a battered old McDonalds ashtray my great uncle stole a million years ago. "It's nothing to do with me."

A flush of adrenaline hits me from out of nowhere, and I feel the room spinning. I ignore it, because if I let this man get to me when he's not even trying, I really will be pathetic beyond all measure.

"Fine," I spit. "As long as we're not going to have a problem."

Another lazy shrug, and he eyes me up and down casually.

"Ain't no problem. But next time you want to have a temper tantrum you can keep me out of it. Don't think I won't teach you a lesson if you keep giving me attitude like this. I'll still give you the belt, grown or not."

I bristle, because it fucking irks the shit out of me when he talks to me like a little kid.

"Bitch please, I out-matured you in the fifth grade. Don't act like you've ever been sober enough to give me the fucking belt."

Silas, who has been a silent, stable presence behind me this whole time, squeezes my hip.

"Cade," he whispers in my ear, a clear warning to calm my shit down.

It's intimate, though. His warm breath on my ear, his chest pressed to my back, and the way Dad's watching us while he does it is making me itchy. I feel exposed, even though his expression is relatively impassive. Like seeing his son get manhandled is no big deal.

The tension stretches out, until we're interrupted by the sound of the door swinging open.

Mom is standing in the doorway, taking in the scene with an appraising eye.

"Cade," she says. "Silas. What are you boys doing here?"

I want to spit back something pissy, but Silas squeezes me again in warning.

Fuck me. I don't know why I agreed to this. I don't know what Silas was hoping to achieve.

"What?" I ask him, turning around. "Seriously, what? Why are we here, if you don't want me to fight with them? Fighting is the only thing they understand. Did you think I was just going to come here and come out to him and we'd all cry and hug or something? I genuinely don't understand what you're trying to accomplish here. Every interaction I've had with this man in my life has pissed me off at best, and added a scar to my collection at worst. This was never going to be any different."

A small, petty part of me was hoping the spiteful words would land, but Silas looks as placid as ever.

"I thought you could talk," he says, his voice hushed. "Maybe tell everyone what you're so angry about."

That makes me laugh. It's a loud, braying sound that disturbs the tension filling the trailer, and everyone stares at me slightly wide-eyed.

"I'm not fucking angry," I say, very aware that the venom in my voice says otherwise, but unwilling to lose any conversational ground right now. "What could I possibly be angry about? He doesn't even care. We came, and we did the thing, and he knows now, and he doesn't fucking care. It's all fine. Let's go."

Dad finally contributes to the conversation by sighing loudly and flicking more ash off his cigarette.

"You've always been such a drama queen. Always making a big deal out of nothing. I don't want to hear you talking about scars, because I never fucking hit you. Nothing more than a normal spanking, at least. You can't go ruining my reputation around town just because I'm not here and you think you've turned into hot shit now that you're grown."

My eyes widen while my body stays stock still, and for a second I think I might genuinely stroke out.

I move all at once, pulling myself out of Silas's grip and stomping toward Kyle, who still looks comfortable in the arm chair.

"No fucking scars? What about this?" I half-yell before pushing my hair up to show him the old, faded scar that runs along my hairline on the tight side. "When you tried to throw a bottle at your friend who pissed you off, but you missed and hit me instead. And made me lie to the doctor and social services, and then gave me a beer afterward as a reward. I was eight."

Dad's eyebrows raise, but other than that he stays still.

"Or this one?" I pull up my sleeve and flash the inside of my wrist, where silvery flesh is partially covered in a tattoo. "When I was trying to cook, but then your drunk ass tried to help and you ended up accidentally pushing me against one of the pots. When you saw, you put some butter on it and told me to be a man about it. I was thirteen."

There's a flicker of some kind of expression on his face, but that's it. Other than that, he's just staring at me.

Realization dawns on me all at once.

"You don't..." I whip my head around to look at Silas, who genuinely looks like he's about to cry, and then look back at Kyle. "You don't even remember? I carry around all these shitty memories every day, and you don't even fucking remember. You don't even care."

Kyle doesn't quite wince, but almost. It's something. Something that makes me think real, genuine words are about to come out of his mouth. I still don't know what I want him to say, but I need him to say fucking something.

"Look, kid, that was a long time ago. It sounds like you need to let it go. None of it matters. You grew up good, got yourself a good job, and a Silas—" I have no idea if he sneers as he says it or if my anger is manifesting "—and no one here wants to hash all that shit out over and over. Being a kid sucks. It sucks for everybody. You know exactly what your mother's childhood was like. And don't forget, I spent Christmas on a fucking bus one year because my parents kept trying to pass me off on each other. It doesn't mean anything. Grow up and forget about it, like the rest of us."

I'm going to fucking hit him.

It's only the pain in my splinted fist when I try to curl it that gives me the tiniest tether to reality, and makes me think of exactly how pissed Silas will be if I fight my dad again in less than 48 hours. I focus on taking a deep breath instead, and don't look him in the eye.

"Cade?" My mom sounds wary, and I hear her stepping up behind me. The thought of her touching me right now makes me cringe, so I take a big step to the side, away from both of them, and then turn to face Silas.

"We're leaving. Fuck this."

Silas doesn't move for a few seconds, then he nods and reaches for my hand. I don't reach back, because I can't right now.

I don't look at my mom. I definitely don't look at Kyle. All I have the capacity to do right now is march my ass out the door and hope Silas follows me.

No witty one-liners to close me out, just a storm of impotent anger leaving the house and folding myself into the truck. Into the passenger seat this time, because my pride is smarting too much to care about who fucking drives. I already feel stupid for caring about it before.

My face is hot, with a familiar pressure behind the eyes, but I refuse to give into it. I can't look Silas in the eye or touch him when he gets into the cab. All I can do is hunch in on myself and stare out the window at nothing.

"He doesn't even remember," I say.

I didn't mean to say it, it just slipped out, and my voice cracks in the process. That pressure builds, but I can't give into it.

"Cade—" Silas starts to say, but I take a deep breath and cut him off.

"Let's just go."

I think I see him reach toward me out of the corner of my eye, but when I curl myself up tighter, he stops. A few seconds later, the engine rumbles and we start to pull away from the fucking trailer to go home.

Finally.

CHAPTER FIFTEEN

SILAS

By the time we get home, Cade has returned to being perilously quiet. Our home has become a seething, brittle place. Every inch of his body is coiled tight, and I'm tense like I'm expecting him to snap.

Which doesn't really make sense, because even though Cade has a terrible temper sometimes, he's never, ever been that way with me.

Not once. Not even when we argue. He always has some kind of control, and I can see him being careful in how he holds himself towards me: his tone, his words, everything. For the first time, I think I realize how much effort that must take for him, when he's normally on a hairtrigger with the rest of the world.

It always comes back to him changing himself to what? Placate me? Keep me calm?

The more I look at the picture of our relationship that's suddenly appearing in my head, the more I realize how blind I've been. I don't know what any of this means, but it can't be good.

Cade kicks off his boots a little too loudly, and I flinch. I catch him looking at me out of the corner of my eye as he freezes, totally still as he watches me for a second, guilt curling into his expression like smoke.

"Sorry," he says, sounding gruff and distant.

"It's fine. You're fine."

I turn to face him. The urge to show him I'm here for him is so strong, but I don't know how to get that across without saying it. And I'm pretty sure if I said it, he'd accuse me of babying him again, as if he hasn't been babying me for our entire relationship. I'm the only one allowed to be weak, apparently.

"Do you wanna sit down and talk about it?"

The words sound awkward, even to my ears.

Cade's eyes widen for a second, then he shakes his head.

"Nope," he says, popping the p.

I start to sigh, but before I can figure out what to say next, he's moving deeper into the house, pushing past me without another glance, moving faster than his aching body probably wants him to. He beelines to the fridge, first reaching in with his bad hand, wincing, then switching to the other. He moves some things around—I've developed a really unfortunate habit of overshopping when it comes to food. My therapist says it's normal for people who grew up with food insecurity, which I don't get, because I always had food. Dad made sure I had exactly the right food I needed to perform at my best, and nothing else to distract me. Even when we were living out of shitty motel rooms, I would have my specific, carefully planned meals waiting for me.

She just gave me a long look when I said that, which makes me think we'll be revisiting the topic at some point. Right now though, Cade is crashing through a bunch of vegetables I crammed in there, cursing under his breath as he can't find what he's looking for.

"Fuck," he finally snaps, closing the fridge door harder than he needs to. "I'm going out."

There's a single-minded determination as he avoids my eyes, heading for the door and struggling to put his boots back on.

"Where are you going?" I ask, even though I know the answer.

"Liquor store."

He grunts with pain as he manages to tug one boot on, biting the tip of his tongue as he works to cram his other foot in and lace them both up with clumsy, swollen fingers. I'd helped him when we left the house the first time. He'd let me, without complaint, even if he'd made a stink about driving afterward. I have the feeling the suggestion wouldn't be well received now.

I hold my tongue. By the time he stands up and reaches for the door, my brain has spun half a dozen possibilities for how this could play out, each one worse than the last.

I can't forbid him from going. He's an adult. And I understand the need for a little relief after the conversation we all just had. I just wish he could find relief in something less fucking fraught.

"Cade," I start, just as he opens the door. He whips around to look at me. "You'll come back, right? Come home and drink here. Don't go to a bar or something and then drive yourself home."

Because he's normally pretty responsible about that stuff, but not always when his mood has gotten the best of him. I should probably be telling him not to drink when he's this upset, but I can't get into that right now. All I can think about is him getting hurt because he didn't feel safe coming home to me and spiraling in our home.

Cade's entire posture is piano-wire taut, but after he blinks a couple of times, I see him soften, like all the air was let out of him at once.

"Yeah, baby," he says softly. "I'll come home. I'll only be a few minutes. I just—" he chews on his lip for a minute and waves his hand vaguely around. "I'll be home soon."

There's a note of finality to it, and he doesn't give me the chance to say anything else before he slips outside and shuts the front door behind him, the keys to the truck in his hand.

It'll be fine. He'll go pick up some beer, come home and relax, and everything will calm down. It'll be fine.

Once the truck has rumbled away down the driveway, silence falls over the house. I'm still standing in the living room, unsure of what to do with myself. I have to be overreacting. All this fear is just anxiety. I'm catastrophizing.

Cade is fine. He's tough. He's been through so much and he's always fine.

One little argument with his dad won't be the thing that pushes him over the edge.

It sounds like a lie, even in the privacy of my head.

This all feels too big. Cade's never been the most stable person internally, but his presence in my life has been rock-fucking-solid since he first pulled me back from the edge of that quarry. He's a constant, and I'm abruptly realizing how much I'd been taking that for granted.

Now that he's spinning out in a way that scares me a little, I don't know what to do.

I need an adult. I know I'm an adult, but not enough of one. It takes all my energy just to get through the day sometimes, and as much as I want to swoop in and have all the answers, right now I don't have shit. My brain has run so far with all the terrible possibilities that I don't even know what's realistic anymore.

Cade drunk-crashing the truck.

Cade getting into another bar fight and losing.

Cade deciding he's sick of taking care of everyone in his life and finally leaving.

Images flash through my mind one after the other like a flip-book from hell, and then I'm picking up my phone with shaking hands before I even consciously make the decision.

It only rings twice before he answers.

"What's wrong?"

Normally, Tristan is someone who doesn't leap to dramatics. But I don't think I've ever called him unless it was a five-alarm crisis. He normally talks to Cade, and sometimes I happen to be there. We don't seek each other out.

"Um," I start, not sure what to follow up with.

There's a brief pause before he talks, and I immediately recognize the calm, even tone he uses with his patients. It's the same tone Cade has learned, and uses on me when I'm unraveling. Which I'm only just realizing I'm doing right now.

"Silas, take a breath for me. In for two... three... four... now out slowly."

I do as he says, my heartbeat pounding too loudly to let the pending embarrassment settle in yet.

"Where are you?"

"I'm at home," my voice sounds reedy, so I clear my throat and try again. "I'm at home."

"Is everyone okay? Is anyone hurt?"

"No," I say quickly. "I, um—"

I can almost feel the patience seeping into me from the other side of the phone as he waits for me to finish. Literally the only time he can be still seems to be if the world is on fire. It's baffling to me.

"We went to see Kyle. I was hoping they might be able to talk. Clear things up a little. But of course they just fought, even though they weren't really fighting about anything. And Cade's just bottling everything up more and more. I—" There's a pause while I gather myself and try to decide if I'm really, legitimately worried, or just overreacting. "I'm really scared. He seems off. He needs to blow off steam sometimes and I know he tends to avoid his shit, but this just feels different. I don't know what to do." Another pause, filled with the sound of my harsh breathing. "Tell me what to do, Tristan."

Tears abruptly fill my eyes, but I blink them back. I have to focus.

Tristan exhales slowly through his nose, sounding like a bull about to charge.

"Okay, let's go back. Start from the beginning, and tell me everything this time. What the fuck has been going on?"

And that's all it takes for me to spill my guts.

I'm not sure how long I was on the phone to Tristan. Not that long, in the grand scheme of things, but enough talking to completely exhaust me.

I don't think I even told him anything coherent. It was mostly just rambling about the weird ways I've noticed Cade seeming off and how worried I am about the fall out from the fight. I hate his dad being here at all, and how much it seems to eat away at his stability. And I hate even more that we seem to be having a lot of misunderstandings and hurt feelings when we try to talk, for the first time in a long time.

Tristan didn't say much, but it still helped a little to spew it all out to him. He reminded me to stay calm and communicate clearly and not bottle shit up but also not turn a disagreement into a *tit for tat* kind of thing, which is all stuff I knew, but helped to hear him say, anyway.

I'm barely finished hanging up when I hear Cade opening the front door and stomping back inside. At first, I think he's going to ignore me, but when he walks into the living room and sees me, his eyes light up.

He has a twelve-pack in his good hand and his phone is balanced on his bad. I'm more relieved than I want to be that it looks like he hasn't opened any of the drinks yet. He really doesn't do that, but the paranoia has been totally unleashed in me.

"Oh, Silas!" he says, looking more energetic than I've seen him all day.

I turn to face him, waiting to see what's got him so worked up. Once he knows he has my attention, he heads to the kitchen to start unloading his drinks while he half-yells to me across the open space, until I wake up and move closer to him.

"Hey, so you remember Wyatt from high school? He used to race with us until he enlisted. Anyway, I had to go to the gas station because the liquor store was closed, and I ran into him. And he was telling me about the custody drama he's been having with his daughter. Because he had the kid with Breanna—you remember her, right?—just before he was deployed. But then Breanna ended up relapsing or something and skipped town, and left the baby with her parents. So all while he was deployed her parents and his mom took care of the baby. It sounds like a shitty situation for everyone involved, obviously. I hope Breanna's okay, she always had it rough. But that's not the point."

Now he has a beer in his hand which he cracks the tab on before taking a swig and turning to look at me. He's still animated, using big gestures as he speaks and waving the can in the air. I've seen him get worked up like this a million times before, but normally it's for a reason I at least kind of understand. I still have no idea where he's going with this story. He continues to talk a mile a minute.

"Anyway. So they all made it work for a couple of years and he came back as much as he could, but now he's home because he decided not to re-up, plus his mom's MS has been getting a lot worse so he didn't want to keep putting that burden on her. No one has heard from Bree this whole time. But it turns out that he never realized how fucking churchy her parents are. Like, everyone's parents are churchy. Except mine. But I didn't realize they were *Pentecostal* churchy. Not even the regular Pentecostal church in town, the weird one over on Rt 21 that still does like, snake handling or laying hands or whatever. So they're saying he's a demonic influence and so is his mom, and they're trying to get full custody. Which should be impossible, right? He's the kid's dad and he's home full-time now, apart from reserves shit once a month."

Cade takes another swig, emptying the can before crushing it in his hand and throwing it in the recycling and then grabbing another from the fridge.

"So this whole time—this whole fucking time!—they've been building a case against him. Collecting affidavits and paper records and anything else they can to show that they've been the primary caregivers. It's not like he's a shitty dad, he just wasn't here. But he's here now and according to him, they actually have a case and he has to play fucking catch up. It sounds really stressful. All of a sudden he's launched into this whole legal battle, and that poor little girl is in the middle of it."

There's a long pause while he drinks and looks at me. When no more words follow, I get the feeling I'm supposed to be responding with something, but I'm not sure what.

"That's... really sad?"

It is, but I don't think that's what he wanted to hear specifically.

"Yes, but that's not the point," he says, resting the can on the counter before walking toward me. "It made me realize what I need to do. I think I need to actually start preparing to petition for custody of the girls."

He must see the expression I make, because he immediately shushes me, holding me by the arm and making a placating expression at me like I'm missing something that makes this whole situation not fucked up.

"No, no, no," he says. "It's fine. I know Mom's been doing better and we were hoping everything would turn out okay, but I think Dad showing up has made it clear that things aren't okay. She's kowtowing to him like the old days, sober or not. He's lounging around like he's Harvey fucking Weinstein sitting on a throne, dragging random sex workers after him and fuck what happens to the girls. They were both more than happy to ship Maddi and Sky off with us, as soon as something they thought was more interesting came up. It just makes it clear that they'll never be safe with either of our parents. I finally have a stable job and a real house, I need to just pull the trigger and do it. Fuck them. Fuck their custody. A judge will see that, if I just put the work in. And then they'll be here and I can know that they're safe all the time."

The earnestness on his face is fucking killing me. This isn't the first time I've seen him get swept up in something, convinced that it's going to be the answer to all our problems. But it's normally something less insidious, like buying a blender or trying to buy those crates of unsold Amazon goods and then resell them on the internet. And it's normally not that hard to distract him until he realizes it was a stupid idea.

This is a whole other level.

"Cade, would you really do that to your mom? I know she's not perfect, but she does love them and she's been trying so hard to do good this past year. We're around all the time to make sure they don't slip through the cracks. Your dad will get bored and move on soon. Taking them away from your mom and having a whole legal battle sounds expensive and really painful, for not a lot of gain. I think you need to take a breath."

Cade's expression falls. For a second, I think I've gotten through to him, but then he furrows his brow at me and takes a step back.

"You don't get it. She could snap. He could snap at any minute. They're all one bad trip from becoming a podcast episode about family annihilators. And every time you hear about one of those cases, you're like *oh but there were so many warning signs, how did everyone ignore it?* This is me not ignoring it. I've seen too much happen to too many kids. I'm not picking them up in a fucking ambulance because I was too lazy to do some paperwork."

It's been a tense, tense day. And somehow, this is the most on edge I've felt. There's a thread of logic to what he's saying, but it's also so displaced from the reality of the situation—or at least such a tunnel-visioned way of looking at it—that I still can't believe the words are coming out of his mouth.

"Are you asking me if I think we should do this or telling me that it's happening?"

Cade frowns.

"Neither. I just... I thought you'd agree with me. It seems so obvious."

"To you, maybe. I don't think we should be adopting kids without talking about it first, and especially not when it might ruin your mother's life. I don't want to do this to Kris."

She's not technically my family, but I've been willing to take what I can get, and she really has been working hard on herself since I've been around. I don't want to punish her for that.

Cade sighs, not looking angry exactly, but not happy with my response. As if I was going to automatically be thrilled to launch this whole operation with no thought to our future.

"Look, it's a lot. I sprang this on you. I'll do more research and I'll make a plan. It'll be great, I promise. But I won't do anything drastic without talking to you first, okay?"

I still feel completely side-swiped, but that's better than nothing, so I nod.

"Perfect. Love you," Cade says, stepping in to kiss me fast and hard before turning back around to find his beer.

I'll drop it for now, because this has been a day. But the thought of him getting fixated on this is going to keep me up at night, I can already tell.

Maybe Tristan can talk some sense into him. He's better at that than I am.

Chapter Sixteen

CADE

"I see your ugly ass every day at work. Why do we have to go on a field trip?"

Tristan doesn't rise to the bait of my insult and keeps his eyes on the road, taking turn after turn until I have no idea where we could possibly be going.

"First of all, you haven't been at work, because you're convalescing. Apparently dumbassery qualifies for PTO, now. Second of all, I'm worried about you. I know you're going crazy bouncing around that house by yourself while Silas is at work, and I thought I could take your mind off things for a while."

I can't stop the snort that slips out. Sure, take my mind off things. As if that's possible. I seem to have two states right now—obsessing over the past/freaking out about the future, or completely shutting down. Neither of them is good, but I don't see myself crawling out of that pendulum swing anytime soon.

"I'm fine," I say with a sigh, and Tristan doesn't call me on it, even though I can feel that he wants to. "If we have to go out and do shit, couldn't we just go to a bar like normal? I'm down to kick back and have a beer, you didn't have to literally kidnap me."

Tristan's gaze flicks over to me briefly before returning to the road, and he doesn't say anything. Which is fundamentally against his nature, and makes me feel a little nervous for the first time since getting in the car.

"What?" I ask when the silence gets too much for me to take.

"Oh well will you look at that, we're here."

I don't miss the underlying tension in Tristan's voice as he pulls off the road and into a large gravel lot. It's a weekday afternoon, so it's pretty empty, and we're heading toward a huge ranch-style house, two levels and spread out, surrounded by more gravel lots, empty fields, and a small glittering lake off to one side. It's late enough in the season that the trees are all bare, and the white house, light blue siding, and bare, flat scenery all create a cold, empty image. It feels like we're much farther from home than a thirty-minute drive. It's like we're far from everything right now, with no one but the barren trees to watch us.

"What is this place?" I ask as we both pile out of Tristan's car.

The distant sound of gunfire answers my question before Tristan can. He moves around to the trunk and pulls out a dark equipment bag, slinging it over one shoulder before nudging me and pointing at the house. Just disappearing from sight, I can make out a large wraparound porch. It looks segmented, with little barriers evenly spaced, and the whole thing points towards the tree line. If I squint, I can make out targets at the end, and a few more loud pops of gunfire confirm my suspicions.

"Okay, got it. And why are we at a gun range?" I ask.

Tristan turns and walks toward the entrance, equipment bag in tow.

"Because neither of us knows how to play fucking golf."

I'm a little bewildered, but I fall in line behind him anyway. I'm sure it'll make sense eventually. I don't think I've ever actually been to a gun range. Most of my friends had something slapped together on their land or a neighbor's growing up. We were no exception, with Dad marking out a specific area a couple miles from the trailer where he would drag me out for target practice from time to time.

It was probably the only thing we really did together, other than fight. I haven't really thought about it in a while. This place seems fucking all class in comparison to Dad, a few beers, and the weathered old AK-47 that one of my uncles smuggled home after Desert Storm, which was my dad's pride and joy.

I chew on the memories quietly as we head inside. It's clean and well kept, with a single clerk behind the counter. An older guy with steel gray hair and that tight, controlled body language that seems designed to scream *I served* to everyone he meets.

There are a bunch of *Don't Tread on Me* bumper stickers and shit stuck up around the space, and the first time the clerk glances at me, I feel acutely uncomfortable. Like I don't belong and everyone here is going to know it. Like Sergeant Hartman over here is about to start pointing at me and screaming to everyone else that he spotted my queerness or just the fact that I'm not a fucking libertarian. Normally, that kind of situation gets my blood up. It makes me ready for a fight, and instantly on edge.

I don't know what's different today, but instead of anger, I feel the urge to sink in on myself. But as I show the man my ID and sign in, spacing out through the obligatory safety spiel despite my best efforts, nothing happens.

He doesn't talk to me any differently, and starts walking us outside to a lane like this is all normal. He and Tristan aren't exactly chit-chatting, but there's a level of familiarity there that makes me think this isn't Tristan's first time here.

Does this guy really know who Tristan is? Him and Ford shacking up was wild gossip in this area, influenced I'm sure by Tristan's status as a showy outsider, Ford's reputation as a mysterious recluse, and the fact that they're both so fucking hot. No one admits the last part, but I know it's true.

Maybe he does know, and he doesn't care. I focus on watching Tristan's posture as I follow along behind, and try to let the way he seems utterly at ease with himself and his surroundings rub off on me a little.

After what seems like forever, our lane is declared hot and the dude leaves us alone. I'm waiting for Tristan to say something profound, but he just gets to work loading the small Beretta he pulled out of his sack of wonders before passing it to me.

"What are we doing, Tristan?" I have to shout because we're both wearing ear protection now, even though it's pretty silent here apart from the one other customer standing all the way at the far end of the lanes.

"Shooting," he says, with a look like I'm dense for not understanding.

"My hand—" I start, looking at the splint that's been driving me insane.

"You can watch me shoot if you'd prefer. But your work note is almost finished, I think you can handle a little recoil. And I can't think of a damn thing for us to do that doesn't require your hands, unless you wanna learn to crochet with your toes."

I'm tempted to suggest the bar one more time, because that sounds relaxing as hell right now. But also, so does the range. Now that we're here.

I finally turn and face the target, careful to line up my body and the site the way I was taught, and squeeze the trigger. The sound of it, the smell of gunpowder in the air, the jolt of energy that my body has to absorb as it kicks, it all combines in a way that's so familiar, I feel some of the tension in my shoulders automatically unfurling.

The world gets quiet as I focus on nothing but what I'm doing, emptying the clip methodically until Tristan takes it from me and reloads. Which I appreciate, because my hand is fucking sore and my thumb is not feeling up to the job right now, but the pain is nothing compared to the steady flush of endorphins into my body.

We repeat this three times, with my aim improving each round. Eventually, my hand throbs enough that I have to take a break, so I nod to Tristan to have his turn.

Of course, he pulls out a rifle from somewhere, holding it like it's an extension of his body. He aims for the steel target farther away from us than the one I was hitting. And of course, he decimates me in terms of accuracy. He doesn't even try to hide the cocky smile when he finishes.

"It's not classy to gloat. I got taught to shoot by a meth addict, you got taught by the US fucking Army."

"Bold of you to assume nobody there was on meth," he says, his grin not dampened even a little. "Deployments can get long, and you can only supervise bored meatheads up to a point."

The afternoon continues like that. We don't really talk, just quietly take turns, and by the time we agree to pack up I'm sore everywhere, even though it can't have been more than an hour.

I feel calm, though. The flustered kind of panic I felt when we arrived doesn't return when we finally check out to leave, and the clerk's demeanor hasn't changed one iota as he thanks us gruffly and sends us on our way.

Once we're back in the car with the engine on and the radio tuned to some classic rock station turned low, I finally ask him again.

"So, what was that about? Not that I didn't have fun," I start.

Tristan makes no move to pull out of the parking lot, but runs his hands over the leather of the steering wheel, like a habit.

"I thought you could probably stand to get out of your head for a little while," he says. "And like I said, neither of us fucking golf. What else is there to do around here? You wanna go bowling? Next week I'll take you bowling."

I can't help but snort at the image of Tristan bowling. It seems sacrilegious somehow.

"I would crush you, just so you're aware. That's basically the only family-friendly activity I actually did growing up. My nana was a fucking champ, she used to take us."

Tristan smiles. "All right then, bowling it is. But I know this is something you used to do for fun, and I'm assuming you don't keep guns in the house anymore."

Neither of us speaks, and the mood in the car turns somber. I'm not sure what Tristan is waiting for me to say, but he doesn't push it.

"Nah," I answer. "I got rid of Dad's guns when he left. We needed the money, and it wasn't worth the risk, with the girls around. And now with Silas... Yeah, it's not worth it."

Tristan doesn't say anything, because we both know what I'm talking about. There are a lot of ways to kill yourself, but a gun is well and truly the most effective. It's easy to make an impulsive, devastating decision, which is one more reason I want them well away from my family. Even when you're unsuccessful, Tristan and I have both seen the kind of physical damage that a last-second flinch can leave behind. Surviving something like that doesn't normally mean you get your life back.

Nope. Not happening on my watch.

It was nice to shoot in a controlled environment, though. Bringing back some of my only happy childhood memories, as fucked up as that is. I felt calm, and distant from the issues in my real life. Except for that brief moment when we walked in and the clerk first looked at me, though.

"Don't you get uncomfortable going to places like that?" I ask when I can't take the quiet anymore.

His brow furrows as he thinks about it. "What? You mean because I fuck men? Well, a man."

"Classy, as always," I reply.

"You know what I mean. I don't really think about it. But I guess that's my privilege. This kind of place is normal for me, and I'm not going to change what I do based on what some conservative asswipes think about my sex life. I'm not hiding who I am. And maybe if I keep acting like myself, it'll open their minds to other people who don't blend in as much as I do. Or maybe it won't. It's worth a shot, though."

He pauses, studying me from the other side of the car.

"Does it make you feel weird? You grew up here. If anything, you fit in more than I do."

I chew on the words. He seems to be so effortlessly at home in any situation he falls into. I've spent nearly every day of my life in this fucking county, but I keep finding more and more things that trip me up sometimes. Make me wonder if I still have the welcome I used to.

"It feels like my life is divided into a before and after, sometimes. Silas, I mean. Like he had such a profound effect on everything about me, that I'm a different person now, and everyone can see it."

"Is that a bad thing?" Tristan asks, pulling some Big Red out of his center console that immediately fills the car with the smell of cinnamon as he chews.

My answer is fast, but not as fast as I'd like. "No." I take a breath. "I'm a better version of myself with him, I know that. It's just weird sometimes. And when shit goes down with my dad, I can't tell which version of me he's fighting."

Now it's Tristan's turn to snort, rolling his eyes as he answers. "I think he's fighting the version that's throwing punches. That man does not contain hidden depths. He seems to be taking whatever you're putting up for him to see without a lot of critical engagement."

Yeah, maybe, I think, but hold my tongue.

"Do you think you'd still be queer, if it wasn't for Silas? I'm not gonna lie, it's been kind of nice watching you really get into the whole community aspect of it. It's not something I ever would have considered at your age. And now I'm too old and grumpy to make new friends."

That makes me roll my eyes, but I don't take the bait.

"Oh, I was definitely fucking queer before Silas," I say, shaking my head at my own stupidity. "I just couldn't see it. I wasn't spending a whole lot of time on self-exploration, I guess. I was busy just getting to the next day. But when I look back now, it was all right there, waiting for me to wake the fuck up. It wouldn't change if Silas, you know…" I trail off, unwilling to even say the words. Unwilling to even think them. Like it would tempt the universe to fuck me over.

"Good. So then, did you really change? If you were bisexual all along and just too hard-headed to realize it? Or does dividing the world into some kind of before and after situation really feel necessary?"

I chew on his words for a minute before I answer. My pulse has ticked up a little, and I don't like the way this conversation is going, but I feel obligated to at least reply to Tristan after he dragged me all the way out here as a pretense for this little heart to heart.

"Maybe it hasn't changed. Maybe I just have more to lose now."

Tristan nods slowly, still chewing that gum, his face set in the grimace he always seems to make when he's dishing out his little pearls of wisdom.

"What are you gonna do about it?"

"What?" I reply, blinking.

"You said you have more to lose. I'm assuming you mean Silas. But also I'm guessing there's more. The acceptance you got from your family. Well, most of them. The identity you seem to be cultivating. This new life you've been building for yourself that doesn't revolve around cleaning up your parents' messes. What are you going to do about it?"

I make a few noises, but I don't think any of them qualify as words. The point he's trying to make is lingering at the edge of my consciousness, but I either can't or don't want to really see it.

Another big, cinnamon-scented sigh comes out of Tristan before he gives me a leveling expression.

"Look, I'm not going to pussyfoot around anymore. You are becoming self-destructive." He looks me in the eye and enunciates every word like I'm a child. "You've always been a little off the rails, which I can definitely fucking empathize with, but recently its stepped up a notch. I get it. I like to drink and fight and fuck as much as the next guy. Probably more than the next guy, let's be honest. But when that stuff becomes the thing you need just to feel normal, you have a problem. There's a difference between indulging your baser urges and being crippled by them, you hear me?"

Getting scolded has never been one of my favorite pastimes, and normally kickstarts my anger faster than anything else. The urge to do the complete opposite of whatever that person wants me to do is all-devouring. And especially now, with the words Tristan's saying making it feel like he's peering directly into the most raw part of me. I take in one deep breath after another, resisting the urge to call him an asshole and start a fight so we can stop fucking talking about this.

I'm sure he can tell, but as always, he's unperturbed.

"I'm not giving you a hard time. Remember when my cunt mother showed up to suck me back into her web of misery? I'm telling you, I get it. I get how it feels to be immediately transported back in time into a much more fragile, scared, and angry version of yourself, while everyone around you expects you to keep acting like an adult. My point is that you have to stay one step ahead of that feeling, or it'll consume you. So find some way to work it off. Come here and shoot. Take up fucking boxing once your hand is healed. Run a triathlon like a masochist. Read stories at the peds unit. I don't give a fuck. But you have to put that energy somewhere, or it'll just keep eating at you."

I open my mouth, but he cuts me off before I can speak.

"And no, drinking doesn't count. Neither does riding your bike, unfortunately, as long as you and Silas are still fighting about it. That's just more fuel for the fire."

This time, the mention of Silas's name clicks, and I put two and two together.

I turn to look at Tristan, my expression sharp.

"He talked to you. Didn't he?"

Tristan's face remains impassive.

"What do you think?" he asks.

There's a pulse of anger, but I try to release it before it can take hold, and in its wake I crumple in on myself.

"Yeah," I say, my voice quiet, guilt creeping in from all sides. I can't stop myself from bringing up a thumbnail to chew on, because what's one more bad habit right now, really?

My whole mission most of the time is to make things easier for Silas, and it looks like I've been doing the opposite recently. "Fuck, I'm an asshole. I should never have put him in this position."

Tristan holds one hand up like a stop sign.

"Don't do that. He's your fucking partner. He's supposed to worry about you and hurt when you're hurting. That's normal. You running around pretending to be king shit of mental health and ignoring your issues because you think he's the only one allowed to have problems—that's what's fucking you both over. Come on, you know this. It's common fucking sense."

Oof, this is just one dick-punch of embarrassment after another. "Yeah," I say, because I can't muster anything else. Then I think about it for another few seconds and pull on my big boy pants. "Thank you, Tristan. I know I need a kick in the ass sometimes."

He reaches over and ruffles my hair like we're in the after part of an anti-depressant commercial. It's cheesy and embarrassing, and I yank my head out of his reach even while he grins at me.

"Good talk," he says, reaching to give me another condescending pat before I slap his arm away.

"Yeah, yeah, can we go? I'm hungry."

This time, he actually does start to pull out of the parking lot.

"Sure. I'll buy you some food. But you have to promise me to keep your face out of a liquor bottle for at least a week, until you and Silas sort your shit out. Promise me that and I'll get you the most disgusting, overstuffed cheeseburger we can find."

"I can buy my own food, Tristan, I'm not destitute. Well, not anymore." He stares at me. "Fine, fine, I promise. Let's go."

A little voice in the back of my head reminds me of what Micah said at the hospital, that unburdening myself to Tristan doesn't count as a big enough step in the right direction. As if I can afford therapy after the amount I spent on Silas already. Or, frankly, think about it without immediately getting angry.

I don't need therapy. This is enough. I feel lighter already, and I'm going to apologize to Silas as soon as I get home.

Everything will be fine.

Chapter Seventeen

SILAS

I don't know what I expected when Cade said he was going out with Tristan. After I word-vomited all my worries to his friend, I knew Tristan would do something, I just wasn't sure what. And that was before Cade unloaded all his weird thoughts about custody battles, which we haven't talked about since. Mostly because I hope he's forgotten about it, and I'm scared to remind him.

Either way, Cade coming home sober and relaxed before it even got dark was not what I was expecting today. It is a delightful surprise, though.

He's closing the door behind him just as I reach the entryway. I can hear Tristan's car pulling out of the driveway and taking off, and I immediately do a once over of my boyfriend to get a lay of the land.

There's no smell of liquor, which is nice. There is an acrid, burned sort of smell, but that could be a lot of things. And more importantly, his whole posture is loose and relaxed, even as he struggles to take off his shoes.

Cade looks up at me and his shoulders slump a little, like he's sad. But the smile he gives me is soft and sweet. A real smile, not something he put on for show or when he's desperately trying to make me laugh.

"Hey, baby," he says so softly it's almost a whisper. "Can you help me out here? My hand has given up for the day, I think."

It takes me a few long seconds to process, then I move toward him all at once. I'm not sure what to say, so I focus on bending over and unlacing his boots while he leans heavily into my back. It's awkward and he probably should have sat down first, but I like the feeling of him leaning on me.

It's a little on the nose, but it feels good. I'm only wearing a t-shirt, and I can feel the chill of his wind-chapped skin where he rests his hand on me.

"It's getting cold out there, man. We might be finished with the teeny-tiny window of hoody season and headed straight into real winter," Cade says overhead.

As soon as I get his boots off and stand up, he makes a show of rubbing both his hands together and then wrapping his arms around me.

"Brr," he pretends to shiver. "Warm me up, baby. I need my own personal space heater." His cold hands splay across my back underneath my shirt as he squeezes me a little around the waist and pushes his face against my chest like a cat.

I huff a little, because I do run hot, and he tends to be on the colder side and more than willing to steal my body heat. Also like a damn cat.

"You'd probably conserve your heat better if you weren't always yapping," I mumble, even as I wrap my arms around his shoulders and hold him tighter. "Your mouth is open so often, all the heat zips right on out of you."

Cade chuckles, even though the sound is muffled by my shirt.

"One of us has to yap, or we'd live in absolute silence. It's all about balance, baby. I yap so you don't have to. It's self-sacrificing of me, really."

I rub one hand up and down his back, letting myself truly relax into the embrace for the first time in god-knows how long.

"And what was your excuse for the first 22 years of your life?"

"It was a public service. Just making sure the introverts of Possum Hollow knew they had someone around to pick up their slack. What can I say, robot boy? I was made for you. You just kept me waiting."

He leans back as he says this, looking me in the eye and giving me a crooked grin that makes me want to kiss him more than I want to breathe.

So, I do.

Cade kisses me back, and it's a soft, gentle thing. It feels real, though, and I find myself settling inside more and more with each second that our lips are pressed together.

"Hi," he says when we break apart, almost shy.

"Hi," I reply. "Did you have a nice time on your play date?"

His expression shutters a little, becoming more serious, but he nods.

"I did. I'm glad Tristan took me out. I think I needed that."

"Tell me about it," I say, pulling away from him enough to snag him by the less-injured hand and lead him into the living room.

He follows me easily, letting me pull him onto the couch and arrange us so we're lying down face to face, our bodies interlocked and overlapping everywhere we can. It's not really necessary for this conversation, but I feel compelled by the need to keep him as close to me as possible.

While I manipulate us until it's comfortable, he tells me about the day in bits and pieces. The shooting range; going for food. He tells me that they had a sort of heart to heart, although he downplays it and doesn't use those words. I can imagine what they probably talked about.

"I'm sorry I've been scaring you," he says finally, after a long silence. His voice is small, but his grey eyes are meeting mine without hesitation.

It's difficult to pick what to say. I don't want to minimize it, because he has been scaring me. That's the whole reason I ran to Tristan in the first place. Telling him it's okay feels like telling him he can do it again, and even if this kind of stuff isn't the end of the world, I'd really rather if he never did it again.

"You don't have to apologize," I say, my voice cracking a little from being quiet for so long. "Just don't shut me out, okay? This is supposed to be the happily ever after part." I push an unruly curl back from his forehead, because my fingers are itching to touch him. "I know neither of us has a good template to work from as far as happy endings are concerned, but I'm pretty sure however they work, we're supposed to do it together."

Cade is quiet, and my words seem to sink into both of us like weights through murky lake water. Slowly, but inevitable all the same.

"I'm sorry, " he says again. His voice is thicker now, but his eyes are dry, and there's a tension to his whole body that I'm aching to soothe. "I don't know what's wrong with me."

Cupping his jaw, I hold his face more forcefully than I need to as I look him in the eye.

"Nothing's wrong with you. You deserve this. You deserve to be happy. We both deserve to be happy. Even if it doesn't always feel right, because you're so used to being stressed or miserable that anything else is uncomfortable."

Cade huffs something close to a laugh, but doesn't pull away from me.

"Is that what they teach you in therapy?"

I can't help but smile. "Yeah, dude. That's it. And then we repeat it over and over and over again until it starts to make sense."

He laughs at that, even though it's a wet sound, and I find myself laughing quietly, too.

"We deserve this. I know I still have shitty days sometimes, but it doesn't mean I'm not here for you. We can take care of each other."

"Yeah, where the music plays us off and we kiss in front of the sunset or some shit. A soft epilogue, right? That's what you're picturing?"

I laugh again and kiss him hard, eventually nodding against his mouth. "All we have to do is pretend, and eventually it won't feel like pretending any more."

"I can do that," he mumbles before kissing me again.

I know it's not everything that needs to be said. I know it's not enough. But it's enough for now, and I need to have my hands on him without all these layers between us before I explode.

Our kiss quickly turns from something intimate to something messy and intense. Cade grinds against me, pawing at my t-shirt, and I fumble my way to the hem of his hoody without breaking away from his lips. We roll until Cade's more under me than next to me, and when I tug at that fabric he arches his back with a whine, giving me space to drag up the sweater and whatever shirt he's wearing underneath in one fluid movement. As soon as it's off, I attack his mouth again, and the sensation of him rolling his hips into mine, already half-hard, has me growling into his mouth with a desperate kind of urgency.

I want him.

I need him.

Sometimes I think this desire will consume us both.

My fingers leave ragged, red trails in the skin of his torso as I touch him everywhere I can, stopping only to pinch his nipples roughly, the way he likes, until I pull a ragged noise of pleasure from him. Cade's hands are on me just as frantically, under my t-shirt, the material of the splint scratching against me overheated flesh.

"Please," he whines between kisses, and I quickly reach behind my head to yank off my shirt.

For once, the insecurities about my body that have been eating away at me more and more lately stay silent. Having Cade touch me with nothing between us feels more important right now, and my normal chorus of doubts are quiet.

Cade pushes his splinted hand into the waistband of my basketball shorts, but when he can't comfortably get a grip on my hard cock, he whines in frustration.

This might be my favorite version of him. I mean hell, they're all my favorite. But this Cade is special. He's always in control, hour by hour, minute by minute, even if he doesn't seem like it. But here is where he truly unravels, just for me.

He turns into something soft, pliant and desperate, unable to take care of his own needs and desperate for me to do it all for him.

I'll never get sick of how much he lets himself need me when he's like this.

"Don't worry, baby," I whisper to him. "I've got us. You just relax."

I pull away from him for a second, which earns me another whine, but it's easier to pull off the rest of my clothes followed by Cade's. He lies on his back on the couch, letting me manhandle him, his chest and cheeks flushed from arousal and his mouth open in a quiet pant. His cock is hard and dark, glistening with moisture, and I need him now.

There's no lube down here, and I can't wait that long. I need to be close to him more than I need to be inside him.

"I've got you, baby," I say again as I lay my body on top of his and press our lengths together. I hold my weight on one bent arm, using the other to reach down and fist both of us. One stroke is enough to have Cade groaning, but when I pull back my hand to spit in it before I continue, I see his pupils dilate at the sight.

"I've got you." It's becoming my mantra as I begin to jerk us both together. Cade starts making breathy, bitten-off noises, jerking his hips in time with my movements. His legs spread underneath me, bracketing my hips with his strong thighs as if I'm fucking him, continuing to arch his back up into me.

I pause for a second, grabbing the fingers of his good hand and sucking them into my mouth without hesitation. Cade's breath stutters, and I love that I can still affect him so much even now. I work my tongue up and down his fingers until they're dripping with saliva, and then release them with a faint pop.

"Fuck yourself for me," I tell him. "Fuck yourself for me while I fuck us together."

Cade gasps a little, but doesn't hesitate as he reaches down. He has to hitch his leg, both of us shifting as he finds a good angle and eventually pushes his fingers into his hole.

"Rough, baby. Make it hurt, just like you like."

I barely recognize my voice when I get like this. In the same way that Cade turns into a completely different person, so do I. But I think it's what we both need right now.

Cade must add another finger, because he tenses up and lets out a few squeaky, desperate gasps. I'm continuing to jerk us both off at a steady pace, stopping occasionally to collect whatever moisture is leaking there and spread it around the head of Cade's cock.

"That's it, Cade. Do you feel full? Are you getting fucked just the way you deserve?"

He bites his lip and whimpers, but I see him working his fingers deeper into himself, shuddering with pleasure as I tighten the grip I have on us. My hips are thrusting, helping rub our lengths together, and with every inch of us pressed together and my forehead resting on his, it feels just as intimate as it ever has when I'm inside him.

"Fuck your fingers until you come, Cade. I need you to come all over me. I want to feel your cock pulse and watch you gasp as you tighten around yourself and make a mess. Fuck yourself for me, baby."

His hand is moving faster now, reckless and sloppy, and I tighten my grip, reaching between our cocks to press my thumb against the underside of his head for a second. The air fills with slick, sloppy sounds as I work us both over before shoving my tongue back in his mouth.

Cade starts to whine, desperate little noises punched out one after the other to the rhythm of his fingers inside him and my fists around us both.

"Uh—uh—uh—uh," he gets higher and higher, spreading his thighs further open beneath me, fucking his hips downward with a single-minded desperation.

"Come for me, beautiful," I tell him before putting my tongue back in his mouth, and I'm rewarded by a strangled noise and the pulse of his cock as wetness spurts between us.

I don't stop. If anything, I speed up. I keep milking him for every last drop of cum, but then, as his body starts to relax, I keep going.

Cade's arm relaxes a little, but I keep jerking us both. I'm so focused on him right now, I'm able to hold back the tide of my own orgasm. His cock is softening a little in my hand, but not entirely.

"Don't stop," I say. "Keep fucking yourself until I tell you you're done. Find your spot, and fuck yourself as hard as you can."

Cade whimpers, but I see his fingers start working again with renewed energy. He's shaky, but I can see the shiver of pleasure that's still going through him every time he grazes his prostate, even if he's flinching from my rough grip on his oversensitive cockhead.

We fall into a sort of trance, for a while. I keep jerking us both steadily, Cade keeps fucking himself on his fingers, and gradually, minute by minute, the oversensitivity shifts back to pleasure. By the time he's fully hard again, I can see the deep purple color of his cock, and he's too overwhelmed to kiss me back, instead whimpering meaningless sounds at me between gulped breaths and pawing at my back with his splinted hand.

"That's it, Cade. So fucking good for me. Are you going to come again? Come again all over me like you need to?"

Cade shivers and bites his lip again, but he nods to me, a glazed look in his eye.

This time, his orgasm builds slowly. His body gets tighter a little bit at a time, and each time I think he can't possibly get more tense without exploding, he stiffens up a little more. He's shaking consistently now, and the noises have quieted to just breaths.

"You can do it. Come one more time for me," I say.

I lower my head to his chest and tug his nipple between my teeth, teasing the swollen bud. Cade cries out once, and then what feels like minutes later, he finally comes in my hand.

It's nowhere near as much as before, but he still slicks the space between us with his release.

"Oh fuck, Cade," I mutter, suddenly turned on beyond measure. I release his cock with a gasp, shifting my grip to just mine, and jerk myself frantically, knuckles dragging over Cade's stomach with every movement, our bodies pressed together. My mouth falls against his sweaty skin in an open kiss, and my hips buck into him a few times before I finally spill my own release.

"Fuck," I grunt again as I come, my wetness joining his.

The grip of my orgasm starts to relax, and a rush of emotion seems to flood the space it left behind.

"Jesus, Cade," I say again, pulling our mouths together. "I love you. I love you. Please don't leave me."

I don't know where the words are even coming from, but I can't stop repeating it as I rub my face against his and milk the last bit of pleasure from myself.

Even once I've released my cock, the feeling of intensity doesn't fade. I keep riding his body, moving my hips as we both grow soft, but now touching his face and holding him close to me.

I don't know when he comes back to himself enough to talk, but he starts saying "It's okay," over and over as I tell him how much I love him, and the words are eventually enough to stem the frantic tide that had built up in me.

When I'm finally still, he holds me close, and I let my weight sink into his body, wishing we could combine and knit our cells together, just for a minute.

"I love you," he says, stroking my sweaty hair before pressing a kiss to the top of my head. "We're okay. Everything's okay."

I let out a slow, shuddering breath, and for once, I make the choice to believe him.

CHAPTER EIGHTEEN

CADE

T hings have evened out ever since Silas and I talked. Not that we really got into it in that much depth, but it felt like everything that needed to be said was said.

There was never any doubt that we fucking love each other, things just went off the rails for a minute and I got a little carried away. It doesn't help that my anger at my dad—something I've held onto for over a decade with no fucking issue—has suddenly decided that it's a festering wound, ready to burst open and cover my skin in putrescence for no real reason.

But it's fine. Everything is fine. I will keep my temper under control, I will pay more attention to Silas, my dad will eventually get bored and leave, and everything will go back to normal.

It's fine.

That's been my internal refrain for days. It's kind of holding up.

At least going back to work was uneventful. I got cleared to go back and do basically everything except super heavy lifting, which I'm more than happy to make Tristan do on his own. He spends too much time in Ford's backyard gym now, working on his fucking abs. Might as well make him use that shit for something real. I'm too busy paying bills to finely hone my lifting regime.

If I sound bitter, it's because I am. Things are probably better now in a macro sense than they ever have been, but for whatever reason, that just comes with a mounting sense of pressure to keep providing. This is the first real opportunity I've had to give my sisters a normal life, instead of scraping by all the time. Silas and I combined make okay money. The house is paid off and taxes and shit in this area is not the worst. There's always food and it's not a fucking nightmare to sign off on school trips and new sweaters and all the other shit kids shouldn't have to worry about.

It feels like if I just push a little bit harder, I can give them the kind of childhood I dreamed of. If that's not a motivation to skip working out and keep picking up extra shifts, I don't know what is.

Which is why I'm capping off my normal work week with a twelve-hour overtime night shift. Tristan is off, so today I'm paired up with Sharon—a salty old workhorse of a paramedic who's been employed here almost since before I was born. She's not chatty or maternal, and that suits me just fine. I'm itchy from feeling like Tristan was peering into my soul all week.

I've been good! Zero beers. Zero fights. Minimal thoughts about Dad, and no complaining whenever Silas fed me fucking cabbage. If you work enough hours, you don't have time to have a mental health crisis. This is a well-established law of the universe. It has never, ever backfired.

It's been a less-than-eventful night, which is giving me enough space to let the exhaustion kick in. I'm on my third energy drink, so I'm starting to smell the damn things coming out of my pores, and I could really use an exciting call sometime soon.

Of course, as soon as we get an address, my heart sinks.

It's 5 a.m.. Which is a special time of day when people start waking up and noticing that the people around them are not right, and probably haven't been all night. No one calls an ambulance over bullshit at four or five in the morning.

They call because grandma won't wake up and there's bloody foam coming out of her mouth.

I know this address though, which is what makes it worse. This is Jaden's house. And I know it makes me a shitty person, but I'm crossing my fingers the entire drive there that his dad is really the one that's sick and there was a miscommunication with dispatch.

The house seems still as we pull up. It's late/early in a residential area, so we've got lights but no sirens, and as soon as the blue and red washes over the walls of the exterior, the front door opens. Mr. Halloran looks haggard. I can see that, even through the blue light. He has a cigarette pinched between his fingers, and he waves us in with a peculiar mixture of urgency and fatigue that tells me more than anything else about what we're about to find.

Sharon and I hustle out of the rig and towards the house, stretcher in tow. Neither of us says more than the bare minimum. Inside, most of the lights are still turned off. Jaden's mom is barefoot, wearing an old bathrobe, while the dad looks like he hastily pulled on some jeans and boots. They both look completely drawn. No one's crying.

Sometimes you're too far past the point of crying to get it out.

Jaden is on the couch. He has slow, shallow respirations and his color is terrible. Sharon and I quickly move to the floor so we can move around him and get to work.

"I went to wake him up and he just..." her mom starts. "He just wouldn't wake up. His eyes were open, but he didn't seem right. He'd wet the bed, and I couldn't get him to answer me. Paul brought him out here."

Sharon asks her more questions and makes a couple quick notes while I get his vitals, and then she works on placing an IV.

We won't be here long. He's not responsive, so he's going to a hospital no matter what, and the faster we get him there, the better. Who knows how long he's been having back-to-back seizures for, and because his seizures are non-convulsive, there was no noise or anything to wake up his parents.

Which could potentially have been prevented if he'd been seen by a fucking neurologist the first time I told them.

I take a deep breath and push that thought away. If I let myself dwell on the what-ifs right now, I'll never stop, and I have to focus.

It feels like I'm in a daze the whole time. My hands move on auto-pilot. I answer when Sharon speaks to me, but otherwise I'm her silent assistant, getting Jaden strapped in and loaded into the back of the ambulance as quickly as we can. His mom rides in the back, while his dad decides to take their car so they have it at the hospital.

It takes us 26 minutes to get to the ER. Every minute feels like agony. Jaden doesn't improve or decline. There's not a lot for us to do other than continue to monitor him, give the supportive care we're already giving, and keep communicating with the ER. We don't exactly have an EEG back here, so we can't even run many helpful tests.

His mom doesn't ask many questions, just silently holds her son's hand and tries not to let anything show on her face. I can't imagine how she feels, and I don't want to. The only thing worse than getting pissed right now would be to get empathetic, because I'll end up picturing one of my sisters in front of me and I don't think I can handle that.

The numbness that this is breeding in me is the thing I need to hang on to. And boy, do I. I cling to it when we get to the hospital and all through patient hand off. I cling to it when I see Jaden's pale face disappear into a bay, and I cling to it when I pass his dad in the hallway, avoiding making eye contact as the exhausted, defeated man walks toward what we both know is going to be a shitty ending.

I cling to it through every meaningless, tedious step it takes to eventually close out my shift and get back in the car, ignoring Sharon when she offers to talk about it, because I'd rather just leave.

This isn't the first time I've stood outside of a liquor store waiting for it to open, because sometimes you want to pick up something on the way home and if you're on nights, it's the fucking morning. I've gone to after-shift drinks with coworkers at 8 a.m. on more than one occasion. You're headed straight to bed after, so who cares what time it is?

Right now, this feels dirty. And not just because I'm not waiting alone—I'm standing ten feet from a guy I've picked up for drinking himself unconscious on more than one occasion, rubbing my arms to stay warm as that flinty morning light gets brighter and brighter without taking off any of the chill. Thank fuck the man doesn't try to talk to me.

The liquor store is a squat, broad building with peeling paint and a weathered old sign. It's surrounded on two sides by a gravel lot that's barren right now, except for a rusted-out sixties-style pickup parked up on dead grass, with spiderwebs caked in the wheel rims and weeds growing through the wooden slats of the bed.

We're at a T-junction, and there's nothing else around within spitting distance. Just more dead grass and gravel. Some cheap clapboard houses a ways away, and a couple signs rising up on the horizon; one for the feed store, a taller one for the Dairy Queen.

I try to take all that quiet desolation and pull it into myself. I try to be as still and flat and fucking bleak as the world surrounding me.

I'm not convinced it works.

There's a heavy thunk as the deadbolt comes off the front door, and the owner wordlessly lets me and the other guy in. He's dressed in woodland camo and two days of stubble, holding a styrofoam cup of coffee and showing absolutely no commitment to making eye contact, which I appreciate. I definitely should know his name—I think his nephew was a senior when I was a freshman—but it's not coming to me right now. My brain feels like soup, but I'm still in and out in less than five minutes.

Another blessing of taking so long to get home is that by the time I do, Silas is at work and the girls have been picked up for school. I'd much rather have them here than leave them with the shitshow at the trailer, but it's hard enough keeping a happy face on for Silas all the time. Adding them to the mix makes it even more taxing.

I know Silas doesn't want me to keep pretending everything's chill when it's not. But at the end of the day, he won't understand that the shit I have to complain about is nothing compared to the shit he deals with in his head every day, so I can't be the kind of selfish asshole that puts that on him.

The first beer goes down like water, because I'm dehydrated on top of everything else, and it's ice fucking cold. I feel refreshed as fuck. The second one is almost as good, and I finish it in the shower.

Once I'm clean, comfortably dressed and cradling a glass of room-temperature whiskey in my hand, I can finally relax. I know I should eat something as well, but exhaustion is dogging at my heels so I don't have the energy for more than getting chips out of the cabinet. There's a brief pause while I think about my choices, and I force myself to chug one of Silas's protein shakes as well.

For posterity.

I'm trying not to think about it, but the image of Jaden's ashen skin and vacant eyes feels like it's etched onto my eyeballs. I normally excel at letting this shit go, but sometimes something sticks.

All I can think is what if, what if, what if...

What if I'd pushed his parents harder?

What if I hadn't let Tristan talk me down?

What if they really did have options for getting help, but they were too lazy or defeated to try?

And of course, the question I've been desperate not to ask, what if it was Sky or Maddi?

I don't need to wonder what would have happened if it had been me, because I already know. I would have been dead a long time ago.

I start off by scrolling on my phone, but eventually I boot up my clunky old Chromebook because I need a bigger screen to focus on. I set up shop at one end of the dining room table, hyper aware of how much medical neglect Silas himself has suffered right here in this room, and click through page after page.

It's not easy to say what I'm looking for. I start by looking up services that the Hallorans might have been able to use, but just chose not to. The reality of getting them charged with abuse or neglect is practically non-existent, but I feel the need to prove it to myself. Or Tristan, maybe.

Exploring social services is a mixed bag, but it leads me down one rabbit hole after the other once I start thinking about what I would do in the same situation. I know I'd fucking care, for starters. I go through my own insurance with a fine-toothed comb, now that I have it, and then do the same for the girls' coverage from the state.

I still don't know what I'm looking for, but one click leads to another, which leads to another, and then another. The light in the room shifts as time passes, but it doesn't feel real. I keep switching between beer and whiskey, sipping fast enough to keep my mounting anxiety at bay, but slow enough not to get sloppy.

Well, not too sloppy. At some point, the chips run out. I get up to root through the cabinets for something else to eat, but I keep knocking into the walls as I'm moving around.

Which doesn't make sense, because I feel fine. I feel ass-sober, not even buzzed. Just sleepy enough and cotton-mouthed enough to not let my worst thoughts dig their claws into me, and let each tumbling emotion that attacks me shrug away one by one. I'm fine. So I don't know why the world tilts a little when I sit down again, or why I keep accidentally banging into shit.

I know I should go to sleep. It's probably late, but I refuse to look at the time, as if that can change it. I know I should feel tired, and I do, but I also feel so alive. Like the alcohol has burned away all the bullshit that normally clutters my brain and left the rest of me pure, fast and able to focus.

I don't stop searching.

After the conversation I had with Silas the other day about getting custody of the girls, this is the first time I'm actually consciously looking into it. I'd felt so convicted at the time, but Silas's hesitation really worried me. I didn't abandon the plan, but I did decide to take a breath before I continued down that road. To make sure he and I are on the same page.

But today has reminded me of just how quickly things can change, and how little it takes to let your children slip through your fingers. I have to do something. I have to. I can't just sit here and wait for something awful to go down, I'll never forgive myself. It's bad enough that Sky got burned last winter because I wasn't there to help her. I owe them this.

The sound of the door opening startles me so much I knock my lukewarm beer over, and start cussing as I pick up the laptop, watching my hastily scribbled notes on back of junk mail take the worst of the damage.

"Motherfucker," I hiss, just as Silas, Maddi, and Sky all come into view.

The looks on their faces start off surprised, but quickly settle into some form of scared and/or pissed.

"Uh, hey guys. Sorry, I must've lost track of time, I didn't realize you were about to get home, or I would have cleaned up."

"Cade," Silas says slowly, putting his keys down on the little side table and pulling off his Carhartt without ever looking away from me. "It's 3:30 in the afternoon. Why are you still awake?"

"Um," I start, without having anything to follow. I take a look at my sisters and immediately wish I hadn't. Sky looks stressed, and has grabbed hold of

Silas's hand, while Maddi's face has settled into the same brutal disappointment as when I had that fight with Dad. Yikes. "I just got caught up. Shift ran late," I lie. "I was having trouble winding down."

The bottle of whiskey on the table is more than half empty, I realize, now that everyone is looking at it as well as me, and a tendril of shame curls through me. At some point I'd hit a wall, and the whiskey started tasting like water too, not having any effect on me that I could feel no matter how much I drank.

"It's fine. I'll clean up so you guys can do homework. I should probably get to bed, anyway."

Maddi frowns, and I realize I've listed a little to the side while I was talking, and reach out to catch myself on the table. Except I misjudge the distance and miss, which makes me stagger back a step, and suddenly draw attention to myself and make everything worse.

Shit.

And of course, Silas doesn't even have the heart to look pissed. He just looks sad.

"Why don't you guys go upstairs for a bit while I get your brother in bed," he says, never moving his gaze away from me as he speaks. "I'll make you something to eat in just a minute."

"I can make us something," Maddi interjects, her eyes flicking between us, but Silas is already moving.

He cups one large hand around her shoulder and gives it a reassuring squeeze before kissing the top of her head.

"Don't worry about it. Go relax. I'll take care of everything."

That's supposed to be my line. I can already glimpse the magnitude of how I've fucked up, but it hasn't quite penetrated the alcohol-fog enough to truly settle in yet.

Silas stays calm as the girls drift away, both of them watching me with careful, terse little faces.

"G'night," Sky says, but I notice she doesn't even look like she wants to hug me. Maddi doesn't say anything at all.

"What happened?" Silas asks as soon as they're gone.

"What do you mean?"

Sure, Cade. Play dumb. That's worked so well for you all the other times.

"I mean, why are you shitfaced in the middle of the day? In front of your sisters. Right after you promised not to bottle shit up anymore."

The words are supposed to be a question, but it all comes out flat. Period. No answer expected.

"I—" I swear I had an answer that was about to come out, but as soon as I open my mouth, I think about Jaden again, and this time it feels like a gut punch. The whiskey creeps up on me all at one, and before I know what's happening my eyes are stinging and my throat aches. For one bright, terrifying second, I wonder if I'm about to truly fall apart.

I swallow hard and take a breath, and that's the best I can do right now.

"Cade," Silas says again, but this time it's soft. Like a prayer.

He moves toward me and gathers me into his arms, and I let him. I go slack, allowing the man I love to hold me up, taking deep breaths of the smell of him and burying my face in his shoulder.

"I'm just so tired," I try to say, but it comes out half-sobbed.

"Yeah, I'll bet."

Silas reaches down, and with one sudden movement—and a grunt of effort, because I'm smaller than him but I'm not exactly small—hoists me the fuck up like a little kid. I don't object. Not one little bit. I just slide my arms around his neck and wrap my legs around his hips and let him walk me slowly but steadily toward the bedroom.

"I've got you," he whispers, cupping the back of my head as he walks.

Once we're in the bedroom, already dark from the shades being down, he half-places, half-dumps me on the bed. All I want is for him to crawl on top of me and lean his entire bodyweight into me, but no such luck. Instead, he keeps a blank face as he moves around the room, fussing over this and that. Silas gets me to take my hoody off and my sweats. He brings a wet washcloth in from the bathroom and wipes my face. He turns the ceiling fan on, because I like it on when I sleep, and once I've drunk a glass of water with some electrolyte powder in it, brushed my teeth sloppily and taken a piss, he gets me back on the bed and wrestles me under the covers.

"Please don't leave," I say, my voice sounding small and wounded.

Silas stops, halfway between the bed and the door, then comes back to sit on the bed next to me.

He leans over and kisses me. Just a peck, but it already makes me feel more rooted in reality. Then he brushes back my hair while he speaks.

"I have to go take care of Maddi and Sky. They've had a rough week, and you know better than anyone that this shit stresses them out."

I jerk back as if he slapped me.

"It's just—" I start, but Silas cuts me off.

"Stop. We're not talking about this while you're shitfaced. I don't know what happened today, but we'll talk about it when you wake up. Please sleep. I gotta get them some food and clean up." Silas pauses, studying my face for a second before he sighs. "It's okay, Cade. Everything will be okay. Just sleep. Can you do that for me?"

I nod, feeling a little like a chastened child and not liking it a single bit.

"Stay with me? Just until I fall asleep?"

I know it's pathetic, but that doesn't stop me.

Silas shakes his head. He looks pained, and I hate it. This is the opposite of everything I'm supposed to be doing for him.

"Sleep, Cade. I'll be back in a little while."

He cups my cheek one more time before he stands up, and it feels like there's a glass wall between me and the affection I'm used to getting from him. It hurts more than I want to exist.

Silas slips silently out of the room, closing the door behind him, and it's only then that I let myself start to cry.

Chapter Nineteen

SILAS

I 'm operating on autopilot for the rest of the night. I make the right faces and the right sounds—I think—as I feed the girls and reassure them that their brother is just having a hard time, and not descending into the sort of self-destructive alcoholism that a lot of people would say he was born to.

I don't know who I'm working harder to convince, them or myself. Nobody really seems to be buying it. Everything is quiet between the three of us, moving through the basic routine of homework and showers and a tense dinner in front of the TV. When I tell them it's time for bed, they don't even complain. They both look as worn out as I feel.

Whenever they stay here, they share the bedroom that used to be mine. It's always something I like to see. We really should clear out one of the other rooms still full of junk so they don't have to share, but I've been dragging my feet on that.

I've spent so much time in that room being miserable that having it spackled over with their particular brand of chaos and noise always makes those memories seem like a bad dream. But of course, tonight when I go to make sure they're ready to go to sleep, the old familiar tension of my childhood has seeped back into the atmosphere.

Sky is already out; face slack and a soft snore coming from her. But Maddi is in bed, propped up by a pillow, tapping on her phone as the light from the screen illuminates her face. She's somber, biting her lip slightly as she concentrates in a way Cade does sometimes as well, and only glances at me briefly when I open the door.

"You good?" I whisper, feeling suddenly unsure of my role in this little family drama.

Maddi finishes what she's typing, sighs, and holds the space for a long time before she finally looks at me.

"What are you going to do?" she asks, ignoring my question.

Sky, thankfully, can sleep through almost anything. Still, I walk into the room so I can sit on the edge of her bed and not have to talk across the room. It's hard to look her in the eye, because more than anything I want her to look back at me and see someone strong. Someone who's going to keep her safe. But I don't have any more idea of what to do right now than she does.

"What do you think I should do?"

She snorts, rolling her eyes at me the way she's started doing constantly. I recognize all the prickliness for what it is—a defense—and I don't feel like I have any right to tell her to drop the attitude, considering none of us have been able to be a real defense for her, either.

"Tell him to get his shit together, before he loses everything he has. Just like our dad."

I stare at her, because I wasn't expecting her words to come out with quite so much rage. She's quiet, but now that she's talking, I can see all that anger simmering under the surface. Also just like Cade.

"You don't think it's my job to take care of him?"

Maddi stares at me for a second, but instead of rolling her eyes again, she keeps talking.

195

"Why? Because you love him? He loves us, but look how far that got him. Totally ran himself into the ground. He loves you, but it makes him crazy. It was always going to end up like this. Save yourself the trouble."

She's fighting to keep a straight face, but her cheeks are flushed and I can see all that emotion threatening to surge out. I feel like I'm finally peeking beneath her closed-off facade into darker fears she's always carried, and I hate that I can't tell her she never needed to worry about it.

Words of wisdom aren't my strong suit. And while I've gotten close with Cade's sisters in the year we've been together, it's not the same thing as actually being their parent. I feel pretty adrift when it comes to stuff like this, and Cade's normally the one having meaningful talks and whatever else with them.

"There has to be a way for people to love each other without imploding in the process. That's what I keep telling myself. None of us knows how it works, because we all had garbage-fire childhoods, as Cade would say."

She interrupts me to huff again, but I keep going.

"There are happy people in the world. Including people who had shitty upbringings. There has to be a way to just get there, eventually." I shrug. "Maybe the fact that I love him enough to stay and keep trying to take care of him is what he needs right now. Instead of all of us giving up, assuming he's going to end up the way all our parents did."

I reach toward her, feeling the familial urge to comfort her, but my hand drops as soon as she flinches away.

I can see the fear eating away at her, and I need to do something about it, before we both collapse.

"I'm not going anywhere, Maddi." There's conviction in my voice when I say it, because I'm realizing this might be what she really needs to hear right now. "Even if Cade keeps fucking up. Even if I keep fucking up. We'll figure it out."

She stares at me, her expression flinty with no hint of a reaction for me to read.

I reach out again, but this time I hold my fist at a distance and let her come to me.

More seconds drag by, but she ultimately puts down her phone long enough to fist-bump me back. It's cheesy, but it feels like progress.

"Everything will be okay," I tell myself more than her.

She's not convinced, but I think her features have softened at least a fraction by the time I let myself out of their room.

I feel like the human embodiment of a sigh as I drag myself back downstairs. I'm so lost in my head thinking about all the shit that needs to be dealt with, I jump a mile when I notice Cade isn't asleep, he's standing in the doorway to our room with a shifty expression and a tremble in his hands.

"You're up," I say, like an idiot. I try to force myself back into crisis mode instead of drifting on my internal monologue, but I'm tired and it's not something I've ever excelled at. "You should drink some water."

Cade snorts, a shallow echo of the conversation I just had with his sister. He fidgets a little where he stands, and I realize he's not meeting my eye.

"Why don't you lie back down and I'll get you something to eat. You should probably put something in your body before you pass out."

Blowing out a long breath, Cade still doesn't meet my eye, but starts to walk past me as he speaks.

"Don't worry about me. I'm sure you're tired, you should relax. I'll get out of your hair."

My eyes narrow, because even though the words he's saying sound normal, none of this feels right.

"What—" I break off, before repeating myself. "What? Where are you going?"

It's 9 p.m.. He's slept for a handful of hours after being awake for about 30 and he looks like he's been waterboarded by the devil in his dreams. He stops moving at my question, but still doesn't look at me. Instead, he hangs his head, hands still a little shaky, and speaks to the floor.

"I just need a minute. Can you please leave me be? I need a minute alone, so I can fucking... process everything without my sisters around to see." Cade looks at me, and his face is as wrecked as I feel. "I'll come home later. It'll be fine. I just... I just need a minute."

There's a very good chance my mouth is hanging open. I don't know what to say. I've never seen Cade like this before, and I feel completely out of my element. I want him to stay. But I don't want him to feel chained here, like I'm beginning to think he does. If he believes I'll fall apart every time he leaves, he'll keep putting me first until he finally collapses in on himself in a state of eternal decay.

"Cade..." I start, before immediately trailing off, no idea what I was going to follow that up with.

He stops moving and stands in the entryway, his body sagging, not making eye contact with me.

"What happened?" I ask.

Something had to have happened. Something is happening right now, I just don't understand it.

He exhales loudly, still not turning to look at me.

"I just need a minute," he says, almost too quiet for me to hear. "I promise I'll be back."

There's a split-second where I wish I knew what to say to stop him, but then he picks up the keys and disappears through the door before I can find the words.

CHAPTER TWENTY

CADE

I regret having so much to drink last night.

Well, today, really. But I slept, so it feels like last night. Now I'm awake again and the thought of lying in the dark with my own thoughts was enough to immediately propel me to my feet, cotton mouth, aching bones, roiling nausea, and all.

I better not hurl. I'm not going to hurl. I just need something in my stomach, and a little space to breathe.

When I stopped at the gas station for fuel after leaving the house, I picked up a bag of Funyuns to settle my stomach, a Gatorade and a Monster to chase them with, plus a cherry-flavored sucker to help keep the dry mouth at bay. I wish I had a goddamn IV, but the snacks and caffeine and electrolytes will have to be close enough.

It all gets consumed in the parking lot, each item methodically inhaled like it's the solution to all my problems until it's just me and the sucker against the world, and I can finally get back on the road. I'm going to a bar, because where the fuck else is open that isn't home right now? But that doesn't mean I have to drink.

As long as I can sit in peace without Silas's worried gaze and my sisters' disappointment trailing me, I'll be fine. I need to escape the weight of my own inadequacies for a hot minute, and I'm not letting anyone stop me.

The drive to the Feral Possum all happens on auto-pilot, and by the time I'm testing my suspension over the pot hole-ridden parking lot, I wonder if this is a mistake. Sure, this is probably the place where I have the most friends at any given time in this town. Real friends, that is. Not the kind of friends I had at school who all stayed permanently at arms' length, because I had way too many secrets to let any of them in.

Except for Wish, obviously. The first person to karate-kick down my defensive walls, whether I liked it or not.

At least she won't be here. Thank fuck for the tattoo expo that's kept her not just out of state, but too damn busy to needle me about things the way she normally does. But that doesn't mean the others won't be watching me, waiting for me to go nuclear or whatever they're all doing lately.

Fuck it. Maybe I do need a drink, after all.

I get out of the car, shivering briefly against the chill. There's no snow on the ground, but the gravel underfoot has that particular kind of crunch that tells me snow isn't far off, and the trees surrounding the lot seem to shrink in on themselves, closing ranks in a dark blur that makes this place seem even more isolated than it is. Even the animals are quiet tonight, only a distant sound of frogs piercing the noise humming from the bar.

For a brief, singular moment, I miss living in the trailer with an aching kind of fierceness. I miss the darkness, and the way it felt so full of life, the amount of wildlife on our doorstep constantly buzzing and thrumming with their existence at all hours of the night. The sounds of coyotes yipping on top of cicadas on top of the hum of Mom's TV set permanently to home shopping, on top of Sky and Maddi shuffling around to go to the bathroom or get a snack.

200

I love Silas as much as I've ever loved anyone, but I didn't expect living with him to leave me feeling so alone.

These are not the kind of thoughts I should be entertaining at 9 p.m. in a parking lot. Not when there are a couple of smokers 20 yards away starting to give me weird looks, I'm assuming for the loitering. I shove my hands into the pocket of my hoody to ward off the chill, set my eyes on the ground, and follow one foot with the other until I'm inside where it's warm.

The warmth hits me like a wall, complete with the smell of too many people in a too-small space, and the sickly sweet rotting lime smell from the bar runners that I know you can't get rid of, no matter how much Gunnar cleans. He's nowhere to be seen right now, and neither is Tobias, which makes me breathe a sigh of release. It's just Sav and Kasia behind the bar, and they're both judgey motherfuckers but at least they'll keep shit to themselves.

I walk up to the bar on instinct, taking up an empty barstool and studying the taps, despite the fact that I told myself I was going to just chill by myself in a corner.

Fuck it.

"What'll it be, pretty boy?"

The words sound like they should be a compliment, but something about Kasia's wry tone and permanently disdainful expression makes it clear the nickname is an insult. I'll take it anyway.

"Draft and a shot, please," I say, trying to not look ashamed as I say it.

I don't think I succeed, because she arches an eyebrow at me before quickly deciding she doesn't care about whatever shifty shit my expression is doing. That's probably a key part of surviving as a bartender, at least in a small town like this. Distancing yourself from the shit you know everybody gets up to.

"You care what it is?" she asks.

"Whatever. Well."

I really, really don't care. I just want to arrest the momentum in my spinning brain for a hot minute.

Of course, Kasia makes me regret this choice immediately, because she pours me an IPA—why do they even have this? Who the fuck drinks this by choice, it tastes like beer soup—and a shot of sambuca.

It's fine. I probably deserve this.

Even if there's no way they keep *well* sambuca on hand and this is just her fucking with me for fun. I take half the shot, try not to grimace too much and fail, based on her bemused expression, and chase it with the beer soup.

"Another?" she asks.

"I'm good for now. Thank you for your hospitality."

There's a split-second where I think the Funyuns weren't enough and my stomach lurches, but a couple deep breaths suppress the issue and I go back to my beer.

Fuck it. I just pour the rest of the sambuca in the IPA. It can't make it any worse.

"Make sure your appreciation is reflected in your tip," she says, before walking away to serve someone else.

I already over-tip her, because I'm a little afraid of what she'd do if I didn't. Just like everyone else in here, I assume.

The drink I've made is disgusting, but it's strong, at least, so it goes down smoother than I'd feared. By the time I'm finishing the glass, my head is pleasantly swimmy and I'm feeling the tug of sleepiness again. Maybe this was enough. A little space was all I needed. Maybe I should go home and go back to bed.

Or maybe if I wait until it's late enough, Silas will be asleep and I can just sneak in, putting off any potential conversation until the morning.

Yeah, I'll shower, crawl into bed and then snuggle the shit out of him in his sleep. I think we both need that right now. Less talking, more human blanket.

There's a dark, discomfiting feeling shrouding me all of a sudden, and my sleep-deprived brain takes longer than it should to realize Sav is standing in front of me now. Not saying anything, just standing in Kasia's section, looking down at me like some kind of stone guardian in a fantasy movie.

When I look up, he stares me down, and it's just as uncomfortable as I imagined. I honestly don't get how he and Micah work, and I feel like their sex life is probably terrifying. I don't know why I think that, just vibes.

"No buddies, today?" he asks in a neutral tone.

Is he getting at something? Or is this because the last time I was in here I started a huge fight and got the cops called?

"Uh, no. Why?"

Sav shakes his head and crosses his arms, and I get the feeling this is done specifically to intimidate me. Well, his biceps are huge and he's covered in tattoos that are definitely gang shit, so yeah.

Consider me suitably intimidated.

I came out here to get away from feeling judged, and instead I'm being stared down by the pit bull of Possum Hollow. It's causing a creeping unease in my gut that feels too close to what guilt feels like, and I don't fucking care for it.

In fact, that feeling combines with the liquor enough to make me surly.

"Do you have something to say, Sav? Or can a man not have a fucking drink in peace?"

I think I sound tough when I say it. He arches an eyebrow at me in an echo of the way Kasia did a minute ago, not saying anything, and it pisses me the fuck off. Why does everybody keep looking at me like they're seeing something I don't know?

Sav finally speaks after an awkward silence, his voice a quiet rumble across the bar.

"Make sure it stays peaceful. This is Gunnar's place, and he doesn't deserve you tearing it up. He's put up with enough from this town."

I don't know what he's specifically talking about. Well, I can guess. I've been called here on the job to some less than savory situations, more than one of which involved Tobias and all the shit he never deserved. But still, it's nice to know I make one goddamn mistake and everybody writes me off as a problem.

"No drama from me. Can I get a beer?" I was ready to pack up shop before, but now he's irritated me and I need to calm down again before I go home to Silas. "And not whatever the fuck Kasia gave me. A normal beer. Please."

"Coming right up."

He pulls a glass off a stack and brings it to the tap. The entire time the glass is filling it up, he stares at me. His face is carefully neutral, and I'm used to being around Silas who has absolutely no internal gauge for what is an appropriate amount of eye contact. That doesn't bother me, because it's just how he is.

This feels pointed and deliberate. It's also possibly the most Sav and I have ever interacted. I don't know what he's trying to accomplish here, but it's clearly something.

The stink eye continues as he places the full glass in front of me, a little sloshing out to slide down the side. At this point, I'm determined not to let him know he's getting to me, so instead of looking away, I stare right back at him and ostentatiously lick the spill off the side before taking several gulps. His eyes narrow, like he's not sure what I'm trying to do here—*newsflash buddy, me neither*—but there's a slightly uncomfortable shift to his posture and he finally looks away.

I take a few more deep sips, letting it calm me and walk myself back from this weird interaction. I just need to reclaim the peacefulness I was beginning to feel before, and then I'll be good to call it a night.

"Cade!"

The voice that pierces the general din of the crowd and music is one that I'd recognize anywhere. I keep the glass to my face, intently swallowing the rest of it before a very tiny tornado of affection slams into me.

"I didn't expect you to be here!" Wish says a hair too loud, like she's already drunk herself.

Abort. Abort. Abort.

I move to throw some cash on the bar and bounce, but then realize I'm an idiot with empty pockets and I'll need to take the time to pay by card.

"Can I close out?" I ask Sav quickly, and he eventually nods and goes to get my check.

"I'm not here. I just wanted a quick drink after work, I gotta get home."

When I finally turn and look Wish in the eye, her head is cocked to the side and she's looking me up and down.

"Are you okay?" she asks, her voice sinking as her whole demeanor shifts to something serious.

Putting a smile on my face feels like clawing out a piece of skin from my insides to slap it over my outsides, but I do it. I think it's even convincing. One megawatt, charming smile to throw the emotional bloodhound off my scent.

I follow it with a big yawn, which is only a little fake.

"Yeah, I'm just tired. I've been on nights."

Wish looks from side to side, taking in my lack of company.

"Where's Silas?"

"At home. We have the girls right now. My dad's in town and he's shacked up at the trailer with my mom and a literal hooker who apparently bankrolled his attempt to flee Alabama. It's a whole thing. I would have told you about it, but I didn't want to distract you from your big expo debut. How was it?"

"Awesome," she says, enthusiastic for only a second before her brows dip and she ingests everything I said. "Shit, is everything okay? I can't believe you didn't tell me. You know you could have interrupted me for this. I only got into town this afternoon, I was going to hit you up tomorrow."

Another wrung-out fake smile flits across my face, and I reach out to squeeze her shoulder in an attempt to sell it.

"Nah, it's not a big deal. You know what he's like, it'll blow over soon. We're all good."

She doesn't look convinced, but Kasia interrupts to put down the check that Sav obviously couldn't be fucked to walk back over here, and ask Wish if she wants a drink.

"Whiskey soda, please," she says, eyeing my check.

I cover it quickly with my debit card and slide it to Kasia before she can walk away. The last thing I need is Wish getting on me about having two fucking drinks—okay, two drinks and a shot, but sambuca doesn't count—and driving, as if two-thirds of the people in here won't be driving themselves home tonight.

Just because it's normalized doesn't mean it's normal.

It's been her favorite phrase for a while, and I hate it. Just because she's right doesn't mean it isn't exhausting. I love my best friend, but the thought of being near her when I'm trying to unravel is too much. Too much goodness. I just need to be alone.

Fuck it. There are other bars in this town. Ones where I won't run into anyone who cares about me, and I'll be left alone. I just want one more drink, and then I'll go home. And I'll eat something.

Just a little more time to clear my head.

CHAPTER TWENTY-ONE

SILAS

I t's 1 a.m.. Cade is still not home, and he stopped answering my messages over an hour ago.

This is absolutely not what we agreed on. I get that he's going through something, and if he was spending the night with Wish or something just to get away, I would understand. I'd hate it, but I'd understand. But I can't just not know where he is or if anything has happened to him.

Bars legally have to close in half an hour, which means he's most likely about to get kicked out of wherever he is. In which case, he's going to either drive home drunk, or be stranded somewhere with his car. If someone responsible was with him and planned to give him a ride, they would have texted me.

A worse-case scenario is that he's met up with someone who isn't responsible and is planning to go to some kind of afterparty. Or that he's at one of the shittier bars around here that locks the doors at 1:30 but keeps serving their regulars under the table.

I don't like any of those options. I've done every breathing exercise and calming logical bullshit I can manage, but it's a lot more difficult to ease my anxiety when the root of it is so very real, and the danger so very immediate. The girls are asleep upstairs. I can't leave them, but I also don't want them to wake up and see he'sl not here, and not have any answers about it. They don't deserve that.

Fuck it. *I* don't deserve that.

After pacing a hole in the carpet, I decide to ask for help.

Silas

> Are you awake? Please be awake or I'm going to have to call and wake you up.

Tristan

> I'm awake. What's wrong? Don't call unless it's an emergency, I don't want to wake up the beast sleeping next to me.

Silas

> I don't know if it's an emergency. It feels like it but I might be overreacting. Cade went out at like 9 p.m. and he still isn't home.

> I know he's an adult but he seemed so upset and he's not talking to me and he's not answering and I don't know where the fuck he is or if he's safe.

Tristan

> Woah, hold up. Slow down. Did you guys have a fight?

Silas

> No? I don't think so. I came home from work this afternoon and found him absolutely shit-faced. He never slept after his shift. We didn't fight about it because I wanted to talk about it when he was sober, but he only slept for a few hours before getting up and saying he was going out.

> He said everything was fine but he just needed a minute.

> Fuck, he probably wasn't even sober enough to drive then.

> I never should have let him go.

> Fuck fuck fuck.

> I need to find him.

My spiral is interrupted by the phone buzzing in my hand. I swipe to answer, but I don't know what to say, so no words come out of my mouth when I lift the phone to my ear.

"Okay," Tristan says without prompting. "I'm here. We'll sort it out. To start with, did he tell you where he was going? Even just vaguely?"

"No," I answer.

Tristan isn't whispering, and the rustling in the background tells me he's already woken Ford up. I'll feel bad about it later, but right now I'm too distracted.

"Do you wanna go look for him? I can come with you, we can check a few places he might be. I'm guessing you've called Wish and Gunnar and everyone already."

"I, uh..." I trail off. "I haven't. It's late, I didn't know if it was worth waking people up. I was waiting and waiting and then it got too late and I started to freak out. I want to go look for him, but I don't want to leave his sisters here alone. I know they're old enough to be alone, but it seems unfair. If they wake up they'll be scared... They've had to take care of themselves so much, y'know?"

"Do you want me to go out and look for him?" Tristan asks.

I get that his heart is in the right place, but the thought of continuing to sit here and not do anything makes my heart pound so hard I'm worried it might burst in my chest.

The words to explain that don't come to my mouth, though, so instead we both sit in silence for longer than anyone should ever have to. Thankfully, Tristan seems to speak neurodivergent even though he doesn't seem like he would, and he puts together what's going unspoken.

"Okay, new plan. We're on our way over. Ford can stay with the girls just in case they wake up, and you and I will go hunt down Cade and beat some sense into him if necessary."

"Um—"

"I'm kidding about the beating, obviously," he interrupts me. "Mostly."

"I didn't mean to like, put you guys out though. I'm sorry."

"Silas, you called me in the middle of the night because you were scared and needed help. Do you need help?"

"Yes."

"Okay, then you have to let us help you. We'll be there in a few minutes, try not to freak out in the meantime. Drink a glass of water and text anyone who might be with Cade to see if they're still awake. Got it?"

I let out a big breath, because just having a series of tasks given to me along with a semblance of a plan has really chipped away at all of that mounting anxiety.

"Okay. Thank you. Really, thank you."

Tristan hangs up without saying anything else, and after I take a few deep breaths, I get to work on doing what he suggested.

Wish doesn't answer. I'm assuming she's asleep, and when I think about it, I realize she might not even be back in town from her trip yet. Gunnar does answer, which makes sense. After a few minutes of tense silence, he tells me that Cade was at the Feral Possum tonight, but left hours ago and seemed mostly sober. Or at least sober enough that no one felt the need to investigate.

I text his mom, I text anyone from high school whose number I still have, which isn't a lot of people. I even text Micah, whose number I am surprised I have, but who says he hasn't seen him in the ER tonight but will keep an eye out. Which was a long shot, but still eases my worry a little.

I've barely gotten through the list by the time I hear the rumble of a car engine in the driveway. I throw open the door so they don't wake the girls by knocking, and watch them both lumber up the driveway and into the house. The night air is colder than it's been all year, and I start shivering right away.

Tristan looks as bright-eyed as usual, dressed in his day clothes. Ford looks half-asleep and is wearing sweats and a hoody with his feet shoved into unlaced boots.

For a second, adrenaline dumps into my veins wholesale when a series of anxious thoughts hit me.

I'm selfish for pulling them over here.

Everyone's going to be pissed when this turns out to be nothing.

I don't know how I'm supposed to express how grateful I am for their help.

I'm going to shut down because I'm uncomfortable, and that'll make them even less aware of how grateful I am.

Nothing I say will be effusive enough for them to understand, and it's going to be weird no matter what.

None of these thoughts help me, so I kind of freeze up as they walk inside and don't really say anything at all. The guys don't seem to mind, though. Ford nods at me in passing, while Tristan claps me on the shoulder. As soon as they're inside, I close the door and start to mumble something, but Tristan cuts me off again, thank fuck.

"No time for thank yous. You can be eternally in our debt later. Did anybody you texted answer?"

I give him the rundown of the little I know, and he nods solemnly the whole time.

"A'right," he starts, before being interrupted by Ford yawning ostentatiously, making him smile. "This big fucking teddy bear is going to sleep on your couch so the children have someone around if they wake up. Hopefully they won't, but fortunately for all of us, Cade's sisters are about the only people in town who are not just *not* afraid of him, but actually think he's fun to be around. Which shows they have the same poor judgment as their brother, but whatever."

The fact that Tristan's teasing Ford while we're all whispering in my entryway in the middle of the night helps ease my tension even more. Ford fake glares at him, Tristan laughs and then pushes him toward the living room, and it all feels so mundane. Like the world can't be ending if everyone's cracking jokes.

"Thanks," I say to Ford, signing at the same time, before running to grab him a blanket and a pillow.

I'm going to fuss more, but he waves me away before he throws his phone onto the table, collapses his big, bulky body onto the couch with a sigh, and closes his eyes. Tristan jerks his head toward the door, so I grab my jacket and follow him out the front door.

In the car, we talk a little about what happened in the past couple of days. Well, I talk, while he asks prompting questions. It goes on for a while before I realize I don't even know where we're going.

"Do you have a plan, or are we just driving?"

Tristan *pfffft's* me loudly.

"Do I have a plan? Who do you think you're talking to? I'm the eldest child of an historically undiagnosed bipolar mother. I'm a scenthound for finding people in crisis who don't wanna be found. You can just relax and eat some popcorn over there, I've got this taken care of."

It's so nonchalant, I almost smile. If I weren't still so scared about the Cade-dead-in-a-ditch scenario, I probably would have laughed.

"Okay, I'm sorry." I raise my hands in surrender. "Where are we going?"

"Honestly, it's a small town. There's only so many places he can be. We'll swing by that shithole dive bar out near the fucking mafia farm and see if the lights are on there, and if that's a bust, we'll try The Last Glass. Worst case scenario, we'll start checking all the parking lots that the high school kids go to do whippets, in case he's trying to relive his glory days."

I don't say anything, because my brain is telling me we should be checking all the backroads for his body, but I'm aware that logic isn't my strong suit when I feel like this.

Tristan stays silent for a minute, before softening his entire self and turning toward me.

"Don't worry. We'll find him, and whatever's going on, we'll figure it out. I promise."

It's meaningless, because Tristan doesn't control the universe, but it makes me feel better anyway. I never would have guessed how much of a difference it makes to not feel alone. I let out a shaky exhale, meet his eyes for a second, and then force myself to relax.

Thankfully, Tristan was right. I try not to inflate his ego more than necessary, but we only had to check two places before we found him.

The Last Glass had too much light and too many cars in the lot to truly be closed for the night, despite what the sign on the door says. Tristan pounds on it for a few minutes, yelling loud enough that they need to let us in or he'll call the cops, and it doesn't take long for the door to open a crack.

Of course, it's a shotgun muzzle, not a person, that sticks through.

"Stop that, Rolla," Tristan snarks, seeming totally unperturbed. "Haven't I done enough for you? Aren't we buddies? You know I'm not really gonna narc, but I need you to let me in. I think you have something of mine in there, and I'm here to retrieve him."

I raise an eyebrow at Tristan, because that's a weird way to phrase it, but he just shrugs.

There's rustling for a minute, like something was blocking the door, and then it finally opens. The woman standing behind it looks pissed, but she still gestures for us to go inside.

"He's in the back. If you're kicking him out, you might as well get his friends while you're at it, I'm about ready to go to bed and they're not spending enough money to keep me awake."

She yawns for effect and Tristan only nods.

I feel so young and so out of place as I trail behind him, being led through the dingy, underlit bar. There are a couple of older guys still sitting on stools, but the only real noise is coming from a booth at the back. It has ripped seats, a scarred-up table covered in mostly empty glasses, and is surrounded by people I actually recognize.

And Cade. The love of my life, shit-faced and laughing with a fucking cigarette in his hands, no less.

All the fear I've been holding onto drains almost immediately, and the only feeling that replaces it is the feeling of being fucking *pissed*.

Again, thank fuck for Tristan, because I have no idea what I would say if I tried to talk right now.

"Alright, party's over, boys. Time to go home."

They all stop talking, finally noticing us as they all look up at once. A couple of them look surprised, but generally speaking, they don't seem that worried.

I went to high school with all of these motherfuckers. Of course, Cade was actually friends with them, while I only knew them vaguely because we all trained at the same track. And now they're all staring at me, and I'd probably feel crippling embarrassment if I weren't so goddamn angry.

"Silas!" Cade shouts, stubbing out the cigarette and throwing his hands up in the air with a smile in a way that makes him sway to the side. "You remember the guys, right? Bennie and Junior and Chris. Guys, you remember Silas? Didn't he grow up fucking hot?"

He keeps grinning at me, his expression goofy in a way that I usually enjoy, while I tense up. The guys all laugh at the words spilling out of him, but it doesn't seem like it's in a mean way.

I think.

"Yes, bro. Congratulations. Your boy is very hot," Junior says, which makes Bennie laugh even harder and elbow him in the stomach.

"Well, now that this Algonquin Round Table is coming to an end..." Tristan arches an eyebrow at them with an air of authority that instantly seems to sober everybody up. "Come on, guys. Up! Up! Up!" He gestures at them to stand the fuck up. "Time to go home. Please tell me you fuckwads have a ride."

They all grumble unintelligibly as they start the slow, painful process of crawling out of the booth. Some of them have the sense to throw cash down on the table, but I couldn't care less if this place gets paid, to be honest.

When the surge of sweaty bodies finally spits Cade out, he immediately stumbles, crashing into me and throwing his arms around my neck. I grab him to steady him, but lean back at the same time. He smells like whisky, and I'm so far past angry at this point, I don't know how to describe how I feel.

Tristan starts snapping his fingers in everyone's faces when nobody answers.

"Words, boys. Answers. Do you have a ride?" he enunciates.

Chris squints at him like he doesn't understand why he's so loud.

"Yeah, man. Chill. Bennie's wife is on her way."

Tristan huffs. "Bennie's pregnant wife, you mean. At two in the fucking morning. All class, guys. You're all class."

There's a general sound of grumbling, but nobody has the balls to argue with him about it, clearly.

"Silas, Silas," Cade's oblivious to the tension, bouncing on his toes while he leans into me like he's still full of energy. "You gotta hear about the plan. We have the best plan. We're gonna race on Tuesday. Just a few of us, the old crew from high school. Chris's uncle is going to let us use his track after dark. The whole thing will be off the books, he's going to take bets and the winner takes the pot, minus his cut. Come on, you should race with me. We'll destroy them, and I can use the money for like, lawyer fees and shit. Get the girls. It's perfect, right?"

The conflicting surge of emotions reaches my maximum capacity and then immediately surpasses it, so I do what I do best and shut the fuck down. Blank face, dead eyes, not really looking at him but keeping him from falling on his ass.

The amount of times I've done this for Dad is immeasurable. At least Cade isn't telling me all the ways I suck in the process.

Tristan is pushing the three other guys toward the exit, half-listening to Cade talk. He's tense, I can tell, but he isn't saying anything. I don't even know if I want him to. Instead, though, he starts yelling at the lady who let us in, telling her that if she lets any of these dumbcunts drive home he really will call the cops.

Once there's a little distance between them and us, Tristan turns around and moves toward Cade.

Cade still hasn't noticed that he is failing to match everyone else's vibe with his good mood, but as soon as Tristan reaches for him, his eyes go wide and he leans back on instinct.

Tristan doesn't stop. He grabs Cade by his hoody, fisting it with both hands and yanking him out of my grip. Then, with a lot less struggle than I would have expected, he pins him against the nearest wall with a rough shove, high enough for Cade to be on his toes.

"Hey!" Cade gets out, but it's mostly an explosion of air from his lungs and it's followed by a cough. "What the fuck?"

Bennie, Junior, and Chris also turn like they're about to intervene, but one look at Tristan's face makes them think better of it.

"You have clearly elected to be done with kid gloves. So I'm telling you very fucking directly right now," Tristan says in a quiet, dangerous voice. He's holding Cade in place as he leans into his space to keep talking. "You have fucked up. You have been fucking up, and it has gotten worse, and now you're hurting people with it. I know you're hurting, too. Sharon told me about Jaden."

Tristan gets a little quieter as he says it, while Cade abruptly turns away from him and doesn't answer.

"And I'm sorry," he continues. "But you don't get to use that as an excuse to go off the rails. You're not your fucking parents, no matter what you keep telling yourself. So you are going to dry out, apologize to absolutely fucking everybody, and then find a constructive way to deal with your shit or I swear to god, I will drag your ass to rehab kicking and screaming the whole way."

The silence in the bar is almost painful, and I can't let myself think about how everybody must be staring at us.

Cade lets his mouth hang open for a minute, unable to find the right words as he stands on his tiptoes, held tight in Tristan's grip. Finally, when the tension has reached fever pitch, he speaks.

"I'm sorry," he says to Tristan before turning to me. "I'm sorry, Silas, I wasn't trying to... You didn't need to come down here. I had a ride. Everything's cool."

I can't even look at him right now. The parallels between him and his dad and my dad are all too painfully clear, and I've heard this shit too many times to buy into it.

"Apologies don't mean much when you're still sweating acetaldehyde. You're going to hydrate, and sleep, and then face the consequences of your actions. Understood?"

Cade nods, and it looks like the gravity of the situation is finally sinking in.

I don't know what to do with myself. I'm hollow right now, having carved out all my insides and placed them somewhere else in time and space to deal with later. I know Cade is staring at me, looking for absolution or something, but I don't have anything to offer him right now.

Tristan finally lets him go, and Cade sways again before finding his balance. He looks at the ground, and out of the corner of my eye, I think I see him blinking too much, like he's trying not to cry.

My heart would break if I had one.

"Let's go," I say, still not looking at him. My voice is raspy as hell, and I have no idea why, but right now all I want is for this to be over.

Cade slumps as he walks, but he doesn't reach for me and stays upright on his own. Tristan follows behind us silently, and I can feel him watching us. Nobody else in the bar says much either as we all pile out into the parking lot.

Tristan offers to drive Cade if I drive Cade's car. I think he thinks I'm upset, but he doesn't know how little I can truly feel, or just how much practice I've had doing this.

"It's fine. He can ride with me. I know you need to pick up Ford, so I'll see you at the house, yeah?"

Tristan nods and pauses. For a minute, I think I'm about to get some mind-altering pearl of wisdom, but nothing comes out of his mouth other than a sigh.

"Yeah," he says. "I'll see you in a minute."

I don't say anything as I lead Cade to the car and take the keys from him. Clearly, he takes his cue from me, because he doesn't say a damn thing the whole ride home, and for once, I'm grateful for it.

CHAPTER TWENTY-TWO

CADE

I would tell myself I regret having so much to drink last night, but this time I feel like I'm too far gone for regret.

I was selfish. As soon as I left the house, I felt so free. Which is a horrible thing to think, and not something I would ever say to Silas out loud, because I don't mean free from him. Every night the girls sleep with our mom, a part of me is worried about them. There's no way for me to be totally at ease unless they're with me, or now with Silas.

So, for them to be safe with him, for everything to be safe with him, so I could unravel in private gave me the most intense rush of liberation I think I've ever felt. It was so goddamn heady that I didn't even spiral in the end. Once I'd escaped the beady eye of Sav and Wish and everyone else who knows me too well, I just relaxed and started to enjoy myself.

Staying out so late was stupid. And not texting Silas was even worse. I feel as terrible as I should. But in that moment, hanging out with those idiots, it felt like a do-over of every high school party I couldn't enjoy because I knew what a mess I had waiting for me at home.

The contradictions swirling in my mind are nearly crippling, and I lie in bed, pretending to still be asleep, for god-knows-how-long after I wake up.

I can hear Silas checking on me from time to time, and I know I don't deserve it. In the end, my shame edges out my capacity for inner exploration, and dehydration drives me out of bed.

Once I have enough clothes on to be decent and I've brushed my teeth, I make my way to the living room. It's been quiet all morning, and I was wondering if the girls were even here. Or Silas, I guess. He has work today, I think. Which obviously makes me feel even guiltier for making him run around after me in the middle of the night, but that's becoming a scope of guilt I can't look directly at. Like the sun. Or my mom when she's on drugs. I just need to graze my eyes over it quickly and pretend it doesn't hurt.

Convinced I'm at least able to stew in my guilt alone, I head to the kitchen and pour myself a glass of water. So when Silas steps up behind me, quiet as a church mouse, I nearly jump out of my skin.

"Jesus Christ," I say, sputtering water over the counter after failing to swallow. "You scared the shit out of me. I thought you were at work."

Silas stares at me for a long time. Long enough to make me sit in my discomfort.

"Ford told me to take the day off, after we were all up late last night. I asked your aunt to take the girls after school so they don't have to be here for whatever today turns into."

Oh, fuck, I guess we're doing this first thing.

I let out a huge sigh, curling in on myself like it can protect me from the specter of guilt and shame that surrounds me. It doesn't work, and when the threat of it seems like it might cripple me, I feel myself shutting down.

It's too much. It's all too much. I can't process this without getting angry, and I can't ever get angry at Silas. Not for real.

Which is why I know the words sound wooden and insincere coming out of my mouth, but can't do anything to stop it. Fuck, I can barely even look at him while I say it.

"I'm sorry. I'm sorry, Silas. I was an asshole. I didn't mean to make you worry, I should have called, I should have... I should have done a lot of things different. I feel terrible."

Silas stares at me, and nothing between us softens.

I don't even know what I want him to say. His forgiveness seems like the only thing I need, but also I'm so hyperaware of the fact that I don't deserve it, it wouldn't feel real if I had it.

Maybe it's a blessing in disguise that he doesn't even bother.

"Is it going to happen again?" he asks, arms crossed over his chest and a painful foot and a half of space between us.

"No. No, it won't."

I hang my head like a scolded child, even though he's barely said anything.

Part of me wants to scream, and beg him to fucking touch me.

But I don't deserve it, so I stay quiet.

"You scared me," he says, his voice still flat.

I can't answer. My throat is twisting itself into a knot, so it's all I can do to swallow and nod.

The silence between us drags on and on. Silas doesn't move away, but he looks to the side, staring out the window for a long time, like the answers to his questions are in our barren front yard.

I glance at him, then again, then I let myself look properly, as a little of my apprehension recedes.

He's not crying. His face looks completely impassive, if you didn't know him. But I do know him. I know him better than anyone else in the world, and I know that all that blankness is masking too much for him to express.

God, I'm such an asshole, focused on my own feelings instead of him, just like last night.

"Jesus, Silas. Come here. Please?" I ask, holding out my arms to him but stopping just shy of physical contact.

Silas works his jaw for a few seconds before he turns, then closes the distance all at once, wrapping his arms around my chest and burying his face in my neck. I circle his neck and squeeze him even tighter to me, running my fingers frantically through his short hair as we cling to each other and both take deep, shaky breaths.

"I'm sorry," I whisper, kissing him on the neck and the side of the face—whatever I can reach.

He doesn't say anything, so I repeat myself. And again, and again, and again.

Silas shudders underneath my hands, and continues to breathe deep, like he's trying to suck me into his lungs and keep me there.

We stand there for a long time like that. I'm aware that there are a lot of things left to say, but right now, Silas feels fragile in my arms and I just want to hold him close to me. Plus, my brain feels fuzzy as hell and I'm not exactly eloquent on my best days.

"Hey," I whisper, pulling back a little so I can see his face. See how blotchy and sad his face is, unfortunately.

"I know we have more stuff to talk about, but I feel like ass. And I love you, but you look like ass. Both of those things are my fault, but could we just chill for a little while? Let's play fucking GTA or something else mindless. We can both relax, eat some food, maybe take a nap, and then do big talks later. Deal?"

Silas looks at me, and although he's still quiet and tense, I feel like the hostility from before is gone.

I give him the most charming smile I have in me right now.

"We can even throw in blowjobs later, if you're into it. Hmm?"

I chuck him on the chin like we're in an old-timey movie and study his face while he processes.

"Yeah, sure," he says, eventually.

"Yeah to video games and blowjobs or just video games?"

There's a ghost of a smile. It's small, but it's there.

"Let's start with GTA. We'll take it from there. Why don't you go shower first and I'll make you something to eat."

"You don't have to do that, I can make myself something," I start to say, but when Silas raises an eyebrow at me, I lean down to sniff myself. God, why the fuck did I think it was a good idea to have a cigarette. Yikes. "Oh yeah. Let me go shower. I'll be right back. But I can make my own food, I swear."

I don't let myself linger and stare at him the way I want to, forcing myself to turn and go. This is fine. Everything is normal. I did a bad thing, I will apologize again and make it up to him any way he'll let me, and we can all move on. It doesn't have to be a big deal.

Silas's hand is still on my hip when I turn, and his fingers drag across the skin slowly, like he's just as reluctant to let me go as I am.

Everything will be fine. I can take care of him like I'm supposed to, and fix what I broke. By tomorrow, everything will be back to normal.

"Fuck you, robot boy, why are you so good at this?"

That actually gets a soft laugh out of him. It feels like I've been teasing the happiness to the surface for hours, and it's finally making a difference. All we needed was a little distraction.

"Because you have the attention span of a hummingbird. You're not that hard to beat, bro."

I scoff. "*Bro*. How dare you address me like you've never fucked me in the ass when you are literally, currently fucking me in the ass!"

Not literally, but that's what it feels like as I throw my controller down on the table in frustration. Silas deposits his gently, with a smile. The difference in mood from this morning is palpable, and I want to savor every minute of it.

With the game paused and the controllers down, I decide now is the moment to introduce some oxytocin to the situation. Because it's worth staving off the difficult conversation a little longer if I can finally make Silas feel good, after putting him through all this bullshit.

We're already close on the couch, only a few inches between us, so it's easy for me to lean over him. I run my hand up his thigh and edge closer until our faces are almost touching, and then wait to see his response.

"I promise I'll apologize some more in ways that involve words, but I'd like to apologize on my knees, too. If you're into it, of course."

The way his mouth pulls to the side and his eyes flick away from my face and back is not the reaction I was hoping for.

"Cade, didn't we just talk about the whole *sex as a punishment for real things* thing? Like a week ago?"

I frown, because I'm not totally sure what he's talking about, but then it comes back to me. Oh, shit. I'd forgotten about that.

Silas doesn't pull away from me. He puts a hand on my waist, holding me close to him, but also lets out an epic sigh.

"Of course, we never actually finished that conversation, either. I just..." He trails off, but I don't say anything while he finds the words. The last thing I need is to start talking over him on top of everything else. "I don't know where your head is at. I feel like all these weird things keep popping up, and then you brush it under the table and act like everything's normal."

When he brings his hand up to push back my hair, I let my eyes fall closed for a minute. My hair really is getting too long, but I'm such a fucking slut for when he touches me like this.

"I promise I'm not dodging you and I'm gonna do better. But can we please not talk about it yet. I miss you."

I push my face further into his hand. Every word I said is true. I'm not trying to avoid it. But Silas has been the one rock-steady thing about my life for the last year, and having this distance between us is making me feel unmoored.

Silas's eyebrows draw together. He looks almost mournful. But he heard me, clearly, because he gently tugs me closer to him until we're finally kissing.

It's a slow, lazy kiss, combined with both of us touching each other everywhere we can. I sink into him a little more every second until I'm basically in his lap, and he takes advantage of the position to wrap his arms around me and hold me in place. It all feels luxurious, and like the world is correct, for the first time in so long.

I get lost in it, and I know Silas does, too. Neither of us tries to push it any further, content in the moment. My body turns syrupy and relaxed, and I finally start to feel like I can have a conversation about my feelings or whatever without all the meat boiling off my bones.

Of course, that's when my phone rings. Well, vibrates. It buzzes on the coffee table, making a hard, sharp noise that interrupts the peaceful mood. We both ignore it, but I can feel the peace slipping away from us.

The buzzing stops and then immediately starts again. All my worries about what could possibly be wrong creep in, until I can't concentrate and pull myself away from Silas. It takes some contortion to reach the phone without extricating myself from Silas's lap, but I manage it. Like an idiot—a hungover idiot—I swipe to take the call without actually looking at who it is.

"Hey man, I have great news about the race. We're so on. And since I got you involved, people are throwing down way more than they should; the betting just got interesting. My uncle wants me to confirm that you're in before it gets out of hand."

"Chris?" I ask, like an idiot.

I can practically hear him roll his eyes.

"Yes, it's Chris. Are you still hungover? Jesus. Eat a burrito or something and get your shit together, because we're racing tonight."

"What?"

I'm so confused. I don't think Silas can hear the other end of the conversation, because he's frowning at me with a question in his eyes, and if he knew what I was talking about he'd probably look more pissed.

I gesture to him to give me a second and then climb off his lap, only barely managing to not fall to the floor in the process. Once I'm standing, it's easier to go to the kitchen and get a little distance so I can pull my thoughts together.

"Wait, what are you talking about tonight? I thought this plan was for like, days from now?"

I'm mumbling, but I don't know if it's enough for Silas to not hear. I'll explain everything to him when I'm off the phone, but I'd like for that conversation to not start as an uphill battle.

Chris answers me, talking super fast and animatedly about his plan and his uncle's buddies and bunch of other shit I half listen to. Apparently tonight is the only night that works with all of our schedules. Which, of course, reminds me that I have fucking work tomorrow night. And then there's something about the quality of the riders and the whole fly-by-night secrecy of it is getting everybody excited, and word has spread that they all need to get their bets in fast.

When he asks me to try and get Silas involved, I don't even bother to pretend, I just say no. There's no way Silas would ride in a competitive context, and I wouldn't want him to. Not when I know how much he hates it.

I'm still not convinced I'm going to do it. It seemed like a great idea last night, but that was when I was farther from the specter of Silas's disappointment and concern.

Then Chris interrupts his monologuing to tell me what the pot is already at, and sweet Jesus fuck. That's a lot of money. More than I expected in such a short amount of time.

That's the kind of money that could make a dent in this custody situation, I realize. And with that thought, I remember all the reasons I was so excited about the idea in the first place, and all the research I've been doing.

It's been a fuzzy couple of days and I've definitely been drinking more than I should, so the details got lost for a while there. But now I remember. And I remember the sheer urgency of the situation. Because it only takes one day or one random event to have Dad change his mind, or Mom to relapse hard, and suddenly my sisters are being taken across state lines into danger by someone I'm not legally able to stop.

I don't have a choice. It's just one shitty race. The race is fine, even if I'm still exhausted and not exactly at my peak. It's managing Silas's anxiety around me riding that I'm worried about.

"Yeah," I say, realizing I've left him in silence for too long. "Yeah, man. I'll be there. I'll see you tonight. Thanks."

I hang up, trying to dig around in my head for the right words to ease Silas's fears. Of course, when I turn around he's standing right there in the entry to the kitchen with a storm cloud of emotion on his face.

It's not exactly what I was expecting. Anxiety, yes. Anger? Not quite.

"So..." I trail off.

"No."

"What?"

"No," Silas repeats himself, arms crossed over his chest. "I really don't like being made to play the role of a nagging housewife, but absolutely fucking not. You are not going to kill yourself over a drunken fucking bet."

"Dude, it wasn't a drunk bet." I step toward him with my hands reaching, but he tenses up so I don't come any closer. "Yes, we were drinking and it was stupid of me to stay out so late. I really am sorry. But I'm serious about the race. This is too much money to pass up, Silas."

Silas pauses, rubbing at the bridge of his nose for a second.

"I know you have a lot of trauma around money. I get it, I really do. But baby, when are you going to get it in your head that we're not fucking broke anymore? We can afford to throw away food that's gone bad, we don't struggle to pay the bills, we have this whole fucking house to live in for just property taxes. We give your sisters enough to make sure they're comfortable. Things are good. I mean, neither of us is going to a four-year college, but I don't think we missed out there. Take a fucking breath. You don't need to keep going like you're fighting for your life every day."

It's possibly the most words I've heard him say in a single string, but it definitely doesn't hit me the way he was hoping.

"First of all, you don't have to *therapy-speak* me. She talks to you that way because you two are in a professional relationship and it makes it all impersonal. When you start talking to me that way, it makes me feel like I'm talking to a chatbot. I'm sorry, I'm not trying to be a dick, but please just talk regular."

I take a breath, vaguely aware that this is not the road I want to start down but it's too late to stop my momentum.

"And second of all, yes, I do have trauma around money. Which is why I know how quickly it can be taken away. Just because we can buy groceries doesn't mean we're safe. Either of my parents could go fucking crazy and make a mess in an instant. Your dad could show up here anytime he wants and fight you for the house. We—" I gesture between the two of us— "are not the kind of people who get taken seriously when the cops get called. Or something goes to court. In fact, people take one look at me and assume I'm guilty of something. It's just who I am. Literally the only thing we can have on our side is more money than the degenerate fucks that raised us. That's it. That's our whole safety net."

Silas's eyes are wide, and he's leaning away from me a little, making me wonder just how unhinged I look right now.

I can't stop, though. I have to make him understand. I *need* him to understand.

"I would never make you do anything you didn't want to. I'm not even asking you to race. I love you, I don't want to see you hurt. But I can't pass up on something so simple that has the chance to get us as much cash—under the table, I should add—as either of us makes in a month! You can't ask me to do that. Not when I need money if I want to get my sisters safe."

Silas's hesitation drops, and he leans towards me again.

"Oh, yeah. I forgot about the genius plan you had to steal your sisters from your mom and adopt two fucking children without even asking me. How stupid of me."

"Don't pretend you don't love them."

I can hear myself getting bitchier by the second, but I'm powerless to stop it, apparently. Silas is the only person I ever let boss me around, apart from the girls, and apparently there's a limit to that, too.

"Of course I love them," Silas says, throwing his arms to the side. "You know I love them. And I'll fight with you to protect them. But I don't think it's protecting them to start what will be a stressful, prolonged legal battle over a *what-if*. I also don't think your mom deserves this when she's been working so hard this year to stay clean. Even if it's just mostly clean. And I really don't think it's okay to make unilateral decisions about *adopting fucking children* when we're supposed to be partners. I've never had a boyfriend before but I thought the lack of surprise children was supposed to be one of the perks."

"How are you only funny when you're being a dick to me?" I'm not changing the subject. I'm not. "Explain to me how that works."

"Explain how I'm being a dick to you. Please." Silas is looking more desperate by the second, and it's making my anger back down incrementally. "I love you. I'm scared that you're hurting yourself right now because you won't fucking talk about what's really bothering you. And I don't want you to race—illegally, hungover, and on a whim—just to potentially make some money that we can get safely. Please stop."

I throw my head back, covering my eyes with my hands. I know he's making sense, and I know he's only doing this because he cares. But it's like the part of me that understands that and the part of me that's in charge right now refuse to fucking talk to each other, and I'm just a passenger, trapped behind a glass wall.

"I'm so sick of hearing 'please stop'. You, Tristan, Mom, everyone. Nothing is wrong. My dad being in town is making me a little antsy but it's not the end of the world. I caught a sad case at work and went out to drink about it. I like rough sex, but until a few days ago, so did you. I'm not doing drugs, I'm not driving drunk or shotgunning beers to get out of bed or going to work with anything in my system. I got in one fucking ill-advised fight with Dad, and that was a long time coming, in the grand scheme of things. Why is everyone so bent out of fucking shape right now? I'm—"

"So help me god, Cade, if you tell me that you're fine right now, I will go sleep at Ford's. I'm telling you to stop because you're so caught up in this weird, self-destructive momentum that you can't even see it anymore. And you're not listening to me."

I force in a deep breath, then blow it out. Then another, then another. I continue to tilt my head back with my eyes closed until I can wrangle all the anger and other emotions coursing through me into some kind of submission, because as pissed as I am, I still never want to fight with Silas. Especially because I know how much he hates conflict. If I want to argue with someone I can go yell at Mom.

When I finally ease up a little, I look at him again and see him taking stock of my face and posture, and I do my best to bring down the tone.

I speak softly, and take a small step toward him.

"I'm sorry. I'm really, really sorry. I didn't think any of this was going to upset you like it did, or I would have been more careful. I will be more careful. But I don't want to pass on this money just because we're fighting. Especially when we're really fighting about a bunch of other stuff. Please just come with me? You can watch, I'll win some cash, we'll go home. We'll sleep all this anger off,

I'll stop doing stupid selfish shit, and in a week it'll all feel like a bad dream. And I promise we'll talk about the custody thing more before I do anything, because you're right, I did spring that on you. But please, right now, can you come with me? I don't want to ride thinking about how angry you are at me."

I wince, because I didn't mean for that to come out all manipulative and shit. I was shooting for honesty.

"You don't have to," I say as a quick correction. "If you don't want. I'll be fine. But I would like it if we could go together. And we'll talk more when I get home, no matter what."

"Yeah, because talking in the middle of the night is going to be so helpful."

"Please, Silas? Will you please do this for me?"

There's a long, scary silence before he finally answers.

CHAPTER TWENTY-THREE

SILAS

I hate everything about this.

The stupidity of it is that I'm not sure why. I've always had anxiety about Cade riding, that's not new. But never like this. It always felt like an isolated fear that was largely irrational, and I knew that. Sure, it's a sport where you can get injured. But my fears were always so outsized.

If Cade had done this race a few weeks ago, before things started to get weird between us, I would have been worried a normal amount, but also optimistic. Now though, it feels so ominous. Like we're fucking doomed, and this is just highlighting how much worse things have gotten ever since his dad showed up.

Kyle hasn't even done anything. It's so fucking nuts how much he can get under Cade's skin and make him spiral just by existing, but at the same time, I know that if it were my dad, I'd be the same. Not spiraling in the same way, of course, but I'd still be spiraling.

I don't know what to do. I don't know how to stop this terrible momentum that we seem to have gained, but the only thing worse than watching this stupidity would be sitting at home, waiting to get a call when Cade hurts himself or gets into a fight or does any of the things he does to misplace all that anger he won't even acknowledge.

This whole situation is a shitshow. I'm standing here with the fifty or sixty other people who came to see the carnage. Because this is all illegal and we're trying not to attract the cops, only a couple sodium lights are on, and none of the really big overhead ones. We're surrounded by forest and one single dirt road leading away, and the small track already seems dwarfed by all this darkness.

I considered asking Tristan or anyone else I can trust to come with us, but then I realized I'd be putting them in danger if this whole thing gets busted up by the cops. It seemed too selfish.

So it's just me here, waiting to see what happens and how bad it ends up being. I'm trying to brace myself, but it keeps shifting to numbness, instead.

"Wish me luck?" Cade asks.

He's only standing a foot away from me, all of his gear on except the helmet and googles dangling from his long fingers. It feels like a bigger gap, though. It feels astronomical.

"Do you need luck?"

The flash of hurt on his face hurts me too, but it's too late to take the words back. I realize I've got my arms crossed and my shoulders up around my ears, my body thrumming with tension, and force myself to relax. A little.

"I just mean... make good choices. You're the best rider here. We both know that. But you have to ride smart and clean."

Cade chews on his bottom lip for a minute, staring at me before he eventually nods.

"I don't like how dark it is. It seems too risky," I continue, as if I can still change his mind.

"It's still light enough to see. I'll be careful, I promise."

He keeps staring at me, but doesn't move any closer to me. I can hear by the shift in the noise around us that everyone's getting ready to start.

Cade's riding against four other guys—the three from the bar last night, plus a man I don't recognize, who looks too old to have gone to high school with us. At least most of them are also hungover, I guess, and Cade's on roughly even ground with them.

Or maybe the collective hangovers will just make it all more sloppy and dangerous. I've given up trying to predict what's going to happen. I know, deep inside myself, that whatever it is will be bad. Now I just have to wait.

I catch Cade's eye one final time, and notice the way he's shifting his weight from one foot to the other, not turning around to go. I feel like an idiot when I realize what he's waiting for. We normally try to keep PDA to a minimum when we're in any kind of public space, but I also don't want to leave things between us feeling like this.

It only takes one step to put myself in Cade's space and wrap my hand around the back of his neck, holding him firm. He sinks into me when I kiss him on the lips. It's chaste; mouths closed, but it feels like we're saying everything that we haven't said. I lean my forehead against his when I break the kiss, taking a deep breath of the scent of him and closing my eyes for one more moment of peace.

Cade brings both his hands to hold my face and keep me close. When he speaks, it's quiet, and his voice is a little choked.

"I love you. I don't want to fight anymore, okay? I just need to do this. You have to let me take care of you and the girls."

I can't help but sigh, because this really is what it always comes back to, but there's no point in getting into that conversation again right now. I've given up on trying to stop him.

"I love you, too. Please just be safe."

I feel him nod against my forehead, and I don't make any moves to pull away. Maybe if I keep my eyes closed and my face next to his, nothing has to change.

Cade is the one to pull away first. He leans back, still holding me in place, and presses a hard kiss to my forehead. By the time I open my eyes again, he's walking away from me. He doesn't look back, and I get it. I wouldn't want to, either.

I don't let myself look at the people scattered around me, because I don't know whether they were looking at us with disgust or some kind of pity, and I don't care. I'm just trying to breathe.

The riders all line up at the start, and a controlled cheer goes out from the crowd. A lot of people parked up tailgate style, and people are drinking, smoking weed out in the open, acting like it's a big party. Adrenaline starts to blur my vision.

The track is a cross between a backyard set-up and something more professional. It's mostly berms and smaller jumps, but there's enough space for them to get up some real speed in places, and the final jump of the track is big enough to qualify as a booter. They can get some serious air time there, if they go for it.

Air time in the dark. Perfect.

I'm so consumed by my tension, I don't really clock the start of the race. I just hear the sudden roar of the engines, smell the octane in the air, and then see Cade—a pink blur—eating up the track. I haven't decided if I want to watch him closely or just close my eyes and hope for the best. I can't believe I agreed to stand here for thirty fucking minutes of this.

Like always, a rhythm descends on the arena. The engine noise pitches and ebbs as they move around the track, the conversation falls to a general kind of chatter, and everyone seems pretty content to just relax and watch the ride. Once in a while a cheer goes up for one of the riders, and I think they're mostly for Cade. He's obviously the favorite to win.

Without making a conscious decision about it, I realize my eyes are trained on him and I'm not willing to look away. To save myself some pain, I focus on studying his technique. Where he's holding his weight, when he accelerates and slows, how he gets past or falls behind the other riders. It's closer matched than I expected—all of them still huddled together more or less—but Cade is also slower than I've ever seen him. Not just slow on the bike, but slow in his reactions. I suspect he's been pretending to feel a lot better than he did today.

The other guys might be hungover, but Cade is coming off a what? Nearly 24-hour bender with only a few hours of sleep here and there, plus a lot of stress about it?

All he ate today was fucking potato chips. God, this is a nightmare.

I wince as Cade lands hard from a jump and fishtails a little, but he gets it under control and keeps going.

This is out of my control.

This is out of my control.

This is out of my control.

I have a strong urge to talk to my therapist, which has never happened to me before. I guess if I had a parent I was close to, I might have an urge to talk to them instead, but that's not something that's ever going to be a part of my life.

I'm shocked out of that thought by a sudden series of noises. They're harsh—metal on metal—and accompanied by a gasp from the crowd.

I'm calm. It's like the waiting was worse than the event, and I always knew this was coming. The world is moving in slow-motion around me as I finally latch my eyes onto what everyone else is looking at.

Or course. Of course it's Cade.

Someone must have been passing someone else and lost control, because Chris's bike is on its side as well as Cade's, and both riders are tangled together in a pile, several feet away. My lungs are frozen as I wait for them to move, to try to get up.

If this were a real race, the EMTs would already be out there, but of course it's not, so instead we have some confusing yelling coming from different sources and the other riders, clearly oblivious, still moving around the track.

Cade still isn't moving.

I think someone—probably Chris's uncle—is moving closer to the track, yelling and waving his hands, but it's too slow. I wall off every emotion I have into somewhere very far away, and start to run. There aren't any real fences or barriers, it's all just open, so it's easy for me to get on the track and start waving off the other riders.

One stops, then the rest, getting their feet on the ground and looking around to see what's going on. I'm past them now, though. Just as I reach the crash, I can see Chris pushing himself to his feet on one hand, the other held protectively close to his chest. His helmet is still on until he pulls it off and throws it to the side, but Cade still isn't moving.

Fuck. The panic and emotion I've contained is clawing at the door, but I manage to keep holding it back. I ignore Chris, because he seems okay and I hear other people running up beside me. My knees hit the dirt next to Cade and I lean down to look at him, remembering at the last possible second that I shouldn't move him, in case he fucked up his spine.

The word *spine*, crystallized in my own mind, hits something raw inside me and I make a wheezy, pained noise without meaning to. Not crying. Something more uncontained.

Cade looks small. He's on his side, one arm trapped beneath his body, the face of his helmet pushed into the dirt. I want to fucking do something. I want to pull off his helmet and see that his face is intact and maybe his eyes are open, but I can't, so I kneel close to him but not touching, my hands hanging uselessly in the air between us and my entire body vibrating with fear.

"Cade?"

I know it's stupid to say. If he were conscious, he'd be moving. But I don't know what else to do.

Eventually, I start to touch him gently, looking for blood or broken bones without moving him. My hands are shaking so much now that I can barely use them, but I have to keep trying. I think I might keep saying his name over and over, but I'm not sure.

Behind me, people are yelling. I can hear them running around. Shit, I should be calling an ambulance. But trying to fish my phone out of my pocket with my shaky fucking hands is a waste of time.

Someone comes close up behind me, and I lean over Cade protectively on instinct. But when I look up, it's Chris's uncle. I can't remember his name right now, but I always recognize him because he has two teeth missing from the top row, a little to the left, and it makes him easy to pick out of a crowd.

He puts his hand on my shoulder and leans over to talk to me.

"It's okay, I called an ambulance. They're like ten minutes away. Everyone else is bailing. I gotta get out of here before the cops show up, I'm going to drive Chris to the hospital myself after we get him changed out of his gear. If anybody asks, just tell them I let you guys use the track whenever you want. Nobody else was here, Cade was training and had an accident. They'll know there's no point in digging harder, it's not like anyone's gonna talk to them."

I nod. I'm probably supposed to say something, but none of this feels real. I can wait here for an ambulance. That's something I can do.

Uncle Missing Teeth keeps holding my shoulder and stares at me for a second, like he's trying to decide if it's really okay to leave us. I must look more capable than I feel, though, because eventually, he gets up and jogs away.

There's more shouting, but I don't bother looking. I know I'll just see everyone who was here to profit off of Cade running away from him, now that he's hurt.

Don't move him. I have to remember not to move him.

There's nothing else I can do. Not like this. I've been scared of this happening for so long, and now it's here and it doesn't feel real. Or maybe it feels like I summoned it here with all my stupid thoughts.

Nothing matters. I only have to wait.

Holding onto that thought, I lay down in the dirt a few inches away from him, my shoulder tucked under and my face turned to the side, my body a mirror image of his. I stare at the helmet, trying to see through the mud and the darkness to catch if he opens his eyes. I watch his chest keep rising and falling in shallow breaths.

I don't move when the ambulance shows up. I hear it, and there's some flashing from the lights, but I don't need to look. They can see exactly where we are. There might be cops here, too, but that seems like a later problem. I continue to lie here, studying every inch of Cade that I can, with my fingers curled loosely around his gloved ones. I focus my energy on pushing back against the thought that once he gets into that ambulance, I might never see him again.

Their voices come to me like we're all underwater, but eventually someone tugs me away from him and gets me sitting on my ass. I can see one of the medics putting down a backboard next to Cade while the other gets in my face.

I've met both of them before, I should remember their names, but just like with Uncle whatever, I can't find the information in my brain.

It's an older woman talking to me.

"Are you hurt? Were you both in an accident or only him?" she asks me in clear, articulated sounds.

The underwater feeling drifts away, and more ambient sounds come to my attention.

"I'm okay," I answer, too slowly.

That seems to be enough for her, because she turns her attention back to Cade.

They both move in a blur of color and straps and things I can't identify, until Cade is strapped onto the board, his helmet still on, and they both hoist him into the air.

"Come on," the woman half-shouts at me. "Time to go. You can't just sit here all night, you can ride with us, Silas."

I should feel worse that she remembers my name and I don't remember hers, but that seems like a lot right now. I focus on getting up on my feet, and then following them as they carry Cade over the dirt mounds that make up the track. It's difficult, and I think about offering to help them, but I would probably be in the way more than useful.

No cops in the parking lot. Just my truck, and the lingering beer and weed smell from everyone who ran away. It's quick getting him into the ambulance, and when the lady says something to me I don't hear, she seems to give up and politely manhandles me into the back and straps me into a little folding jump seat.

I want to reach for him, but I'm scared to get in the way. I want to stop shaking. What I want most of all is to feel something other than the finality of all that impending doom, but none of the tracks in my mind feel like they're lining up correctly this time.

"Don't be scared, hun. We're gonna take care of him," the woman says, her voice sounding disembodied and coming from somewhere.

"Thank you."

It doesn't seem like enough, but I don't have anything else to say.

CHAPTER TWENTY-FOUR

CADE

Everything is light and sound and nothing else for a while. I'm not sure how long, but it feels like days. I keep heaving my eyes open to see what's happening, but it takes so much effort every time, and I still can't piece together the things around me more than the basics.

I was in the race. I think there's a brief flash of memory of being in an ambulance and seeing Silas. But I wasn't sure if I was the patient or he was. He looked terrible. Pale and dirty and hunched in on himself. I tried to reach for him, but my hand wouldn't do what I was telling it and my head felt thick and fuzzy.

Then it was the hospital. Which feels real. I don't think it's a dream. My eyelids are still heavy, but there's the persistent sound of beeps and people walking quickly down hallways that's so familiar. An IV pump alarm is going off somewhere close to me, and it's driving me insane. I keep trying to open my eyes and reach for it. Probably just a little air bubble or a kink in the line. I want to fuck with the patient's arm in case it's positional, but that makes the realization that I'm probably the patient swim slowly up into my consciousness.

Everything goes dark and quiet again. This endless tug of war with my awareness goes on and on, until one time, I'm able to open my eyes, and I feel rooted in my body enough to look at the world around me.

I didn't realize how much I wanted to see Silas until I look around and he's not here. No one's here. I can tell I'm in one of the inpatient rooms, not the ER, but other than that, the room is empty.

Wait. Not totally empty. When I arch my neck enough, I can see someone sitting in a chair wedged into the corner of the room. It takes long, syrupy chunks of time for me to figure out who it is, but eventually it comes to me.

The girl that came with Dad. K-something. Krista?

Krystal. That's it.

"What happened?" I try to ask, but it comes out as more of a rasp.

Krystal looks up from her phone at the sound of my voice. She's silent for a minute, then untucks her legs from beneath her, drags the armchair up the edge of the bed and folds herself back into it.

I almost suspect that time is moving wrong for me still, but finally she speaks. Her Arkansas drawl is thick as hell, more than I noticed the other time we met, but she's not yelling at me. Which is probably more than I could ask if Silas were here.

"You crashed your bike. I don't really know the details, but Silas called your mom, and we were with her at the time so we all came down. Her and Kyle were here a minute ago but they couldn't stop fighting, so I told them both to get until they could behave themselves. Said I'd sit with you. We were all waiting for you to wake up."

God, everyone must be so fucking mad at me.

I'm so fucking mad at me.

"How long has it been?"

It takes me a couple of tries to get the words out though, because my throat is so raspy and it triggers a weak coughing fit. I realize there's an oxygen cannula under my nose, and do my best to breathe some O2 in.

242

Krystal passes me a plastic cup with a little water in it and helps me drink. Her expression is flat, but something about her presence is more maternal than I would have expected. Or maybe I'm just so starved for it, I'd enjoy a hug from a wire sculpture, at this point.

"Not long," she says. "You came in late last night, it's only just gone morning now."

She pauses, and I feel like she's waiting to say something else.

"Your throat hurts because they had to put a tube in it when you weren't breathing enough on your own. Something about a cracked rib and a little hole in your lung. You scared your momma half to death."

My throat clenches and my heart rate picks up, but I don't know what to say back to that.

"I'm sure your head hurts, they said you busted it pretty bad."

This time I turn to look her in the eye, my mouth hanging open.

"No way," I start. "I had my helmet on like always. It should be fine."

Krystal taps long, coffin-shaped acrylics on the arm of the chair a few times before she answers.

"The helmet was still on when they brought you, I think. I wasn't here yet. But they were talking about your brain bouncing around in your skull. There was a fancy word for it, but I don't remember. Coo-something."

I drop my head back into the pillow and look at the blank ceiling, already tired from turning to look at her.

"Coup-contrecoup."

I can see her snap her fingers and point at me out of the corner of my eye.

"That's the one. Sounds like you really fucked yourself up. They weren't sure how long it would take you to wake up."

It's hard to stop trying to look around, even though it makes my head throb and the low light in here is still too bright.

"Shouldn't you be telling the nurse I woke up, or something? If everyone was so worried, how come nobody's in here?"

I sound like a little kid, but I can't bring myself to be fully ashamed right now. Krystal takes her time to answer.

"I can get the nurse. Seems like you're doing alright, though, and they're stretched pretty thin around here. You had your scans; doctor told us it was just a matter of waiting, to try not to worry. You'd have a lot more people in here if they weren't all so worked up right now."

I'm scared to ask, but I do it anyway.

"Where's Silas?"

My eyes well up embarrassingly fast when I say it. God, I'm so scattered. I'm terrified that he hates me. He would be right to, I know it. But if it's true, I'm not sure I'm ready to face that reality yet. I blink back the tears, hoping she's about to tell me he went to the bathroom or something.

"He was having a hard time. One of y'all's friends showed up and they said they were going to go get your bike and truck from the track. I think he might have just needed a minute."

A tear slips out without me being aware of it. It feels like all I've done is cry lately. When the fuck did I become this much of a mess?

Krystal tilts her head at me, and even though her expression stays blank, it feels sort of sympathetic. She lets out a big sigh, like all of this is an imposition on her—which I guess it is, she doesn't fucking know me—and then reaches out to run her fingers through my hair.

The gesture almost makes me crumble. I want to crawl into her lap and hang onto her like a little kid, as pathetic as that is. I take a few gulping, shaky breaths and get myself under control, though. Crying about it isn't going to help anything right now.

"It's okay to be sad, hun. But I'm sure he'll be back soon. He's upset, but anyone with a set of eyes can see how much he adores you. It'll be okay. You should probably try to stop doing stupid shit though, like getting into accidents or starting fights all the time."

244

That makes me laugh a little, even though it sounds wet and the action makes my headache worse.

"I'm honestly surprised you're being so nice to me," I tell her.

"Yeah, well." Her fingers keep stroking my hair, and she shrugs like it's no big deal. "If my kid was alone in the hospital, I'd want somebody there to be sweet to him, if it couldn't be me. He's had a hard go of it, just like you. Gets angry a lot, just like you. It doesn't cost you anything to show someone a little kindness."

My forehead creases and I keep studying her as I listen.

"If you have a kid, what are you doing slumming around with my shitty dad?"

That almost drags a smile out of her, but if it counts as one, it's bittersweet.

"I had some shitty stuff happen to me. And I did some shitty stuff to myself. Made a lot of bad choices, so the state finally took him. He's twelve, and *behavioral*," she makes air quotes as she says the word. "So they put him in a group home. I have a court date for it soon, but I needed to get away for a little bit, as long as I wasn't allowed to see him. I couldn't stand being at home without him. Your dad and I happened to meet at a mutually convenient moment."

I'm watching her, trying to figure out what to say, because stories like that always hit me where it hurts.

"I'm sorry."

She shrugs, and starts stroking my hair again. "I'll get him back. Jump through their hoops, make better choices. Find some safer ways to work, so I don't catch any more solicitation charges. Maybe I can start one of those *OnlyFans* accounts and get famous."

Now she really does smile, teasing me a little, and I can't help but laugh.

"Anything sounds better than hanging out with Kyle and bankrolling his dumb road trip."

Krystal looks at the ceiling for a moment, like she's thinking.

"Hey, I'm not looking for your pity. Kyle's not that bad, anyway. Not really. I'm sure he was a terror when you were little, I'm not saying any of that isn't true. But in my experience, men like him tend to either mellow as they age and let the fight drain outta them, or they let everything else drain out and become all fight. All hard edges all the time. Those are the ones you need to stay away from."

"I guess," I say, chewing on my lip out of habit.

"Trust me, you don't wanna be around that guy, and you don't wanna become that guy. Don't let your anger get the best of you. Not even your dad turned into that angry, bitter old man, but that doesn't mean you won't if you're not careful. There are plenty of ways to hurt the people who love you without physically hurting them, if you see what I mean."

I know she's talking about Silas, but when I try to say anything about it, it's like my throat clenches shut.

"You seem like a sweet kid, Cade. And you've got somebody who loves you. Don't let that go if you can help it."

I huff, forcing myself to keep it light.

"Hey, you're like, five years older than me, max. I don't think you can really call me a kid."

"Yeah, well I've still got all my body parts intact and you're the one who bruised his brain and punctured his lung going bike riding at night, so I'll call you whatever I want."

Valid. Everything hurts right now, and I'm acutely aware of my own shameful, self-centered stupidity.

"So, what? You were just sent here by the heavens to dispense your street-walker wisdom and show me the error of my ways?"

The fingers that were previously stroking my hair pause to flick me on the nose. Not hard enough to hurt, but enough to make me feel like a scolded puppy.

"Don't be a smart mouth. You're not so injured I can't slap the shit out of you. No, I'm not your fairy fucking godmother, but I am the only person left sitting here, so I thought it was worth a shot. Everything I said is common fucking sense, anyway, not exactly wisdom from the almighty. Which you would see, if you could pull your head out of your ass for a minute. I barely fucking know you and I can see that the solution to a lot of your problems boil down to *stop being a dumbass.*"

She takes a deep breath, and goes back to stroking.

"Besides. Chances are I fucked my kid up so bad I'll be lucky if you're what he grows up to be like. I'm doing my best to cut that shit off at the pass, but I could stand to shore up as much good karma as I can find."

Again, I'm hit with the urge to cry, and barely hold it back. I'm trying to find an appropriate way to thank her, when familiar voices interrupt.

Mom and Dad, walking towards my room and still bickering with each other, as far as I can tell.

"Oh, shit on a shamrock, you're awake. Thank god," Mom says from the doorway before rushing over.

"There he is," Dad says. "See? Told you he'd snap out of it. He's a strong kid."

He doesn't rush over, but he does step closer, and I tense up without meaning to. I don't want to look at him yet. I feel like my nervous system is being fried from every angle.

Of course, Krystal is still sitting right next to me, and she's watching my expression shift with a calculating gaze. She nods at me briefly, and holds my gaze as she raises her voice to talk to him.

"Kyle, my court date got moved up. I gotta get back home, and you promised you'd drive me. We should get out of here. I'm sure the cops have gotten bored of looking for you over some bullshit charges, at this point."

No one speaks for a second.

"Um, alright I guess. Kid, are you okay if I take off?" he asks me, as if he's ever been there for me before.

I don't turn and look at him, keeping my head twisted in Krystal's direction, squeezing my eyes shut and pushing it into the pillow. My right hand feels functional, at least, so I raise it in the air and wave goodbye at him without a word.

More silence, but everyone seems to eventually get it that I'm not going to say anything to him.

Krystal stands up, making enough rustling noise that it breaks the tension.

"Alright, well. Feel better. Be good to your mother," is the last thing he says to me, making me huff into the pillow.

He and Mom mutter together for another minute, but I very deliberately don't listen to what they're saying.

Once Krystal and Kyle are gone, a lot of pressure eases out of the room, and I can hear Mom approaching me. I still don't turn around to look at her, though. It's all too much right now, I just want to lie here, suspended in time.

"Has the doctor or anyone been in since you woke up? I think they wanted to run some tests."

"No. It's only been a minute."

"Alright," she says. "I'll get somebody. You hang tight." She squeezes my shoulder gently before she turns toward the door, probably expecting me to look at her, but I stay as I am.

The only person I want to talk to right now is Silas, but after everything I've put him through, I guess I owe it to him to be patient.

I can wait.

CHAPTER TWENTY-FIVE

SILAS

P ulling into the hospital parking lot, it takes me a few minutes before I can even turn the engine off. I probably look like a crazy person, running through every grounding exercise I've learned and touching all the different textures in my truck, but it helps a little.

I'm grateful that Tristan showed up when I texted him and drove me to the track to help rescue my truck and Cade's bike. I was exhausted from pacing around the hospital all night, trying to keep Cade's mom from freaking out, and stonewalling the cops when they briefly showed up to ask questions. And all through it, Cade didn't wake up. Things got real scary real quick in the ambulance, and then they were doing so many tests and stuff that I couldn't even see him for hours once we got to the ER.

They keep telling me that there's no reason for him not to be fine, he just needs to heal, but it doesn't feel like it. Not when I haven't heard the sound of his voice for so long.

I take a final, steadying breath and climb out of the truck, feeling each of my feet as they hit the asphalt. Tristan pulls into the parking lot a couple spaces down and walks over to join me.

"I appreciate the ride, but you don't have to walk me in, I'm fine," I say.

"Yeah but I want to see the kid. I'll be fast though, I gotta sleep before work tonight."

Tristan claps his hand on my shoulder, but I flinch because I forgot he has work in a few hours—just like Cade was supposed to—and not only will he not have his normal partner, but he's spent the morning running around town to help me out.

Guilt seeps into my bones, but it's a familiar feeling so I let myself numb to it.

"I'm sorry, man. I shouldn't have called."

"Are you kidding? You know I love to play the big savior. Always call. I gotchu."

We spend the rest of the walk in silence, heading through the busy, buzzing hospital until we get back to Cade's wing.

Tristan is the one that breaks the silence before we get to the room.

"I'm proud of how you're holding it together, by the way. It's been a fucked-up couple of weeks, and you've handled all of it," he says.

I blow out a breath. "I don't feel like it. If anything I feel like I've just made things worse. Or at least not done enough to make them better."

A wave of emotion pinches at my face while I speak, but I push it back down.

"Nah, that's bullshit. A year ago? You would have been a wreck. No offense, but it's true. You and Cade were still so messy you were running away from each other instead of talking. At least now you're trying. You've come a long way this year, you should give yourself credit. You're making the best choices you can in the circumstances, trying to manage your emotions, you even let me feed you this morning. That's nothing to turn your nose up at. That's progress."

He says it all in a too-light tone, which somehow makes the words easier to swallow. But then he gets more serious.

"You—and the rest of us trauma babies, let's be real—will never be what most people think of as normal. These problems will always be a part of you. But you can get it to a place where it's manageable, and let that be your new normal. You're already well on your way. So don't give up."

We pass Kris talking animatedly to someone at the nurse's station and I hope she's not being rude but I don't have the energy to check right now. But from the few words I overhear, it sounds like Cade's awake, which makes both me and Tristan pick up speed on the way to his room. As soon as we get to the open doorway, though, I freeze.

It's not panic that sets in, or anxiety. It's something heavy. Something that tells me the world is changing around me too fast, and if I just pause for a minute, I can delay the inevitable. There are so many possibilities for what could happen when I walk into that room and see how Cade is, and I'm not ready to face a single one of them.

"You okay?" Tristan asks.

"I need a minute. You go in."

The words come out in a whisper, and I force myself to stand with my back to the wall, taking one deep breath after another.

Tristan nods and heads inside. He leaves the door open, though, so I can hear everything that gets said once he's inside.

"Hey," Cade says. "Are you here to yell at me?"

His voice sounds rough, but strong. And calm, which possibly relieves me most of all.

"Do you want me to yell at you?"

There's a pause, and I can picture Cade fiddling with whatever's in his hands while he thinks.

"Kinda. I know I deserve it."

"Well then I'm not going to yell at you, because you'd take it as some kind of absolution. It sounds like you're finally waking up to how bad things have gotten and maybe it'll be good for you to sit with that for a while," Tristan responds.

Another pause.

"Is Silas okay?" There's a lot of emotion packed into those three words, and it makes me feel… something. Less despair, I guess.

"Yeah, he's okay. He's tougher than you think he is, y'know. He'll be here in a minute."

There's a much longer silence than I think I could handle in a conversation, but waiting here is bringing me a little calm.

"What do I need to do?" Cade asks.

Tristan sighs dramatically.

"I love dispensing pearls of wisdom, but hell, Cade. I've been trying and you're not listening, so maybe you need to figure this one out for yourself. But I bet actually listening to Silas when you talk to him will do you a lot of good." He hesitates before continuing. "Give him what he's asking for, not what you think he needs. And for the love of fuck, remember that in the last 24 hours, he's watched you get fucked up in an accident, then get a needle aspiration in the back of an ambulance for a partial pneumo, and then get intubated in the ER because you were barely breathing on your own, and then lay here unconscious for the rest of the night while he could only stand there and fucking wait."

"Fuck, that's so bad. I didn't realize it was that bad."

Cade sounds shaken, which makes me feel better. Like he's finally getting it. Although I hate how bad things had to get for him to wake up.

"Of course you didn't, you were unconscious. But you're lucky Sharon knows her shit," Tristan snaps.

"I'm sorry, T."

"I'm not who you should be apologizing to."

"No, I know. But I also need to apologize to you. I've made you do a lot of chasing me up and babysitting, and I know you have other shit to do. I don't know when I got used to having you around as a safety net, but I obviously got a little too comfortable. I need to remember to take care of my own shit and not lean on you."

Tristan sighs again, and then I hear the bed creak.

"I am here as a safety net. I don't mind it. And as much as I'm pushing you to act like a grown up, you're still patching up all the holes from the growing up you didn't get to do right as a kid. When your parents are addicts, it's like every developmental stage happens way too fast or not at all. So you can cut yourself the teeny, tiniest sliver of slack for that. I'll be here when you fuck up again. But you need to learn from everything that's happened the past couple of weeks instead of making the same mistakes over and over."

Cade doesn't respond, but I can imagine the devastation on his face right now. He hates feeling like he's disappointed someone. He'll never admit it, but he fucking hates it.

I can hear Tristan get off the bed.

"Now, if you'll excuse me, I have to go sleep before shift tonight."

"Fuck. I forgot we have work tonight. Oh man, they're gonna be so mad I'm calling out again after I just went back. Christ, this is bad."

"Well, you're in luck that I'm a workaholic, because I had enough PTO stacked up to donate it to you. They were grateful, to be honest. You know it makes management nervous when you have too many hours banked. So you can afford to take the time to rest up and get your head straight. And heal the hole in your lung, while you're at it."

Tristan's footsteps move back toward me and the open doorway. Cade doesn't say anything I can hear, but Tristan keeps talking as he exits.

"Thank me by fixing it."

Tristan doesn't say anything else to me when he walks out, just nods in silence and then leaves. It's weirdly comforting.

I still don't go in. I keep waiting. Just another minute, and then I can face it.

I'm not sure how long it actually takes, but when I do walk in, it startles Cade. He looks up at me with tear-filled eyes that I wasn't expecting. He always puts so much energy into pushing shit down, it's weird to see him crack. His skin is blotchy and there are dark circles under his eyes, and I can't believe how close I came to losing him, after everything we've been through.

There are a few seconds where we just look at each other, and then something in Cade seems to snap. The shimmering eyes turn into actual sobs, and I cross the room before I know what's happening, sitting next to him on the bed and pulling him close to me.

Cade cries in a way I've never seen from him before. It's all the grief and rage he's been bottling up for fucking years, pouring out into my lap. It should break my heart, and it does, but honestly I'm relieved. It feels like every single problem we've had recently could have been avoided if Cade would fucking allow himself to feel an emotion other than anger. Maybe that's the therapy in me seeing my shit in everyone else, I don't know, but the way he's letting it out right now makes me think it's true.

At some point, Kris and the nurse poke their heads through the door, probably because of the noise. Luckily, Cade doesn't see them, and I'm able to wave them away. They also close the door behind them, which feels like a relief.

It can't be good for him to cry like this with a head injury, but I'm not going to try to stop him. We sit together like that for a long time. I don't say anything, because the only thing I could say would be "it's okay," and it's not okay. So instead I sit with him, and let him cycle through whatever he's feeling until he finally calms.

The calm is so short lived I don't get the chance to say anything, because Cade immediately launches into a coughing fit. It scares the hell out of me, but I try to get him sitting upright and make sure the little oxygen tube is in the right position under his nose. Just when I'm about to panic and call for someone, the coughing fades away, and Cade takes some deep, shaky breaths through his nose.

"Dude, can you pass me a tissue or something, please? I'm a fucking mess over here."

Only Cade would call me 'dude' in this moment. It's so ridiculous I almost laugh, but it's intrinsically him.

"Sure," I say, but I grab him gently at the back of the neck and kiss his messy curls before I do.

He blows his nose and swipes at his bloodshot eyes for a second, while I watch him on high alert, certain he's about to start coughing again. I'm trying not to flash back to the ambulance, when he started gasping for breath, barely conscious, and they stuck a giant fucking needle into him to let the air out that was keeping him from breathing.

The memory still claws at me, though, and I realize I'm the one tearing up. God, I hate this.

When I look up again, Cade is staring at me.

"Hey," he says.

His hand, trailing IV tubing, reaches out for mine and I take it gratefully. We hold onto each other, content to sit in silence for a little while longer.

"I'm sorry," he says, breaking the tension. "That sounds stupid and like it's not enough, but I wanted to say it anyway."

I nod, scared to open my mouth because I don't know what will come out. My throat feels tight, and words aren't coming to me.

"I don't want to be like this. I spend all this energy trying to make your life easier and better, and somehow I turned into this giant weight that's just dragging you down. I'm sorry. I never meant for this to happen."

"Cade, don't—" I lose track of what I'm trying to say for a minute.

All I know is that it's great he's acknowledging that he's been shitty, but I hate that he's already acting like some kind of failure to me. Like this is all about me, all the time. I want him to be better for *him*, because he deserves it. But I don't know how to say it.

"Loving you is not a chore, Cade." My voice cracks a little as I say it, but I hold his gaze the entire time. "It's not some kind of horrible burden that you have to pay me back for by taking care of me. I want you to stop doing this because it feels like you're hurting yourself, or taking something out on yourself. And you don't deserve that, because no one does—not because it's an imposition on me."

Cade stares at me with wide eyes, and it's surreal to see my chatterbox stunned into silence.

"I need you to stop hurting the person I love. That's all I want."

For a second, I think he's going to start crying again, but he just sniffs and sits there for a second.

"Okay, baby. Okay. Whatever you want."

Kind of missing the point, but it's better than nothing. Maybe now's the time to say it.

"And I need you to trust me to take care of myself more. I know I'm fucked up, and I probably scare you sometimes. But I hate that it's become your entire life mission. I have help. You worked hard to make sure I did. And I still have weird days, but I am getting better. We always say we save each other but it doesn't need to turn into this kamikaze mission, where I'm anxious so you're stressed and trying to fix it so you neglect yourself which makes me stressed and on and on and on. We have real problems. We don't need to be making more for ourselves."

Cade chews on his lip, nodding absently. I wait for him to process, because I really want to see what he has to say.

"I think I've been being stupid for a long time, huh?"

I sigh. "It's not stupid, Cade. You're hurting. But you pretend you aren't, and it makes it worse."

He looks up at me, and there's vulnerability brimming in his eyes.

"What should I do? Can you just tell me what to do please? I'm so tired, and I don't want to be like this anymore."

"I don't know. But if we can afford all this therapy for me, then I don't see why we can't afford it for you, as well. Maybe just to start."

Cade nods, looking small and fragile in a way that makes me want to scoop him up.

"You know," I keep talking. "Since the day I moved back here, I've heard you talk so much about men being allowed to feel their feelings, and not being like our fathers, and all that stuff. But it feels like you think that's true for everyone except you. Talking to someone might help you figure that out."

"Okay," he says. "I guess I always thought therapy was for rich people, but you're right. It has helped you a lot." Cade stares at me like he just realized something. "Don't let Tristan send me to fucking rehab, though. If he gets the thought in his head, nothing will stop him, and I promise I do not need it. I admit I need help, but not that kind of help. I've just made shitty choices all over this week."

I can't decide whether it's worth disagreeing with him or not. Because yeah, he's been bad this week. But this isn't the only time he's turned to drinking when he's upset. But it's never seemed out of control until the past few days, and maybe if he stops bottling all his shit up, he'll be smarter about that, too.

"Fine," I say. "I'll protect you from Tristan's wrath. As long as you start therapy and take it seriously, and stop screwing around. But I will tell on you so fast if you start acting shady again, y'hear? I am not too proud to run to him for help. We've established that."

There's a ghost of a smile on Cade's face. Then he seems to wilt in front of my eyes.

"Can we talk more later? I'm so tired," he says, and his voice is even weaker and raspier than before.

"Yeah, of course. Hopefully we'll find out soon how long you need to be here for."

I shuffle lower on the bed, stretching out my legs and then gently rearranging Cade until he's lying on me the way he likes.

"Go to sleep, baby. I'm right here."

He snuggles down deeper into my chest, his fingers absently tightening and relaxing against me where he's holding on.

"Thank you for hanging around, even when things were fucked," he murmurs into my shirt.

"Always."

I kiss the top of his head one more time, and stroke up and down his back as he drifts off. It's the first time I've felt any kind of peace in months.

CHAPTER TWENTY-SIX

CADE

"It feels like they let you out really fast. Having a hole in your lung sounds like it should be a bigger deal. Shouldn't they do surgery or something?"

Silas has his arm around my waist to steady me as we finally walk into the house. I don't really need it, I can walk fine, thank fuck, but I kind of want it. I never thought I'd be into being babied other than after some buck-nasty sex, but since we talked yesterday, I've forced myself to accept it and it's actually kind of nice.

Silas is warm and solid and keeps treating me like I'm made of spun glass. It's a hell of a change from running away from him all the time. And only one of those will cause the downfall of the best thing to ever happen to me.

"I'm fine, baby. I spent 24 hours in care, I'm breathing good on room air, it was just a teeny tiny hole and it's already healing itself. Honestly, my ribs hurt way more, but what are you gonna do? And my wrist. And my head. But it'll be fine."

"Yeah," he says, frowning at me. "I'm worried about your head, too. The doctor gave me the head injury instructions by the way, so don't think you can

EMT your way out of it. No TV. No phone. Dim lights. Plenty of rest. I know your poor, understimulated little heart might burst, but it's better than making your brain even worse, so we're following the rules."

"Yeah, yeah." I'm smiling, though, because it feels so goddamn good for him to not be mad at me, anymore. I forgot how good this feels. I will do absolutely anything to keep it. "You're gonna have to read me a bedtime story then, because I'm not going to just sit here in silence like a psychopath."

Silas snorts.

"I sit in silence all the time. We're just on different ends of the weird-brain spectrum. Now sit. I'll get you some water."

Silas deposits me on the couch, leaving all the lights off so it's dim in the cold, afternoon winter light. I reach out and make grabby hands at him though, before he goes into the kitchen.

"I don't want water. Come snuggle with me."

Silas looks at me like I'm being ridiculous, which I am, but hey, he wanted me to be soft and squishy and vulnerable. This is what he gets.

And I know he secretly loves it, because he joins me on the couch in about four seconds and then carefully arranges me until I'm draped over him.

"I don't know any bedtime stories, Cade. And it's the middle of the day."

His voice is gruff, but he gives me another one of those tender head kisses he's been liberal with ever since I got hospitalized.

"We could just talk," I say. "I'll even shut my eyes. It feels like forever since we talked about anything other than sex or arguments or what to have for dinner."

There's a long pause while we both ruminate on what to say, and Silas ends up being the one to break the silence.

"Do you ever want to get married?"

That's not what I was expecting, but Silas isn't always linear, so I've learned to roll with it.

"I never thought about it much, to be honest. When I was younger I thought I would one day, but it was always because I thought I had to, not because I actually wanted to. It never really appealed to me, to be honest. My parents were married. They technically still are. So many people get married and then act like it doesn't mean anything, so I never had a lot of respect for the idea. If you really want to be with someone, why do you have to sign a piece of paper that forces you to stay together, you know?"

I feel Silas nodding against me.

"What about you?"

He takes his time answering. "I think I felt the same way. I didn't think about it a lot, because it seemed like something Dad would probably make me do eventually, so there was no point in worrying about it until then. But yeah, it always hung over my head like some vague future obligation I didn't really want. I guess I wanted to know if it's something you want, so you don't feel like you're missing out on anything."

I shake my head and squeeze his side to reassure him. He flinches the same way he has done so much recently, and I feel guilty for not thinking about it, but then he seems to make the conscious choice to relax. I flatten my hand and move it a little higher, then butt my head against his chest for attention.

"I'm not missing out. I'll do it if you want, but I think one of my favorite things about ending up with a man is getting an excuse to avoid all of these heteronormative things that I don't want to do. Not that you can't also do that with a girl, of course, but you know what I mean. My mom isn't breathing down our necks about grandchildren. If I was with a girl, I think she would be. But like, she doesn't even really care about grandchildren. So she'd only be doing it because she felt like she was supposed to, and the whole thing goes on and on and on. I like stepping out of that cycle."

I think about it for a second, and realize something.

"I bet Gunnar and Tobias will be the first Possum Hollow gay wedding. That man has wanted to wife Tobias since the day he set eyes on him. They're all traditional and shit. It'll be fucking adorable."

Silas laughs, and the sound falls over me like warm rain. I relax a little bit more, ignoring all my stupid aches and pains.

"Oh!" I say, tilting my head back to look at him and tapping at his chest. "I have an idea. If we count our anniversary as the day we moved in together, instead of the day we started jerking off in bed together because we were the bestest bros in the world, that's in a couple months. Which seems like the perfect amount of time to plan a party. What do you think?"

Silas hesitates, and my Silas-mind-reading powers kick into gear.

"No big ceremony, I promise. No vows, nothing where we are the center of attention. But we can get everybody together and they can all watch us being in love. Tobias and Gunnar aren't the only ones who should get to be gay and adorable, I want a piece of that action."

Silas starts to laugh, but he buries his face in my hair to muffle it.

"Okay. That sounds doable. I'm down," he says.

"Yes!" I fist pump to celebrate the plan I've been super excited about for 45 seconds now. "You're on, Rush. Non-wedding it is."

"Anything you want, Cade."

I hesitate, because it's been nice having a light tone between us for once, but I don't want to pass up an opportunity to show him I really do understand the things I've done wrong lately.

"For you too, remember. Anything you want." I look up at him again, studying the line of his face that looks like it's glowing a little in the light. "I'm sorry I tried to steamroll you with all the stuff about getting custody of my sisters. I wasn't thinking straight, and I let all these weird fears get the best of me. It wasn't cool, to just force you into something."

Silas nods, looking at me carefully.

"So no surprise children? Because I love you, but if I come home one day and you've acquired a baby or something I don't think I can handle that."

He's joking, kind of. But there's a serious undertone to the words.

I shake my head.

"Nope. No surprise babies. Honestly, that's another thing that always seemed like a threat hanging over me more than something to look forward to. I've spent most of my life raising my sisters, and they're a long way from being grown. I'm sure we'll talk about it when we're older or whatever, but if you don't ever want to have more family than we have right now, I'm very okay with that. We don't need to put weird pressure on ourselves. Right?"

Silas blows out a breath for a long time, and I can tell he was more stressed about that than he was letting on.

"Right. I like that plan. A plan to not have a plan."

We keep staring at each other, but it feels peaceful for once, instead of intense.

"Honestly," he continues. "I have so much more right now than I ever thought I would. Being with you is better than being alone, and that's not something I thought I would ever experience. And I do love having the girls sometimes, although I'm glad they got to go home, finally. This is all so much and it makes me really happy, even on the worst possible days. I don't need more than this."

I think some people might read something negative into what he's saying, but I get it. Life is hard. All the fucking time. This makes me so much happier than I ever expected, I don't feel the need to add anything else into my life. I don't feel like we're missing anything.

"Same, baby," I say softly. "Same."

We both fall into a comfortable silence, and Silas keeps stroking my back while I tap random patterns into his skin with my uninjured hand.

"Silas?" I ask, feeling suddenly exposed.

"Yeah?"

"Promise me everything's going to be okay. That I can go to therapy and learn to stop being an asshole. And we'll talk more about the things we've been fighting about. I haven't forgotten about the sex stuff, either, and I know we need to deal with that. I'm trying really hard not to shy away from anything or push anything under the rug anymore. But I really need you to promise me that if I keep trying to be better, you'll keep trying too, and we're just going to keep learning to love each other better, and we'll still get the happily ever after part. Right?"

Silas is quiet for so long I start to get a little scared about his answer. But he sounds so sure when he speaks, all that worry melts away.

"I promise, Cade. I'm not letting this go. I promise we'll both get the happy ending we deserve."

When he leans down to kiss me, I can't stop myself from believing him.

EPILOGUE

SILAS

I thought I'd feel more nervous. I really did. But instead, everything seems to have fallen into place.

The party we had for our anniversary was actually nice, and Cade kept his promise about not making me the center of attention. It wasn't deliberate, but the timing of it made the party feel like some sort of test of how much progress we've made. It's only been a couple of months since Cade's accident, so it would have been easy for nothing to really have changed and for us to both be stuck in *we'll get to it* mode.

That was definitely my biggest fear after things fell apart and promises were made. Cade would put off therapy and we'd both put off talking about stuff, and everything would get swept under the rug. But I was totally wrong. Cade launched himself into attacking the problem the same way he used to launch himself into what he thought was taking care of me, and it didn't take long to feel the effects.

He hates therapy, obviously. He was always going to. But he goes and he tries and I do believe it's helped him. And we stopped circling around each other nervously without saying anything, which seems to have helped most of all.

And his dad has stayed the fuck out of town, which hasn't hurt.

So, when it came to the party last night—something well and truly out of my comfort zone—everything going well seemed like confirmation that we were doing the right thing. Cade had a few drinks but didn't lose control of himself. I didn't struggle with the food as much as I used to, because I realized that was more of a side effect of feeling stressed and out of control, rather than the root of the problem.

We hung out with our friends and no one made a big deal about anything, but Tristan and a couple other people quietly said something about how happy they were to see us happy, and it felt like finally coming down the other side of a massive hill.

I think I've lived my entire life walking at an incline, and I never realized how easy things could be until we got here.

Last night was the party, but tonight we're addressing the final thing that has been weird between us—sex. There were so many half-fights and unsaid fears before. We were both nervous after Cade's accident, and between the emotional load and all his fucking injuries, we went back into sex with so much fucking restraint, it didn't feel like us.

It was still nice, obviously. But it felt weird. All disjointed and like we were both afraid to upset the other person. I never really knew if all the rough, desperate sex we had was healthy or part of a bigger problem, and after a while we both had to admit that we needed to address it.

There were conversations during therapy. There was more research. Cade even asked Wish some kink-related questions—I don't want to know how that conversation started—and he ended up joining a fucking BDSM educational Discord.

I took one look at the interface for that and gave it a hard pass, but he seems to like it.

It was freeing to know that there were so many people who also like to have weird, kind of brutal sex, but maintain healthy relationships. I'd read about it before, but there was so much more to consider than I ever realized. And so much to talk about. It was actually exhausting, but if we can get back to normal–or a new normal where maybe the sex is even weirder but we both stop being weird about it–all the awkward conversations will be worth it.

I'm not nervous. We've never done something this... structured before. But it's still just me and Cade, at the end of the day. And I want to make him feel the way he seems to need, without putting either of us at risk.

I've been waiting outside the bedroom for long enough I know he must be freaking out. We talked about all the different things we could do and this is what we agreed on, so I know he's into the concept, but it still feels weird to be out here while he's in there, simmering in his own desperation and arousal.

I finally open the door, and he doesn't move–just like he's supposed to–but I can see the way his body sags a little in relief. Before I left him, he stripped down, got on his knees, let me loosely tie his hands behind his back, blindfold him, get him achingly hard and then put a cock ring on him. I thought leaving him for so long would make his erection go down, but apparently I underestimated how much this dynamic is doing it for him. Or maybe how well the cock ring was going to work.

He's rock hard, and glistening in the low light thanks to how much fluid has been leaking from his tip. When I take a step toward him, Cade sucks in a breath and his entire length flexes in the air. It feels like he's reaching for me, which is ridiculous but also makes me thrum with arousal.

"Did you miss me?" I ask.

"Yes."

The word comes out in a rushed exhalation, and he already sounds wrecked. I fucking love it.

Cade sways a little in my direction, so I get closer to him before crouching down. I'm inches away from him, but not quite touching him, and seeing how affected he is already makes my head spin.

"Are you doing okay?"

We talked about safe words and decided what we want to do doesn't require anything super complicated. Cade already babbles a lot during sex, I'm used to him saying *yes* and *no* and *please* in random, nonsensical orders, but anytime he genuinely wants to stop, he's never had a problem saying something to me that's clear enough to communicate. Just *stop* is enough for me, because it's not one of his preferred babble-phrases.

But I like the structure of checking in. I never thought about it in this way before, but making a point to ask him if it's all good several times really eases up on my tendency to catastrophize and spin out.

"Yes," he says again, still breathy. "Please touch me."

I hum, because I love to tease him when he's compliant for me like this.

"Touch you where?" I whisper, leaning in so he can feel my breath on his cheek.

"Anywhere."

I can practically taste the desperation rolling off him.

His pink, swollen cock is too inviting like this, all trussed up in silicone, and I can't resist. I run my fingertip along the underside, from base to tip, with the slightest pressure I can possibly manage.

The air between us is so electric now that just that bare contact makes Cade groan and fluid pearl at the tip of his cock. He flexes for me again, and his entire body shivers.

"What a good boy," I tell him, because I know it hits him somewhere deep inside. "So beautiful for me. So needy."

"Yes," he says, still leaning like he's trying to find me.

"Bend over for me. Forehead on the floor."

Cade hesitates, because his hands are bound behind his back. But I know he can do it.

I use the excuse of helping him to get my hands on him, pushing his thighs further apart to steady him, then placing my hand between his shoulderblades and gently guiding him forward.

"Slowly. Careful. Use your core, I know you can do this. Forehead resting on the floor for me."

By the time he's done, Cade has his forehead on the floor and his ass in the air, chest held between his knees.

I clearly haven't been taking advantage of how flexible he is. How rude of me.

I can still see his cock bobbing as it points to the floor, but that's not what's getting attention right now. When I first got Cade all worked up and ready to go, I opened him up as well. There's still a smear of lube running down his crack, shining at me. I apply some more and then pull out the vibrating plug that we've had for a while but don't use nearly enough.

Cade takes it easily, letting me work it in and out of him a few times before it sits into place. He sighs again as his body settles around the intrusion, getting more comfortable in his awkward position. I don't say anything for a minute and don't touch him, waiting for him to relax as much as he can.

And then I turn on the vibrations.

A choked noise escapes him, because I turn it to maximum power without warning. He's in a difficult position to move in, but he does arch his back and do a weird shimmy as he adjusts to the toy pulsing deep inside him.

"Silas," he gasps, but doesn't follow it up with anything.

"Mm?"

There's sweat beading on his forehead, and I can't resist the urge to reach out and push his hair out of his eyes, even though they're covered by the blindfold. It's a movement I've done hundreds of times in the last year, and I hope I get to do it thousands more.

"Does that feel good?" I ask.

Cade nods, his mouth hanging open, his lower lip swollen and shiny where he's been chewing at it.

"Do you think you can come just like this?"

He hesitates, and then nods.

It's what I want to hear, but he's not coming anytime soon even if he can do it hands free.

"That's what I thought. So, so needy."

I stroke his hair again, because gravity is pulling it back down, and then kneel beside him. Cade is tense with arousal, but still pliant when I get my hands on him and pull his body towards me.

It's easy to rearrange him on my lap. I get him sprawled over it–face on the floor on one side, legs splayed out on the other side, and his pert, vibrating ass right over my thighs. His hard cock drags against me, making him moan with every new moment of friction, but I continue to ignore it.

"It's very important that you don't come, Cade. Remember that. You're not allowed to come. I know you can be good for me."

Cade shudders again, but nods his face against the carpet as he makes a noise that sounds like agreement.

His ass looks beautiful like this, propped up and begging to be played with. I knead the flesh there, letting Cade rub himself off on my leg a little, but stopping him with a *tsk tsk* whenever he gets too eager. Then, when I feel like we're finally ready, I bring the flat of my hand down on his ass cheek.

It's not as hard as I can hit, but it's pretty hard. Hard enough to jolt his whole body forward and make him yelp. I pause for a second, waiting to see if he's going to ask to stop.

When we talked about this before, Cade was adamant. He said he liked the pain of some of the stuff we'd been doing. He liked feeling destroyed and totally overwhelmed. And while I loved choking him with my cock like we used to, the more research I did, the more convinced I became that it wasn't safe enough. So, we looked for alternatives.

And the blush that took over Cade's face when we hit on spanking as an option was fucking delicious. I knew I wanted to try, and he did, too. And he told me he wanted it to hurt.

Cade doesn't say anything, so I hit him again. And again, and again. He jolts forward with each slap, his skin quickly turning rosy pink everywhere I'm smacking him, and his hips begin to hump my lap in a mindless, desperate way while he starts moaning like he can't help it.

I'm only wearing my underwear, so I can feel how much wetness he's leaking and smearing over my skin, and it's making my arousal so much worse. I keep spanking him, gradually building and building until it's getting overwhelming and Cade is letting out little yelps with every hit.

When it seems like he's getting close to rubbing out an orgasm from the friction, I stop spanking and jerk his hips up in the air.

His cock hangs there, swollen and desperate, dark pink and begging for attention. A thin trail of precum connects the tip with my thighs.

"You want to come, don't you?" I ask.

Cade whines, shivering as I hold him steady.

"Ok, baby. You've done good. You can come whenever you want."

I say the words but I don't move at all, still holding him braced over me. When nothing changes and I don't touch his cock, Cade whines and tries to thrust, but I hold him still. The buzz of the plug vibrating inside him is the only sound in the room other than his ragged breathing.

One of my hands stays on his hip to keep him balanced, but I start to knead his ass again with the other, rubbing the tender, swollen flesh and making Cade cry out this time as the pain flares up over and over again. He's shaking, and every time I look at his cock he looks closer and closer to bursting.

The plug keeps going, and I grab the end for a minute to play with it, grinding the tip harder into his prostate and making him groan.

"Go on. I made you wait long enough, I know you can do it."

Cade rubs his face against the carpet and makes more desperate noises than I've ever heard him make before. His face is wet with tears and drool, and I find it just as beautiful as I always have. It feels so freeing to have this without the tiny kernel of doubt and shame that was lurking inside me for so long.

Time seems to slow down. I sit there for a long time, playing with the plug, watching Cade breathe, keeping him balanced over me and waiting for him to explode.

It builds slowly. If I study his cock, even in the dark, I can see it happening. I can see when the skin gets darker, when the veins get more pronounced and all the little lines and curves of him start to throb with pleasure. Cade's gasps and moans get increasingly louder as it builds, and there's an incredible moment when he's on the precipice, every part of him tense and ready, his orgasm hovering right there, but he can't seem to let go.

"Perfect," I murmur, and finally, Cade lets go.

His cock pulses and his body shakes, and cum releases from him all at once to spray over my lap. It's as slow to leave him as it was to build, and Cade seems like he's gripped by orgasm for a long time after the cum has run out.

Finally, he starts to sag, and I help him gently collapse on top of me. Cade is soft as a rag doll, not able to do anything but breathe. I quickly turn off the vibrations for him but leave the plug in and then pull out my own aching cock.

I let one hand roam over his ass again, clutching at that hot, pink flesh, while I jerk myself with the other. I barely care about getting off, at this point. Watching Cade was fucking transcendent. It barely takes a minute to get myself there, and soon I'm gasping as I shoot my load all over Cade's bare hip and then sink backwards until I'm lying on the floor.

It's clumsy, but I manage to drag Cade up to lie on top of me. He fumbles until his hands come out of the restraints–they were there for show and not really tight–and then pushes off his blindfold. His eyes are hazy when I can look at them, but he looks so relaxed. Everything about him feels squishy and calm as he pushes his face against my bare chest, kissing whatever he can find.

I don't have the energy to lift my head and kiss him back, but I touch him everywhere I can reach, as we turn into a messy pile of limbs and cum.

"Perfect," I tell him one more time, because it's the only thing that feels undeniably true.

BOOKS BY ERIN RUSSELL

POSSUM HOLLOW

Stupid Dirty – *Cade & Silas*
68 Whiskey – *Tristan & Ford*
Running Feral – *Gunnar & Tobias*
Hollow Point – *Cade & Silas*

SINS OF THE BANNA

Savage – *Sav & Micah*
Fallow – *Fallow & Colm*
Lucky – *Coming Soon*

About the Author

Erin Russell is a queer author living in Los Angeles. They love to write hurt/comfort romance about neurodiverse characters. They hate writing author bios, but are extremely candid on social media.

Oh, and they love possums.

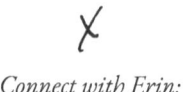

Connect with Erin: